3/24/15 SALE $26.99

THE CINDERELLA MURDER

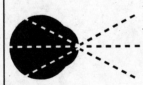

AN *UNDER SUSPICION* NOVEL

THE CINDERELLA MURDER

MARY HIGGINS CLARK
AND ALAFAIR BURKE

THORNDIKE PRESS
A part of Gale, Cengage Learning

GALE
CENGAGE Learning

Farmington Hills, Mich • San Francisco • New York • Waterville, Maine
Meriden, Conn • Mason, Ohio • Chicago

GALE
CENGAGE Learning®

Thorndike Press® Large Print Basic.
The text of this Large Print edition is unabridged.
Other aspects of the book may vary from the original edition.
Set in 16 pt. Plantin.

LIBRARY OF CONGRESS CATALOGING-IN-PUBLICATION DATA

Clark, Mary Higgins.
  The Cinderella murder : an under suspicion novel / by Mary Higgins Clark and Alafair Burke.
    pages cm. — (Thorndike Press large print basic) (Under suspicion ; 1)
    ISBN 978-1-4104-7131-4 (hardcover) — ISBN 1-4104-7131-4 (hardcover)
    1. Television programs—Fiction. 2. Murder—Investigation—Fiction.
  3. Suspense fiction. 4. Mystery fiction. 5. Large type books. I. Burke, Alafair.
  II. Title.
  PS3553.L287C56 2014b
  813'.54—dc23   2014039108

Published in 2014 by arrangement Simon & Schuster, Inc.

Printed in the United States of America
1 2 3 4 5 6 7 18 17 16 15 14

For Andrew and Taylor Clark
The newlyweds —
With love

ACKNOWLEDGMENTS

It is so satisfying to tell another tale, to share another journey with characters we have created and come to care deeply about — or not. And this time to have done it step by step with the wonderful writer Alafair Burke.

Marysue Rucci, editor-in-chief at Simon & Schuster, has been a marvelous friend and mentor. Alafair and I have so enjoyed working with her on this book, which is the first of a series.

The home team starts with my right hand, Nadine Petry, my daughter Patty, and my son Dave. And of course, John Conheeney, spouse extraordinaire.

Abiding thanks to Jackie Seow, art director. Her covers make me look so good.

And many thanks to my faithful readers, whose encouragement and support have made me write yet another tale.

Dear Reader,

My publisher had an idea I loved: with a cowriter, we should use the main characters in *I've Got You Under My Skin* in a series of novels. Working with Alafair Burke, a suspense writer I have long admired, we created *The Cinderella Murder.* In this novel and others to follow, the premise is that witnesses, friends, and family members from unsolved cases will be brought together to appear on a TV show years later in the hope of finding clues that were missed in the earlier investigations. I hope you enjoy the story.

Mary Higgins Clark

1

It was two o'clock in the morning. Right on time, Rosemary Dempsey thought ruefully as she opened her eyes and stirred. Whenever she had a big day ahead she would inevitably wake up in the middle of the night and start worrying that something would go wrong.

It had always been like this, even when she was a child. And now, fifty-five years old, happily married for thirty-two years, with one child, beautiful and gifted nineteen-year-old Susan, Rosemary could not be anything but a constant worrier, a living Cassandra. *Something is going to go wrong.*

Thanks again, Mom, Rosemary thought. Thanks for all the times you held your breath, so sure that the birthday upside-down cake I loved to make for Daddy would flop. The only one that did was the first one when I was eight years old. All the others were perfect. I was so proud of myself. But then, on his birthday when I was eighteen, you told me you always made a backup cake for him. In the single act of defiance that I can remember, I was so shocked and angry I tossed the one I had made in the garbage can.

You started laughing and then tried to apologize. "It's just that you're talented in other ways, Rosie, but let's face it, in the kitchen you're klutzy."

And of course you found other ways to tell me where I was klutzy, Rosemary thought. "Rosie, when you make the bed, be sure that the spread is even on both sides. It only takes an extra minute to do it right." "Rosie, be careful. When you read a magazine, don't just toss it back on the table. Line it up with the others."

And now, even though I know I can throw a party or make a cake, I am always sure that something will go wrong, Rosemary thought.

But there was a reason today to be apprehensive. It was Jack's sixtieth birthday, and this evening sixty of their friends would be there to celebrate it. Cocktails and a buffet supper, served on the patio by their infallible caterer. The weather forecast was perfect, sunshine and seventy degrees.

It was May 7 in Silicon Valley and that meant that the flowers were in full bloom. Their dream house, the third since they'd moved to San Mateo thirty-two years ago, was built in the style of a Tuscan villa. Every time she turned into the driveway, she fell in love with it again.

Everything will be fine, she assured herself impatiently. And as usual I'll make the birthday chocolate upside-down cake for Jack and it will be perfect and our friends will have a good time and I will be told how I'm a marvel. "Your parties are always so perfect, Rosie . . . The supper was delicious . . . the house exquisite . . . ," and on and on. And I will be a nervous wreck inside, she thought, an absolute nervous wreck.

Careful not to awaken him, she wriggled her slender body over in the bed until her shoulder was touching Jack's. His even breathing told her that he was enjoying his usual untroubled sleep. And he deserved it. He worked so hard. As she often did when she was trying to overcome one of her worry attacks, Rosemary began to remind herself of all the good things in her life, starting with the day she met Jack on the campus of Marquette University. She had been an undergraduate. He had been a law student.

13

It was the proverbial love at first sight. They had been married after she graduated from college. Jack was fascinated by developing technology, and his conversation became filled with talk of robots, telecommunications, microprocessors, and something called internetworking. Within a year they had moved to Northern California.

I always wanted us to live our lives in Milwaukee, Rosemary thought. I still could move back in a heartbeat. Unlike most human beings, I love cold winters. But moving here certainly has worked out for us. Jack is head of the legal department of Valley Tech, one of the top research companies in the country. And Susan was born here. After more than a decade without the family we hoped and prayed for, we were holding her in our arms.

Rosemary sighed. To her dismay, Susan, their only child, was a Californian to her fingertips. She'd scoff at the idea of relocating anywhere. Rosemary tried to wrest her mind away from the troublesome thought that last year Susan had chosen to go to UCLA, a great college but a full five-hour drive away. She had been accepted closer to home at Stanford University. Instead she had rushed to enroll at UCLA, probably because her no-good boyfriend, Keith Ratner, was already a student there. Dear God, Rosemary thought, don't let her end up eloping with him.

The last time she looked at the clock, it was three thirty, and her last impression before falling asleep was once again an overwhelming fear that today something was going to go desperately wrong.

2

She woke up at eight o'clock, an hour later than usual. Dismayed, she rushed out of bed, tossed on a robe, and hurried downstairs.

Jack was still in the kitchen, a toasted bagel in one hand, a cup of coffee in the other. He wore a sport shirt and khakis.

"Happy sixtieth birthday, love," she greeted him. "I didn't hear you get up."

He smiled, swallowed the last bit of the bagel, and put down the cup. "Don't I get a kiss for my birthday?"

"Sixty of them," Rosemary promised as she felt his arms go around her.

Jack was almost a foot taller than Rosemary. When she wore heels, it didn't seem so much, but when she was in her bedroom slippers, he towered over her.

He always made her smile. Jack was a handsome man. His full head of hair, now more gray than blond; his body, lean and

16

muscular; his face, sunburned enough to emphasize the deep blue of his eyes.

Susan was much more like him in both looks and temperament. She was tall and willowy, with long blond hair, deep blue eyes, and classic features. Her brain was like his. Technically gifted, she was the best student in the lab at school and equally gifted in her drama classes.

Next to them, Rosemary always felt as though she faded into the background. That too had been her mother's appraisal. "Rosie, you really should have highlights in your hair. It's such a muddy brown."

Now, even though she did use streaks, Rosemary always thought of her hair as "muddy brown."

Jack collected his long kiss and then released her. "Don't kill me," he said, "but I was hoping to sneak in eighteen holes at the club before the party."

"I guessed that. Good for you!" Rosemary said.

"You don't mind if I abandon you? I know there's no chance of you joining."

They both laughed. He knew all too well that she would be fussing around over details all day.

Rosemary reached for the coffeepot. "Join me for another cup."

"Sure." He glanced out the window. "I'm glad the weather is so good. I hate it when Susan drives through rainstorms to get here, but the weather prediction is good for the weekend."

"And I don't like that she's going to be going back early tomorrow morning," Rosemary said.

"I know. But she's a good driver and young enough that the round trip won't be a problem. Though remind me to talk to her about trading in that car of hers. It's two years old, and already we've had too many visits to the garage." Jack took a final few sips of the coffee. "Okay, I'm on my way. I should be home around four." With a quick kiss on Rosemary's forehead, he was out the door.

At three o'clock, beaming with self-satisfaction, Rosemary stepped back from the kitchen table. Jack's birthday cake was perfect, not a crumb astray when she flipped it over and lifted the pan. The chocolate icing, her own recipe, was relatively smooth, with the words HAPPY 60TH BIRTHDAY, JACK, written carefully, word for word.

Everything is ready, she thought. Now, why can't I relax?

3

Forty-five minutes later, just as Rosemary was expecting Jack to walk in the door, the phone rang. It was Susan.

"Mom, I had to work up the courage to tell you. I can't get home tonight."

"Oh, Susan, Dad will be so disappointed!"

Susan's voice, young and eager, almost breathless, said, "I didn't call before because I didn't know for sure. Mom, *Frank Parker is going to meet me tonight,* about maybe being cast in his new movie." Her voice calmed a little. "Mom, remember when I was in *Home Before Dark,* just before Christmas?"

"How could I forget?" Rosemary and Jack had flown to Los Angeles to watch the campus play from the third row. "You were wonderful."

Susan laughed. "But you're my mother. Why wouldn't you say that? Anyhow, remember the casting agent, Edwin Lange, who said he'd sign me?"

"Yes, and you never heard from him again."

"But I did. He said Frank Parker saw my audition tape. Edwin taped the performance and showed it to Frank Parker. He said that Parker was blown away and is considering me for the lead in a movie he's casting. It's a movie set on a campus and he wants to find college students to be in it. He wants me to meet him. Mom, can you believe it? I don't want to jinx myself, but I feel so lucky. It's like it's too good to be true. Can you believe that I might get a role, maybe even the lead role?"

"Calm down before you have a heart attack," Rosemary cautioned, "and then you won't get any role." Rosemary smiled and pictured her daughter, energy exuding from every bone in her body, twisting her fingers through her long blond hair, those wonderful blue eyes shining.

The semester's almost over, she thought. If she did get a part in this movie, it would be a great experience. "Dad will certainly understand, Susan, but be sure to call him back."

"I'll try, but, Mom, I'm meeting Edwin in five minutes to go over the tape with him and rehearse, because he says Frank Parker will want me to read for him. I don't know how late it will be. You'll be having the party, and you'll never hear the phone. Why don't I call Dad in the morning?"

"That might not be a bad idea. The party is from six to ten, but most people linger on."

"Give him a birthday kiss for me."

"I will. Knock that director off his feet."

"I'll try."

"Love you, sweetheart."

"Love you, Mom."

Rosemary had never become used to the sudden silence that followed when a cell phone disconnected.

When the phone rang the next morning, Jack popped up from reading the newspaper. "There's our girl, bright and early by a college student's standards for a Sunday."

But the caller wasn't Susan. It was the Los Angeles Police Department. They had difficult news. A young woman had been found just before dawn in Laurel Canyon Park. She appeared to have been strangled. They didn't want to alarm them unnecessarily, but their daughter's driver's license had been retrieved from a purse found fifteen yards from the body. A mobile phone was clutched in her hand and the last number dialed was theirs.

4

Laurie Moran paused on her way to her office at 15 Rockefeller Center to admire the ocean of gold and red tulips blooming in the Channel Gardens. Named after the English Channel because they separated the French and British Empire Buildings, these gardens were always brimming with something lush and cheerful. Tulips were no match for the plaza's Christmas tree, but the discovery of new plantings every few weeks in spring always made it easier for Laurie to say good-bye to her favorite season in the city. While other New Yorkers complained about the throngs of holiday tourists, Laurie found cheer in the brisk air and festive decorations.

Outside the Lego store, a father was photographing his son next to the giant Lego dinosaur. Her own son, Timmy, always had to loop through the store to inspect the latest creations when he visited her at work.

"How long do you think it took them to make this, Dad? How many pieces do you think there are?" The boy looked up at his father with a certainty that he had all the answers in the world. Laurie felt a pang of sadness, remembering the way Timmy used to gaze at Greg with the same anticipatory awe. The father noticed her watching, and she turned away.

"Excuse me, miss, but would you mind taking our picture?"

Thirty-seven years old, Laurie had learned long ago that she came across as friendly and approachable. Slender, with honey-colored hair and clear hazel eyes, she was typically described as "good–looking" and "classy." She wore her hair in a simple shoulder-length bob and rarely bothered with makeup. She was attractive but un-threatening. She was the type of woman people stopped for directions or, as in this case, amateur photography.

"Of course I don't mind," she said.

The man handed her his phone. "These gadgets are great, but all our family pictures are from an arm's length away. It would nice to have something to show besides a bunch of selfies." He pulled his son in front of him as she stepped back to get the entire dino-saur in view.

"Say cheese," she urged.

They complied, flashing big, toothy smiles. Father and son, Laurie thought wistfully.

The father thanked Laurie as she returned his phone. "We didn't expect New Yorkers to be so nice."

"I promise, most of us are pretty nice," Laurie assured him. "Ask New Yorkers for directions and nine out of ten will take the time."

Laurie smiled, thinking of the day when she was crossing Rockefeller Center with Donna Hanover, the former first lady of New York City. A tourist had touched Donna's arm and asked if she knew her way around New York. Donna had turned and pointed and explained. "You're just a couple of blocks from . . ." Smiling at the memory, Laurie crossed the street and entered the Fisher Blake Studios offices. She got off the elevator on the twenty-fifth floor and hurried to her office.

Grace Garcia and Jerry Klein were already busy at their cubicles. When Grace saw Laurie, she sprang up from her seat first.

"Hi, Laurie." Grace was Laurie's twenty-six-year-old assistant. As usual, her heart-shaped face was heavily but perfectly made up. Today, her ever-changing mane of long, jet-black hair was pulled into a tight ponytail. She wore a bright blue minidress with black tights and stiletto boots that would have sent Laurie toppling over face first.

Jerry, wearing one of his trademark cardigan sweaters, ambled from his seat to follow Laurie into her private office. Despite Grace's sky-high heels, long, lanky Jerry loomed over her. He was only one year older than Grace but had been with the company since he was in college, working his way up from intern to valued production assistant, and had just been promoted to assistant producer. If it hadn't been for Grace and Jerry's dedication, Laurie never could have gotten her show *Under Suspicion* off the ground.

"What's going on?" Laurie asked. "You two act like there's a surprise party waiting in my office."

"You could put it that way," Jerry said. "But the surprise isn't in your office."

"It's in here," Grace said, handing Laurie a legal-sized mailing envelope. The return address read ROSEMARY DEMPSEY, OAKLAND, CALIFORNIA. The seal had been opened. "Sorry, but we peeked."

"And?"

"She agreed," Jerry blurted excitedly. "Rosemary Dempsey's on board, signed on the dotted line. Congratulations, Laurie.

Under Suspicion's next case will be the Cinderella Murder."

Grace and Jerry took their usual places on the white leather sofa beneath the windows overlooking the skating rink. No place would ever feel as safe to Laurie as her own home, but her office — spacious, sleek, modern — symbolized all her hard work over the years. In this room, she did her best work. In this room, she was the boss.

She paused at her desk to say a silent good morning to a single photograph on it. Snapped at a friend's beach home in East Hampton, it was the last picture she, Greg, and Timmy had taken as a family. Until last year, she had refused to keep any pictures of Greg in her office, certain that they would be a constant reminder to anyone who entered that her husband was dead and his murder still unsolved. Now she made it a point to look at the photograph at least once a day.

Her morning ritual complete, she settled into the gray swivel chair across from the sofa and flipped through the agreement Mrs. Dempsey had signed, indicating her willingness to participate in *Under Suspicion*. The idea for a news-based reality show that revisited unsolved crimes had been Laurie's. Instead of using actors, the series offered the victim's family and friends the opportunity to narrate the crime from a firsthand perspective. Though the network had been wary of the concept — not to mention some flops in Laurie's track record — Laurie's concept of a series of specials got off the ground. The first episode had not only aired to huge ratings, it had also led to the case's being solved.

It was nearly a year since "The Graduation Gala" had aired. Since then they had considered and rejected dozens of unsolved murders as none had been suitable for their requirements — that the nearest relatives and friends, some of whom remained "under suspicion," would be guests on the program.

Of all the cold cases Laurie had considered for the show's next installment, the murder twenty years ago of nineteen-year-old Susan Dempsey had been her first choice. Susan's father had passed away three years ago, but Laurie tracked down her mother, Rosemary. Though she was appreciative of any attempt to find out who killed her daughter, she said she had been "burned" by people who had reached out to her before. She wanted to make sure that Laurie and the television show would treat Susan's memory with respect. Her signature on the release meant that Laurie had earned her trust.

"We need to be careful," Laurie reminded Grace and Jerry. "The 'Cinderella' moniker came from the media, and Susan's mother despises it. When talking to the family and friends, we always use the victim's name. Her name was Susan."

A reporter for the *Los Angeles Times* had dubbed the case "the Cinderella Murder" because Susan was wearing only one shoe when her body was discovered in Laurel Canyon Park, south of Mulholland Drive in the Hollywood Hills. Though police quickly found the other near the park entrance — presumably it had slipped off as she tried to escape her killer — the image of a lost silver pump became the salient detail that struck a chord with the public.

"It is such a perfect case for the show," Jerry said. "A beautiful, brilliant college student, so we have the hot UCLA setting. The views from Mulholland Drive near Laurel Canyon Park are terrific. If we can track down the dog owner who found Susan's body, we can do a shoot right by the dog run where he was heading that morning."

"Not to mention," Grace added, "that the director Frank Parker was the last known person to see Susan alive. Now he's being called the modern Woody Allen. He had quite a reputation as a ladies' man before getting married."

Frank Parker had been a thirty-four-year-old director when Susan Dempsey was murdered. The creator of three independent films, he was successful enough to get studio backing for his next project. Most people had first heard of him and that project because he had been auditioning Susan for a role the night she was killed.

One of the challenges for *Under Suspicion* was persuading the people who were closest to the victim to participate. Some, like Susan's mother, Rosemary, wanted to breathe new life into cold investigations. Others might be eager to clear their names after living, as the show's title suggested, under a cloud of suspicion. And some, as Laurie had hoped would be the case with Frank Parker, might reluctantly agree to go along so they appeared to the public to be cooperative. Whenever whispers about the Cinderella case arose, Parker's handlers liked to remind the public that the police had officially cleared him as a suspect. But the man still had a reputation to protect and he wouldn't want to be seen as stonewalling an inquiry that might lead to solving a murder.

Parker had gone on to become an Academy Award–nominated director. "I just read the advance review for his next movie," Grace said. "It's supposed to be a shoo-in for an Oscar nomination."

Laurie said, "That may be our chance to get him to go along with us. It wouldn't hurt to have all that attention when the Oscars come along." She began to jot notes on a pad of paper. "Contacting the other people who were close to Susan is what we have to start on now. Let's follow up with calls to everyone on our list: Susan's roommates, her agent, her classmates, her lab partner at the research lab."

"Not the agent," Jerry said. "Edwin Lange passed away four years ago."

It was one less person on camera, but the agent's absence wouldn't affect their reinvestigation of the case. Edwin had been planning to run lines with Susan prior to her audition but got a phone call that afternoon informing him that his mother had had a heart attack. He had hopped immediately into his car, calling relatives constantly on his cell phone, until he arrived in Phoenix that night. He had been shocked to hear of Susan's death, but the police never considered the agent a suspect or material witness.

Laurie continued her list of people to contact. "It's especially important to Rosemary that we lock in Susan's boyfriend, Keith Ratner. Supposedly he was at some volunteer event, but Rosemary despised him and is convinced he had something to do with it. He's still in Hollywood, working as a character actor. I'll make that call and the one to Parker's people myself. Now that Susan's mother is officially on board, I hope that will convince everyone else. Either way, get ready to spend time in California."

Grace clapped her hands together. "I can't wait to go to Hollywood."

"Let's not get ahead of ourselves," Laurie said. "Our first stop is the Bay Area. To tell Susan's story, we have to get to know her. Really know her. We start with the person who knew her the longest."

"We start with her mother," Jerry confirmed.

5

Rosemary Dempsey was Laurie's reason for moving the Cinderella Murder to the top of her list for the show's next installment.

The network had been pressuring her to feature a case from the Midwest: the unsolved murder of a child beauty pageant contestant inside her family's home. The case had already been the subject of countless books and television shows over the past two decades. Laurie kept telling her boss, Brett Young, that there was nothing new for *Under Suspicion* to add.

"Who cares?" Brett had argued. "Every time we have an excuse to play those adorable pageant videos, our ratings skyrocket."

Laurie was not about to exploit the death of a child to bolster her network's ratings. Starting her research from scratch, she stumbled onto a true-crime blog featuring a "Where are they now?" post about the Cinderella case. The blogger appeared to have simply Googled the various people involved in the case: Susan's boyfriend was a working actor; her college research partner had gone on to find dot-com success; Frank Parker was . . . Frank Parker.

The blog post quoted only one source: Rosemary Dempsey, whose phone number was still listed — "Just in case anyone ever needs to tell me something about my daughter's death," she said. Rosemary told the blogger that she was willing to do anything to find out the truth about her daughter's murder. She also said that she was convinced that the stress caused by Susan's death had contributed to her husband's fatal stroke.

The overall tone of the blog post, filled with tawdry innuendo, left Laurie feeling sick. The author hinted, with no factual support, that Susan's desire to be a star may have made her willing to do *anything* to land a plum role with an emerging talent like Parker. She speculated, again with no proof, that a consensual liaison may have "gone wrong."

Laurie could not imagine what it would have been like for Rosemary Dempsey to read those words, written by a person she had trusted enough to confide her feelings to about the loss of both her daughter and her husband.

So when Laurie called Rosemary Dempsey about the possibility of participating in *Under Suspicion,* she had understood precisely what Rosemary meant when she said she'd been burned before. Laurie had made a promise to do her very best, both for her and her daughter. And she told Rosemary how she knew from experience what it was like not knowing.

Last year, when the police had finally identified Greg's killer, Laurie had learned what people meant when they used the word "closure." She didn't have her husband back, and Timmy was still without his father, but they no longer had to fear the man Timmy had called Blue Eyes. It was closure from fear but not from heartbreak.

"That damn shoe," Rosemary had said about the "Cinderella Murder" nickname. "The irony is that Susan never wore anything so flashy. She'd bought those shoes at a vintage store for a seventies party. But her agent, Edwin, thought they were perfect for the audition. If the public really needed a visual image to hang on to, it should have been her necklace. It was gold, with the sweetest little horseshoe pendant. It was found by her body, the chain broken in the struggle. We bought it for her on her fifteenth birthday, and the next day, she landed the lead role as Sandy in her high school's production of *Grease.* She always called it her lucky necklace. When the police described it, Jack and I knew we'd lost our baby."

Laurie had known at that moment that she wanted the murder of Susan Dempsey to be her next case. A young, talented girl whose life had been cut short. Greg was a brilliant young doctor whose life had been cut short. His murderer was dead now. Susan's was still out there.

6

Rosemary Dempsey juggled two overflowing brown paper grocery bags, managing to close the hatchback of her Volvo C30 with her right elbow. Spotting Lydia Levitt across the street, she quickly turned away, hoping to slip from the driveway to her front door unnoticed.

No such luck.

"Rosemary! My goodness. How can one person eat so much food? Let me help you!"

How could one person be so rude? Rosemary wondered. Rude, and yet at the same time so kind?

She smiled politely, and before she knew it, her across-the-street neighbor was at her side, grabbing one of the bags from her hands.

"Multigrain bread, huh? Oh, and organic eggs. And blueberries — all those antioxidants! Good for you. We put so much junk into our bodies. Personally, my weakness is jelly beans. Can you believe it?"

Rosemary nodded and made sure Lydia saw her polite smile. If Rosemary had to guess, she'd have said the woman was in about her midsixties, though God knows she didn't care.

"Thank you so much for your help, Lydia. And I'd say jelly beans are a relatively harmless vice."

She used her now-free hand to unlock the front door of her house.

"Wow, you lock your door? We don't usually do that here." Lydia set her bag next to Rosemary's on the kitchen island, just inside the entryway. "Well, about the jelly beans, tell that to Don. He keeps finding little pink and green surprises in the sofa cushions. He says it's like living with a five-year-old on Easter Sunday. Says my veins must be like Pixy Stix, filled with sugar."

Rosemary noticed the message light blinking on her telephone on the kitchen counter. Was it the call she was waiting for?

"Well, thank you again for the help, Lydia."

"You should come down for the book club on Tuesday nights. Or movies on Thursdays. Any activity you want, really: knitting, brunch club, yoga."

As Lydia rambled on about the various

games Rosemary could be playing with her neighbors, Rosemary thought about the long road that had led her to this conversation. Rosemary had always assumed she'd remain forever in the home where she had raised her daughter and lived with her husband for thirty-seven years. But, as she had learned so long ago, the world didn't always work precisely as one expected. Sometimes you had to react to life's punches.

After Susan died, Jack offered to quit his job and go back to Wisconsin. The stock in the company that he had accumulated over the years and the generous pension and retirement benefits meant that they had plenty of money to take care of them for the rest of their lives. But Rosemary had realized that they had built a life in California. She had her church and her volunteer work at the soup kitchen. She had friends who cared so much about her that they kept her freezer full of casseroles for months, first after she said good-bye to Susan, then to Jack.

And so she'd stayed in California. After Jack died she did not want to stay in their home. It was too large, too empty. She bought a town house in a gated community outside Oakland and continued her life there.

She knew that she could either live with her grief or fall into despair. Daily Mass became a routine. She increased her volunteer work to the point where she became a grief counselor.

In retrospect, she might have been better off with a condo in San Francisco. In the city she would have had her anonymity. In the city she could buy multigrain bread and organic eggs and carry her groceries and check that urgent, blinking phone message without having to fend off Lydia Levitt's attempts to recruit her into group activities.

Her neighbor was finally wrapping up the list. "That's what's nice about this neighborhood," Lydia said. "Here at Castle Crossings, we're basically a *family*. Oh, I'm sorry. That was a poor choice of words."

Rosemary had first met this woman sixteen months ago and yet it wasn't till this moment that she finally saw herself through Lydia Levitt's eyes. At seventy-five years old, Rosemary had already been a widow for three years and had buried her only daughter two entire decades earlier. Lydia saw her as an old woman to be pitied.

Rosemary wanted to explain to Lydia that she had made a life filled with activities and

40

friends, but she knew the woman had a point. Her activities and friends were the same as when she had been a San Mateo wife and mother. She had been slow to allow new people into her world. It was as if she didn't want to know anyone who didn't also know and love Jack and Susan. She didn't want to meet anyone who might see her, as Lydia apparently did, as a widow marked by tragedy.

"Thank you, Lydia. I really appreciate it." This time, her gratitude was sincere. Her neighbor might not have been tactful, but she was caring and kind. Rosemary made a mental promise to reach out again to Lydia once she was less preoccupied.

Once Rosemary was alone, she eagerly retrieved her voice mail. She heard a beep, followed by a clear voice that hinted at a tone of excitement.

"Hi, Rosemary. This is Laurie Moran from Fisher Blake Studios. Thank you so much for sending back the release. As I explained, putting the show together depends also on how many of the people involved in the case we can sign up. Your daughter's agent, unfortunately, has passed away, but we have letters out to all the names you gave us: Frank Parker, the director; her boyfriend,

Keith Ratner; and Susan's roommates, Madison and Nicole. The final call gets made by my boss. But your willingness to participate makes an enormous difference. I truly hope this happens and will get back to you as soon as I have a final answer. In the meantime, if you need me —"

Once Laurie began reciting her contact information, Rosemary saved the message. She then dialed another number from memory as she began unloading groceries. It was the number of Susan's college roommate Nicole.

Rosemary had told Nicole that she had decided to go ahead with the program.

"Nicole, have you made a decision about the television show?"

"Not quite. Not yet."

Rosemary rolled her eyes but kept her voice even. "The first time they made that kind of special, they ended up solving the case."

"I'm not sure I want the attention."

"It's not attention about *you.*" Rosemary wondered if she sounded as shrill as she felt. "The focus of the show would be on Susan. On trying to solve her case. And you were close to Susan. You've seen how when someone brings it up on Facebook or Twitter, there are dozens of opinions, not least of which among them is that Susan was some kind of slut involved with half the men on campus. You could help to erase that image."

"How about the others? Did you speak to them?"

"I haven't yet," Rosemary said honestly, "but the producers will make their choice based on the level of cooperation they get from the people involved in the case. You were Susan's roommate for nearly two years. You know that *other* people won't want to cooperate."

She didn't even bother speaking their names. First up was Keith Ratner, whose wandering eye Susan had forgiven so many times. Despite his own transgressions, his possessiveness of Susan and unjustified jealousy had always made him Rosemary's top suspect. Next was Frank Parker, who had marched on with his fancy career, never giving Rosemary and Jack the common courtesy of a phone call or sympathy card for the loss of their daughter, whose only purpose in going to the Hollywood Hills was to see him. And Rosemary had never trusted Madison Meyer, Susan's other roommate, who had been only too happy to step into the role that Susan was supposed to audition for that night.

"Knowing Madison," Nicole was saying, "she'll show up with hair and makeup done."

Nicole was trying to defuse the tension with humor, but Rosemary was determined to stay on message. "You'll be important to the producers' decision."

The silence on the other end of the line was heavy.

"They'll be deciding soon," Rosemary nudged.

"Okay. I just need to check on a couple of things."

"Please hurry. The timing is important. *You're* important."

As Rosemary clicked off the phone, she prayed that Nicole would come through. The more people Laurie Moran could enlist, the greater the hope that one of them would inadvertently give himself or herself away. The thought of reliving the terrible circumstances of Susan's death was daunting, but she felt as though she were hearing lovable, wonderful Jack's voice saying, *Go for it, Rosie.*

Lovable, wonderful Jack.

7

Twenty-eight miles north, on the other side of the Golden Gate Bridge, Nicole Melling heard the click on the other end of the telephone line but couldn't bring herself to hit the disconnect button on the handset. She was staring at the phone in her hand when it started to make a loud beeping sound.

Her husband, Gavin, appeared in the kitchen. He must have heard the sound all the way from his home office upstairs.

He came to a halt when he spotted the phone, which she finally returned to its base. "I thought it was the smoke alarm."

"Is that a critique of my cooking?" she asked.

"Please, I know better." He gave her a kiss on the cheek. "You are absolutely the best cook — make that *chef* — I have ever known. I'd rather eat three meals a day here than go out to the finest gourmet restaurant in the world. And besides that, you're beautiful and have the disposition of an angel." He paused. "Is there anything I forgot?"

Nicole laughed. "That will do." Nicole knew that she was no beauty. She wasn't unattractive, either. She was just ordinary, her features unremarkable. But Gavin always made her feel like, in his eyes, she was gorgeous. And he was gorgeous in her eyes. Forty-eight years old, always trying to lose a few pounds, average height, starting to bald. He was a dynamo of brains and energy whose stock picks for his hedge fund made him a formidable figure on Wall Street.

"Seriously, is everything okay? It's a bit troubling to find my wife standing in the kitchen staring at a phone off the hook. Honest to God, you look as though you just received a threat."

Nicole shook her head and laughed. Her husband had no idea how close this joke came to the truth in her case.

"Everything's fine. That was Rosemary Dempsey."

"She's doing okay? I know you were disappointed when she didn't accept your invitation to join us for Thanksgiving."

She had told him about the possibility of

this program. But she certainly hadn't told him the full story about where she was in her life when she had shared a dorm room with Susan.

She hadn't meant to conceal anything from him. She really had managed to convince herself that she was a different person now than she was before she met him.

If this program happened and someone dug deeply enough, would it be better to have told him the truth now?

"Do you know that show called *Under Suspicion*?" she began.

His expression was blank, then changed. "Oh sure, we saw it together. Sort of a true-crime reality show; the Graduation Gala Murder. Got lots of attention. It even ended up solving the crime."

She nodded. "They're thinking of featuring Susan's case for the next one. Rosemary really wants me to be a part of it."

He plucked a few grapes from the crystal bowl on the kitchen island. "You should do it," he said emphatically. "A show like that could break the entire case open." He paused, then added, "I can only imagine what it's like for Rosemary — not knowing. Look, honey, I know you don't like the limelight, but if it could bring some kind of closure for Rosemary, I'd say you owe it to her. You always tell me that Susan was your best friend." He grabbed several more grapes. "Do me a favor, hang up the phone at the end of the next call, okay? I was afraid you'd fainted."

Gavin took the stairs back to his home office. He had the luxury (and curse) of being able to run a hedge fund wherever he happened to be as long as he had a phone and Internet connection.

Now that she had spoken the possibility aloud, Nicole knew that, of course, she had to be part of the show. How would it look if Rosemary asked Susan's college roommate to help solve Susan's murder, and she refused? How could she sleep at night?

Twenty years was so long ago, but it felt like a minute. Nicole had left Southern California for a reason. She would have moved to the North Pole if necessary. In the Bay Area, with Gavin, she had a wonderful husband. With the marriage, she had also changed her last name. Nicole Hunter had become Nicole Melling. She had started over again. She had found peace. She had even forgiven herself.

This show could ruin everything.

8

"Good afternoon, Jennifer. Is he in?"

Brett Young's secretary looked up from her desk. "Yes, just back in from lunch."

Laurie had worked with Brett long enough to know his routine: telephone calls, e-mails, and other correspondence in the morning; a business-related lunch (preferably from noon to two); then back to his desk for creative work in the afternoon. Until a few months ago, Laurie would have needed to schedule an appointment to see her boss. Now that she was back on top with *Under Suspicion,* she was one of the lucky few who could pop in unannounced. If she was really lucky, he may have indulged in a glass of wine or two at lunch. It always helped his mood.

Cleared by his guard, Laurie tapped on Brett's office door before opening it.

"Got a sec?" she asked.

"Sure, especially if you're here to tell me

you've decided to take on the little beauty queen case."

He looked up. Sixty-one years old and handsome by any standards, his expression was sealed in a permanent façade of extreme displeasure.

She took a seat on a recliner next to the sofa where Brett had been reading a script. Laurie thought her office was nice, but Brett's made it look like a cubbyhole in comparison.

"Brett, we went through that case. There's nothing new to say about that investigation. The whole point of our show is to get first-person accounts of people who were real players in the case. People who could possibly have been involved."

"And you'll do exactly that. Sic Alex Buckley on them and watch the witnesses squirm."

Alex Buckley was the renowned criminal defense attorney who had presented the first volume of the show about the so-called Graduation Gala Murder. His questioning of the witnesses had been perfect, ranging from gentle empathy to grueling cross-examination.

Since then, Laurie had seen him regularly. In the fall he'd invited her, Timmy, and her father to Giants football games and in the summer to Yankees baseball games. All four of them were ardent fans of both teams. He almost never invited her out alone, perhaps sensing she was not ready for a definitive progression of their relationship. She needed to complete the mourning process, to close the chapter on her life with Greg.

And she was too keenly aware that he was mentioned frequently in gossip columns for escorting a celebrity to a red-carpet affair. He was a very, very desirable man about town.

"Not even Alex Buckley could solve that case," Laurie insisted, "because we have no idea whom to question. DNA evidence has cleared the girl's entire family, and police never identified any other suspects. End of story."

"Who cares? Dig out those old pageant videos and glamour shots, and watch that Nielsen needle jump." It wasn't the first time Brett had lectured Laurie about the importance of ratings, and it wouldn't be the last. "You need something new? Get a scientist to conduct facial progression. Show the viewers what the victim would look like now."

"It simply wouldn't work. A technologically enhanced photograph could never tell the story of a life lost. Who knows what the future could have held for that girl?"

"Listen to me, Laurie. I happen to be a *successful* man. I know what I'm talking about. And I'm trying to help you keep your show on a roll. Some would say you got lucky the first time around and have just been riding it out since then." It had been nearly a year since the first *Under Suspicion* "news special" had aired. Since then, Laurie had been an executive producer on several of the studio's run-of-the-mill series, but Brett was eager to build on the *Under Suspicion* brand. "You gotta try to re-create the magic of the first time."

"Trust me. I went back to the drawing board and found a great case. It's perfect for *Under Suspicion.* The Cinderella Murder."

She handed him a photograph of Susan Dempsey, a professional headshot she had used for auditions. When Laurie had first seen it, she felt like Susan was looking straight through the camera, directly at her personally. Susan had been blessed with near-perfect features — high cheekbones, full lips, bright blue eyes — but the real beauty was in the energy of that stare.

Brett barely glanced at the photograph. "Never heard of it. Next! Seriously, Laurie, do I need to remind you of the flops you had before this thing came along? You of all people should know: success is fleeting."

"I know, I know. But you've heard of the case, Brett. The victim was a UCLA college student, found dead in the Hollywood Hills. Supposedly she no-showed for an audition that night."

Now he bothered to look at the headshot. "Wow, she was a knockout. Is this the Frank Parker thing?"

Had Frank Parker not gone on to become famous, people might have forgotten entirely about the Cinderella Murder by now. But every once in a while, usually after Parker released a new film or got nominated for another award, someone would mention the onetime scandal in the director's younger life.

"The victim's name was Susan Dempsey," Laurie began. "By every account, she was a remarkable girl: smart, attractive, talented, hardworking."

He waved his hand for her to get on with it. "We're not handing out medals. Why is this good TV?" Brett asked.

Laurie knew Brett Young would never understand her determination to help Susan's mother. Instead, she enthusiastically recited all of the features that made the case so appealing to Grace and Jerry.

"First of all, it's a terrific setting. You've got the UCLA campus. The glitz of Hollywood. The noir of Mulholland Drive."

It was clear that Brett was now listening carefully. "You said the right word: 'Hollywood.' Celebrities. Fame. That's why people would care about that case. Wasn't she found near Parker's house?"

Laurie nodded. "Within walking distance, in Laurel Canyon Park. He says she never showed up for the audition. Her car was found parked on campus. Police never determined how she got from UCLA to the hills."

"Parker knew she was a student. If her car was at Parker's house, and he had anything to do with it, he could have arranged to move it back on campus," Brett observed slowly.

Laurie raised her eyes. "Brett, if I didn't know better, I'd say you're beginning to sound interested."

"Will Parker participate?"

"I don't know yet. I've got Susan's mother on board, though, and that will make a difference. She's motivated. She'll convince Susan's friends to talk on air."

"Friends, schmends. Family and friends won't get people to set their DVRs. An Academy Award–nominated director will.

And get that actress, the one who landed the role."

"Madison Meyer," Laurie reminded him. "People forget that in addition to getting the role Susan was auditioning for, she was also one of Susan's roommates."

According to Frank Parker, when Susan failed to appear for the audition, he called Madison Meyer, another student from the UCLA theater department, and invited her to audition at the last minute. When questioned by police, Madison vouched for Parker's timeline, saying she was with him in his living room at the time of Susan's death.

"Pretty strange he just happened to give the role to a novice actress who provided him a convenient alibi," Brett said, rubbing his chin, a sure sign that he was on board.

"This is a good case for the show, Brett. I feel it. I *know* it."

"You know I love you, Laurie, but your gut's not enough. Not with this kind of money at stake. Your show ain't cheap. The Cinderella Murder is just another cold case without Frank Parker. You lock him down for the show, and I'll give you the all-clear. Without him, I have a surefire backup."

"Don't tell me: the child pageant queen?"

"You said it. Not me."
No pressure, Laurie thought.

9

Frank Parker looked down at Madison Square Park from fifty-nine stories above. He loved New York City. Here, looking north out of the floor-to-ceiling windows of his penthouse apartment, he could see all the way to the top of Central Park. He felt like Batman watching over Gotham.

"I'm sorry, Frank, but you made me promise to nudge you about some of those to-do items before the day ended."

He turned to find his assistant, Clarence, standing in the entryway of the den. Clarence was well into his thirties but still had the body of a twenty-year-old gym rat. His clothing selections — today a fitted black sweater and impossibly slim slacks — were obviously intended to highlight the muscles he was so proud of. When Parker hired him, Clarence had volunteered that he hated his name, but everyone who heard it remembered him because of his god-awful moniker. So it worked for him.

The entire flight from Berlin, Clarence had been trying to get Frank's attention about interview requests, phone messages, even wine selections for an upcoming premiere party. On the one hand, these were the kind of nitty-gritty details for which Frank had no patience. On the other hand, the people who worked for him had learned by now the types of decisions that could send him over the edge if someone made the wrong call. He had a reputation as a micromanager. He assumed it was what made him good at his job.

But as poor Clarence had begged for Frank's attention on the plane, all Frank could do was continue reading scripts. The chance to read in peace on the private jet had been the only part of the trip he enjoyed. Though it made him sound provincial, he hated leaving the United States. For the time being, however, foreign film festivals were all the rage. You never knew what tiny gem you might find to remake into an American blockbuster.

"Don't you know by now, Clarence, that when I make you promise to interrupt me about something in the future, it's simply my way of delaying a conversation?"

"Of course I know that. Feel free to send

me on my way again. Just don't snap at me tomorrow if the sky falls because you wouldn't let me relay these messages."

Frank's wife, Talia, paused in the hallway outside the den. "For Pete's sake, stop picking on poor Clarence. We'd probably have the lights cut off if he didn't keep life running for us. If you wait until we're back in Los Angeles, you'll end up getting too busy once again. Look out your pretty window and let him do his job."

Frank poured an inch and a half of scotch into a crystal highball glass and took a spot on the sofa. Clarence got settled into a wing chair across from him.

First up on Clarence's list was the studio's insistence that he sit down for a lengthy interview for a feature magazine article to promote his summer film release, called *The Dangerous Ones.* "Tell them I'll do it, but not with that wretched Theresa person." One of the magazine's writers was known for presenting her subjects in the worst possible light.

Next was a reminder that an option he had on last year's hottest novel was about to expire. "How much are we paying?"

"Another quarter of a million to extend the additional year."

He nodded and waved a hand. It had to

be done.

None of this seemed urgent enough for Clarence to have been bothering him all day.

Clarence was looking down at his notes, but when he opened his mouth to speak, no words came out. He let out a long breath, smiled, and then tried again. Still nothing.

"What's gotten into you?" Frank asked.

"I'm not sure how to raise this."

"If I could read minds, I wouldn't need you, would I?"

"Fine. You got a letter from the producers of a television program. They'd like to meet with you."

"No. We'll do publicity closer to release. It's too early now."

"It's not about *The Dangerous Ones.* It's about you. The past."

"Isn't that what I just agreed to on the magazine article?"

"No, Frank, I mean the *past.* The show is *Under Suspicion.*"

"What's that?"

"I keep forgetting that you're a genius about film but refuse to learn anything about television. It's a crime show. A news special, really. The concept is to reconstruct cold cases with the help of the people who were affected by them. You were involved in the Susan Dempsey case, and they want you to be part of their next special."

Startled, Frank turned his head and looked again out the window. When would people stop associating him with that awful event?

"So they want to talk to me about Susan Dempsey?" Clarence nodded. "As if I didn't talk enough back then to police, lawyers, studio executives — who, incidentally, were on the verge of dropping me . . . all I did was talk about that damn case. And yet here we are again."

"Frank, I had been waiting for a good time to speak to you about the letter. Now the producer — her name is Laurie Moran — has somehow gotten my number. She has called twice today already. If you want, we can say you're too busy doing edits on *The Dangerous Ones.* We can even redo a couple of aerial shots in Paris if we have to make you unavailable."

The tinny sound of a pop song played from Clarence's front pants pocket. He pulled out his cell phone and examined the screen. "It's her again. The producer."

"Answer it."

"Are you sure?"

"Did I sound unsure?"

"This is Clarence," he said into the phone. Frank had gotten where he was by trusting his instincts. Always. As he heard his assistant recite the familiar "I'll give Mr. Parker the message," he held out his palm. Clarence shook his head, but Frank leaned forward, more insistent.

Clarence did as instructed, voicing his displeasure with a loud sigh as he handed him the phone.

"What can I do for you, Ms. Moran?"

"First of all, thank you for taking my call. I know you're a busy man." The woman's voice was friendly but professional. She went on to explain the nature of her television show. Having just heard a similar description from Clarence, Frank was beginning to understand the reenactment concept. "I wanted to make sure you got my letter inviting you to tell your side of the story. We can work around your schedule. We'll come to Los Angeles or whatever other location is most convenient. Or if for some reason you're uncomfortable discussing your contact with Susan, we'll of course make a statement during the show informing viewers you declined to be interviewed."

Clarence had accused Frank of knowing nothing about television, but he was expert enough about entertainment generally to realize this woman could be bluffing. Would anyone really want to watch a show about the Cinderella Murder if he wasn't part of it? If he hung up now, could that stop the production in its tracks? Perhaps. But if they went forward without him, he'd have no control over their portrayal of him. They could place him at the top of their list of people who remained "under suspicion," as the show was called. All he needed was for ticket buyers to boycott his movies.

"I'm afraid I did not learn of your letter until just now, Ms. Moran, or I would have gotten back to you sooner. But, yes, I'll make time for your show." Across the table, Clarence's eyes shot open. "Have you spoken yet to Madison Meyer?"

"We're optimistic that all the relevant witnesses will appear." The producer was keeping her cards close to her vest.

"If Madison's anything like she was the last time I had contact with her, I'd show up at her front door with a camera crew. There's nothing more compelling to an out-of-work actress than the spotlight."

Clarence looked like he was going to jump out of his chair.

"I'll let you work out the details with Clarence," Frank said. "He'll have a look at the calendar and get back to you."

He said good-bye and returned Clarence's phone to him.

"I'll make scheduling excuses until she finally takes the hint?" he asked.

"No. You'll make sure I'm available. And I want to do it in L.A. I want to be a full participant, on the same terms with all the other players."

"Frank, that's a bad —"

"My mind is made up, Clarence, but thank you."

Once Clarence had left him alone, Frank took another sip of his scotch. He had gotten where he was by trusting his instincts, yes, but also because he had a raw talent for controlling the telling of a story. And his instincts were saying that this television show about Susan Dempsey would be just another story for him to control.

Talia watched from the hallway beyond the den as her husband's assistant left the apartment.

She had been married to Frank for ten years. She still remembered calling her parents in Ohio to tell them about the engagement. She'd thought they would be happy to know that her days of auditioning for bit roles and advertisements were over. They would no longer have to worry about her living alone in that sketchy apartment complex in Glassell Park. She was getting married, and to a wealthy, successful, famous director.

Instead, her father had said, "But didn't he have something to do with the death of that girl?"

She had heard the way her husband had spoken to Clarence and to that television person on the phone. She knew she had no chance of changing his mind.

She found herself twisting her wedding ring in circles, watching the three-carat diamond turn around her finger. She couldn't help but think that he was making a terrible mistake.

10

Laurie was exhausted by the time the 6 train stopped at her local station, Ninety-Sixth Street and Lexington. As she climbed the stairs up to street level, her new Stuart Weitzman black patent pumps still not broken in, she quickly reminded herself to be grateful for her freedom to ride the subway without fear, like everyone else. A year earlier she wouldn't have dared.

She no longer scanned every face in every crowd for a man with blue eyes. That was the only description her son, Timmy, had been able to offer of the man who had shot his father in the forehead, point-blank, right in front of him. An elderly woman had heard the man say, "Timmy, tell your mother that she's next. Then it's your turn."

For five years, she had been terrified that the man known as Blue Eyes would find and kill her and Timmy, just as he had promised. It had been nearly a year since Blue Eyes was killed by police in a thwarted attempt to carry out his twisted plan. Laurie's fears hadn't entirely died with him, but she was slowly beginning to feel like a normal person again.

Her apartment was only two blocks away, on Ninety-Fourth Street. Once she reached her building, she gave a friendly wave to the usual weeknight doorman on her way to the mailboxes and elevator. "Hey, Ron."

When she reached her front door, she slipped a key into the top bolt first, then a second key into the doorknob, and then secured both locks behind her once she was inside her apartment. She kicked off her heels while she dropped her mail, purse, and briefcase on the console table in the entryway. Next was her suit jacket, which she tossed on top of her bags. She'd find time to put everything away later.

It had been a long day.

She headed straight for the kitchen, pulled an already-open bottle of sauvignon blanc from the refrigerator, and began pouring a glass. "Timmy," she called.

She took a sip and immediately felt the stress of the day begin to peel away. It had been one of those days when she hadn't had time to eat or drink water or check her e-mail. But at least the work had paid off.

All the pieces for *Under Suspicion* to cover the Cinderella Murder were coming together.

"Timmy? Did you hear me? Is Grandpa letting you play video games already?"

Ever since Greg was killed, Laurie's father, Leo Farley, had stepped in as a kind of co-parent for Laurie's son, Timmy. Timmy was nine years old now. He'd spent more than half of his life with only Mommy and Grandpa to take care of him.

She couldn't imagine how she would have managed to continue working full-time if it weren't for her father's help. He lived one short block away. Every single day, he walked Timmy to and from school at Saint David's on Eighty-Ninth Street off Fifth Avenue and stayed with Timmy in the apartment until Laurie returned from work. She was far too grateful ever to complain, even when Grandpa allowed Timmy small indulgences like ice cream before dinner or video games before homework.

She suddenly realized that the apartment was completely silent. No sounds of her father talking through a math problem with Timmy. No sounds of Timmy asking his grandfather to repeat all the favorite stories he had already heard from Leo Farley's days with the NYPD: "Tell me about the time

68

you chased a bad guy with a rowboat in Central Park," "Tell me about the time the police horse got away on the West Side Highway." No sounds of videos or games coming from Timmy's iPad.

Silence.

"Timmy?! Dad?!" She bolted from the kitchen so quickly that she completely forgot she was holding a glass. White wine sloshed onto the marble floor. She trekked through it, running into the living room with damp feet. She tried to remind herself that Blue Eyes was dead. They were safe now. But where was her son? Where was Dad?

They were supposed to be here by now. She rushed down the corridor to the den. Her father blinked at her from his comfortable leather chair. His feet were on the hassock.

"Hi, Laurie. What's the rush?"

"Just getting some exercise," Laurie said as she looked over to the sofa, where Timmy was curled up with a book in his hands.

"He was wiped out from soccer," Leo explained. "I could see his head dropping even on the walk home from school. I knew he'd fall asleep the minute he settled down." He looked at his watch. "Oh boy. We're going on two hours. He'll be up all night now.

Sorry, Laurie."

"No, it's fine. I'm —"

"Hey," he said. "You're white as a sheet. What's going on?"

"I'm. It's just —"

"You were scared."

"Yes. For a moment."

"It's all right." He sat up in his chair, reached for her hand, and gave it a comforting squeeze.

She might have been taking the subway matter-of-factly like everyone else these days, but she still wasn't normal. When would things be normal?

"Timmy," her father said. "He said something about wanting takeout Indian food. Who's ever heard of a nine-year-old who likes lamb *saagwala*?"

At the sound of their voices, Timmy's eyes opened. He jumped up to give her a big bear hug. His enormous brown eyes, all expression and lashes, blinked up at her. She bent down to get closer to him. His head was still warm and smelled like sleep. She didn't need a glass of wine to feel like she was home.

Three hours later, Timmy's homework was done, the leftover takeout had been stored away, and Timmy — after enjoying his traditional "nighttime snack" — was tucked into bed.

Laurie returned to the table, where Leo was finishing a second cup of coffee. "Thank you, Dad," she said simply.

"Because I called for takeout?"

"No, I mean, for everything. For every day."

"Come on, Laurie. You know it's the best job I've ever had. Now, is it just my imagination, or were Timmy and I not the only people in this apartment who were a little tired this evening? I swear, sometimes I think you're right about that psychic connection you talk about."

When Timmy was born, Laurie was convinced that she and her son shared some inexplicable link that required neither words nor even physical contact. She would wake up in the middle of the night, certain that something was wrong, only to find dark silence. Invariably, within seconds, the baby monitor would crackle with the sounds of crying. Even tonight, hadn't she had a hankering for chicken *tikka masala* during the subway ride home?

"Of course I'm right," she said with a smile. "I'm always right, about everything. And so are you about my being a little tired.

Only it's more than a little. I had a long day."

She told him about Brett Young's conditional approval of featuring the Cinderella Murder in the next installment of *Under Suspicion,* followed by her phone call to Frank Parker.

"Did he sound like a murderer?" Leo asked.

"You're the one who taught me that the coldest, cruelest creatures can also be the most charming."

He fell silent.

"I know you still worry about me, Dad."

"Of course I do, just like you worried about me and Timmy when you came home today. Blue Eyes may be gone, but the very nature of your show means you've got a good chance, every single time, of being in the room with a killer."

"You don't need to remind me. But I always have Grace and Jerry with me. I have a camera crew. Someone is with me at all times. I'm probably safer at work than I am walking down the street."

"Oh, that's really comforting."

"I'm perfectly safe, Dad. Frank Parker has a huge career now. He's not stupid. Even if he was the one who killed Susan Dempsey, the last thing he's going to do is expose himself by trying to hurt me."

"Well, I'd feel better if Alex were one of those people who was always around you at work. Is he available for this project?"

"I'm keeping my fingers crossed, but Alex has a law practice to run, Dad. He doesn't need a second full-time job as a television personality."

"That's all a story, and you know it. The more he's on TV, the more business he gets for his practice."

"Well, hopefully he'll be on board." Quickly she added, "And not because of your reason, but because no one could be better than he was on the show."

"And because you both like being together."

"I can't get past those detective skills, can I?" She smiled and patted his knee, temporarily putting the issue to rest. "Frank Parker said something interesting today. He suggested that the best way to get Madison Meyer to commit to the show would be to appear at her house with a television crew."

"It makes sense, like waving a needle in front of a junkie. You said her career is all but dead. When she actually sees how quickly she could be back in the spotlight, she might have a hard time saying no."

"And it's Los Angeles," she said, thinking

aloud. "I can probably get a skeleton camera crew on a budget. With Madison, Parker, and Susan's mother on board, I can't imagine Brett not giving me the all-clear."

She picked up her phone from the coffee table and sent texts to Jerry and Grace: "Pack a bag for warm weather. We're heading to L.A. first thing in the morning."

The following afternoon in Los Angeles, Laurie pulled their rental van to the curb and double-checked the address against the one she had entered into the GPS. Jerry and the small production team they'd hired for the day — just a sound guy and two cameramen shooting handhelds — were already jumping out of the back, but Grace asked, "Everything okay? You look hesitant."

Sometimes it gave her the willies how well Grace could read her. Now that they were here, unannounced, at Madison Meyer's last known address, she was wondering if this was an insane idea.

Oh well, she told herself. This is reality television. She had to take risks. "No problem," she said, turning off the engine. "Just making sure we're in the right place."

"Not exactly Beverly Hills, is it?" Grace observed.

The ranch house was tiny, its blue paint

starting to peel. The grass looked like it hadn't been mowed for a month. The weathered planter boxes beneath the front windows contained nothing but dirt.

Laurie led the way to the front door, Grace and Jerry at her heels, the camera crew close behind. She rang the bell, once, then twice more, before she saw a set of red fingernails pull back curtains from the adjacent window. Two minutes later, a woman she recognized as Madison Meyer finally opened the door. Based on the fresh lipstick that matched the fingernails, Laurie guessed that Madison had done a quick touch-up before meeting her newly arrived guests.

"Madison, my name is Laurie Moran. I'm a producer with Fisher Blake Studios, and I want to give you airtime on a show with more than ten million viewers."

The house was cramped and messy. Magazines were strewn randomly around the living room, on the sofa, on the coffee table, in a pile on the floor next to the television. Most of them seemed to be celebrity magazines with important features like "Who Wore It Better?" and "Guess Which Couple Is About to Split?" Two narrow bookshelves that lined the wall by the entryway were packed with memorabilia from Madison's short-lived success as an actress. At the center was the statuette she had received for her first role, the one Frank Parker had gifted her after Susan supposedly never showed up for her audition: a Spirit Award, not an Oscar, but still a sign of a budding career. But from Laurie's research, she gathered that Madison had gone nowhere but down after that one recognition.

"Did you get the letter I sent you, Miss Meyer?"

"I don't think so. Or maybe I did and I just wanted to see whether you'd be following up." She smiled coyly.

Laurie returned the smile. "Well, consider this the follow-up." She introduced Jerry and Grace, who both shook Madison's hand. "Have you heard of the special series *Under Suspicion*?"

"Oh yes," Madison said. "I watched the one last year. I even joked it was only a matter of time before someone came calling about my college roommate. I assume that's why you're here?"

"As you know," Laurie said, "there has been speculation over the years about whether you covered for Frank Parker. You said you were with him at his house at the time of Susan's death."

Madison opened her mouth to speak but then pressed her lips together and nodded slowly. Close up and in person, Laurie could see that Madison had retained her beauty. She had long, shiny blond hair; a heart-shaped face; and piercing green eyes. Her skin was still pale and clear. But Laurie could also see the changes that time had brought to Madison's face, as well as Madison's attempts to forestall them. A telltale stripe of mousy brown revealed she was due for another dye job. Her forehead was unnaturally smooth, her cheeks and lips plumped by fillers. She was still a gorgeous woman, but Laurie wondered whether she'd have been even more beautiful without all the intervention.

"That's true," Madison said. "I mean, the part about people speculating."

"You have nothing to say about that?" Laurie pressed.

"Am I the first person you asked? That letter you mailed seemed pretty generic."

"Ah, so now you *do* recall the letter," Laurie said, arching a brow. "You're right: we did ask others. We try to bring as many people who knew the victim as possible to —"

"So who are the other people? Who has committed?"

Laurie didn't see the harm in Madison's question. "Susan's mother. Your other roommate, Nicole Melling, is interested. Frank Parker."

Madison's green eyes sparkled at the mention of the director's name. "I assume your show pays?" she asked.

"Of course. Maybe not what a studio movie might pay, but I think you'll find the compensation to be fair." Laurie knew that Madison hadn't had any studio film offers for a decade.

"Then I'll have my agent call you to talk terms before I'll say anything on camera. Oh, and you." She looked directly at the two men with cameras. "When it comes time to shoot, the left is my good side. And no backlighting. It makes me look old."

As Laurie made her way back to the rental car, she allowed herself to smile. Madison Meyer was playing hard to get, but she was already talking like the diva of the set.

11

Some people were just creatures of habit.

Not Madison. Heck, Madison wasn't even her name. Her real name was Meredith Morris. How old-fashioned was that? There wasn't even a cute nickname she could make out of it. She'd tried Merry, but people thought she was saying Mary. Then she tried Red, but that didn't even make sense for a blonde. But she always liked the alliteration. When she enrolled at UCLA to appease her parents, she changed her name to Madison Meyer, determined to get discovered by Hollywood.

In various stages of her life, she had been a vegetarian, a gun owner, a libertarian, a conservative, a liberal. She'd been married, and divorced, three times. She had dated actors, bankers, lawyers, waiters, even a farmer. Madison was constantly changing. The only constant was that she wanted to be a star.

But as Madison was to reinvention, Keith Ratner was to habit. Even back in college, he'd flirted, danced, and occasionally snuck off with Madison and other girls. But he always, always, always went back to his beloved Susan. He was loyal in his own crazy way, like a bigamist who insisted his only crime was loving his wives too much to disappoint them.

And just as Madison had always known Keith would never quit his high school girlfriend, she was confident she would find him at his usual haunt, a lounge celebrities liked called Teddy's, in the far front corner of the Roosevelt Hotel. He was even sitting in the same banquette where she'd last seen him here, about six months earlier. She should have called him Rain Man, that's how much Keith Ratner liked a routine. She was even fairly certain she could identify the clear liquid in his glass.

"Let me guess," she said by way of greeting. "Patrón Silver on the rocks?"

His face broke out into a broad smile. Twenty years later, and that smile still sent a chill up her spine. "Nope," he said, jiggling his glass. "I still love this place, but I've been a club soda guy for years. From here I'll hit Twenty-Four Hour Fitness for some cross-training."

Several years ago, at the height of Keith's television career, Madison had seen an interview highlighting his commitment to physical health, volunteer work, and his do-gooder church. It all seemed like a PR stunt to her, but here he was, in his favorite bar, sipping soda water.

"Still trying to convince everyone you're a reformed soul?" she asked.

"Clean body, clean mind."

She waved over a waitress and ordered herself a cucumber martini. "Vodka's clean enough by my standards."

"Speaking of standards," Keith teased, "how did the likes of you get past the red velvet rope?"

Madison's celebrity had taken off before his, thanks to her role in *Beauty Land,* Frank Parker's first major film. But Keith's career hadn't died like hers. If only he knew how close his comment cut to the bone. She had, in fact, slipped the bouncer a twenty to get in.

"I knew I'd find you here," she said.

"So this isn't a chance encounter?"

Keith obviously still knew the power he had over her. Madison recalled the first time she met him, as a freshman at UCLA. She'd shown up to an open casting call for some horrible musical based on the life of Jackson Pollock. Keith was there to audition for Pollock, she for the artist's wife, Lee Krasner. Madison could tell as they read their lines that they were both having a hard time suppressing laughter at the terrible dialogue. They finally burst into giggles when the casting agent declared that they were both "far too good-looking for this project." They headed straight from the audition to a nearby bar, where Keith knew a bartender willing to serve them despite their age. When he kissed her, it was her first taste of whiskey.

She didn't even know that he attended UCLA until she spotted him in Wilson Plaza, holding hands with a girl she recognized from her History of Theater class. Blond, pretty, a less primped version of Madison herself. Madison made a point of befriending Susan Dempsey the very next day, quickly learning that she'd come to UCLA with her high school boyfriend. Keith wasn't happy about his girlfriend's newest friendship, but there wasn't much he could say about it, was there?

Keith had Susan, so Madison moved on to other relationships, too. But they continued their dalliances. When Madison upped the ante by moving in with Susan sophomore year, it only seemed to make their secret rendezvous more exciting.

All that changed after Susan's murder. Keith stopped calling and brushed Madison off when she called him. Not long after she finished shooting *Beauty Land,* he dropped out of college. He told everyone he had landed a major agent who had big plans for him. But whispers in the theater department speculated that he was so broken up about Susan's murder than he could hardly function, let alone attend school or launch an acting career. Supposedly he had found Jesus. Other, less kind whispers suggested that his departure was proof that he'd had something to do with Susan's death after all.

Now, twenty years later, time had been easier on him than on Madison, as always seemed to be the case with men. Somehow the lines on his thin, angular face made him even more handsome. The dark, tousled hair that had pegged him as a rocker type when he was a college freshman now came off as comfortable and confident. He occasionally showed up as a featured guest on a one-hour network drama and had even had a small part in an indie film the previous year. But even so, Madison hadn't seen him in a regular gig since his cable sitcom was canceled four years earlier. Keith needed

Under Suspicion almost as much as she did.

"Not a chance encounter," she confirmed, just as the waitress returned with her drink. She took a seat next to him and smiled.

"Uh-oh. It's been a while, but I know that look. You want something."

"Did you get contacted by a TV producer named Laurie Moran?"

"Oh, I get contacted by so *many* projects, I can't keep them all straight." Now he was the one smiling. He was still a ham, a completely charming ham.

"It's for *Under Suspicion,*" she said. "They want to do a show about Susan's murder. They must have contacted you."

He looked away and took a sip of his drink. When he spoke, the lighthearted tone was absent. "I don't want anything to do with it. What's the point in rehashing everything that happened back then? They're really doing it?"

"Sounds like it."

"Do you know who else is in?"

"Susan's mother, Rosemary. Nicole, wherever she disappeared to. Apparently her last name's Melling now. And the person I think you'll really be interested in: Frank Parker."

When Keith heard that Madison had landed the role in *Beauty Land,* he had shown up outside her dorm. He was drunk and yelled, "How could you? That man killed my Susan, and everyone knows it. All you ever will be is a cheaper, lesser version of her!" It was the only time he had made her cry.

"I'm surprised they got anyone to go along with the show, other than Rosemary," he said.

"Well, I for one am doing it. If we play our cards right, it could help us both. Millions of people watch that show. It's exposure." She didn't add that she also hoped to persuade Frank Parker to find a role for her in his next project.

"I'll think about it. Is that it?"

"What I really need, Keith, is your word."

"And what word might that be? A secret, magical word?" The playful smile had returned.

"I mean it," she said. "No one can ever know about us."

"It was twenty years ago, Madison. We were all kids. You really think anyone will care that you and I played footsie on occasion?"

Was that all I was to him? she thought. "Of course they'll care. Susan was — perfect Susan: smart, talented, the whole package. I was — how did you word it? The other beauty, but *a cheaper, lesser version.* You know that the producers will portray Nicole as the good, loyal friend. I'll be the rival drama queen." Madison knew that the friendship between Susan and Nicole hadn't been nearly as perfect as the media had made it seem in the aftermath of Susan's death. "There are still people on the Internet saying I must have killed Susan or at least faked an alibi for Frank Parker, so I could get the role in *Beauty Land*. If the world finds out I was sneaking around with Saint Susan's boyfriend, they'll really think I did it."

"Well, maybe you did." She couldn't tell whether he was teasing or serious.

"Or maybe you did," she sniped, "just like Susan's parents always thought. It won't look good that you had something going with your girlfriend's own roommate."

"Mutual destruction," he said, staring at the empty glass he was now spinning in his hand.

"So I have your word?"

"Word," he said, pointing at her. "We never happened. Forget all our cozy little get-togethers. Our secret dies with us."

12

Once Madison was out of view, Keith pulled his cell phone from his jeans pocket, scrolled through his favorite contacts, and tapped on the entry listed as "AG." Very few people had this particular phone number. Keith had gotten it five years earlier, and that was after fifteen years of dedicated service. At the time, his career was on a roll. He chose to believe that it was the decade and a half of loyalty, not the fleeting appearance of fame or the financial rewards that came with it, that had led to this privilege.

"Yes?" the voice on the other line said. All these years later, and Keith still thought this voice was one of the strangest he'd ever heard. High-pitched like a child's, but completely confident and controlled.

"I have more information about the television show I told you about."

"Yes?"

"Apparently they are going forward with

production. My understanding is that every-one else is getting pulled in: Frank Parker, Susan's mother, Madison Meyer, Nicole."

"Nicole. You're certain?"

With a source like Madison, how could Keith possibly be sure? That woman would lie, steal, cheat — maybe even kill — to get what she wanted. Wasn't that why he'd been drawn to her back then? She was dark and dangerous — everything Susan was not. But, as much as she'd been trying to ma-nipulate him, seeking him out here at Ted-dy's, he didn't think she was lying about other people's signing on to appear on the show. "Yes, I'm almost positive." He knew to include the word "almost." You didn't get access to this phone number by withhold-ing any tiny kernel of truth.

"Did they say anything else about Ni-cole?" the voice asked.

"Her last name is apparently Melling now. That's all I know."

There was a pause before the voice contin-ued. "It will be better if you participate."

Keith had been afraid Martin would say that. Money in Keith's pocket meant more tithing, not to mention the help Keith could give to the church's reputation if he were back in the spotlight. Keith reminded himself that the church focused on fund-raising to advance its mission of helping the poor, but he really didn't want to do this show.

"Susan's mother has always suspected me of killing her daughter. I can only imagine what she'll say about me. And I've been public about my religion. It could make the church look bad."

"You're an actor. Charm the producers. And be sure to report back with any new information on Nicole."

"She's been off the radar for twenty years. Why the curiosity?"

"You let me worry about my own enemies."

When the line went dead, Keith Ratner was glad that he hadn't made an adversary of the man on the other end of the line. He intended to keep it that way at all costs.

13

Three hundred fifty miles away, in downtown San Francisco, Steve Roman's cell phone rang. The screen identified the caller as "AG."

He felt himself smile. The directive that Steve move to the Bay Area was a sure sign that he was trusted, but he missed seeing Martin Collins in person. Maybe the church would ask him to return to Los Angeles. Or perhaps Martin would be coming north for another big revival.

"Steve Roman," he answered. Steve, like Steve McQueen. Roman, like a gladiator.

"You're well?" Martin never identified himself during phone calls. It wasn't necessary. Anyone who had witnessed one of Martin's sermons knew the distinctive sound of his voice. Steve had first heard Martin's voice when a friend brought him to a revival in the basement of a Westwood tattoo parlor fifteen years earlier. Since then, he'd listened to Martin's preaching for hours — in person, on cassette tapes and then CDs, and now via streaming audio from the Internet.

Over the years, Steve had worked his way closer and closer to the inner circle. Advocates for God used a circle metaphor for a member's relationship to the church. It wasn't a hierarchy. Martin wasn't the top; he was the *center.* And through the center, the word of God could be heard.

"Yes," Steve responded. "Thank you, as ever, for the opportunity."

When Martin decided to expand AG's reach beyond his Southern California megachurch, he had dispatched Steve here. Even though Steve preferred the sunny glow and glitz of Southern California to the gloomy, windy Bay Area, he always expressed gratitude to AG for the opportunity. The church had found a studio apartment for him above Market Street and secured a job for him with a home-alarm company, Keepsafe.

Mostly, he was thankful for his new identity. He no longer used drugs. He didn't hurt people anymore. With the help of Martin Collins and AG, he was on a path to find himself by serving the Lord and the poor. He had even transformed himself physically. Before he ventured into the basement of that tattoo parlor, he had been skinny, with long straggly hair, often unwashed. Now he did a hundred sit-ups and push-ups every single day. He ate healthfully. He kept his hair shaved close to the scalp. He was hard, lean, and clean.

"Do you need something?" Steve offered.

Steve thought of himself as Advocates for God's own private investigator. He gathered dirt on former church members who tried to sully AG's reputation, often by slipping in and out of the homes of Keepsafe's customers unnoticed. When Martin got wind that a federal prosecutor was looking into the church's finances, it was Steve who had conducted the surveillance to prove the lawyer was cheating on his wife. Steve was never certain how Martin handled the crisis, but once he gave Martin photographic proof of the affair, the murmurs of an investigation disappeared.

His work for AG wasn't always strictly legal, but Martin — and Steve — saw it as a necessary evil to keep tabs on people who tried to suppress the church and its good works.

"Yes. I need you to keep an eye on someone. And to send a message when the time is right."

There was something about the way that

Martin said "send a message" that made Steve's skin prickle. Steve closed his eyes and thought to himself, Please, no, not that.

He accepted this life, in a noise-filled studio overlooking a traffic-filled street, in a city where he knew no one, because he was a better person here than he had ever been when he made his own choices. It had been years since he'd inflicted physical pain upon another living being. What if he tried it again and liked it too much? But then he reminded himself not to question the supreme Advocate for God.

"Whatever you need."

14

According to Nicole Melling's GPS, the drive to Palo Alto was supposed to take less than an hour once she hit the Golden Gate Bridge. Clearly her car's computer system hadn't taken traffic into account. She was stuck in yet another stretch of gridlock, this time through Daly City.

She looked up at the endless rows of non-descript houses packed on the hillside above I-280. What was that song someone — Pete Seeger, perhaps? — had written about this suburb? Little boxes, on the hillside, all the same, all made of "ticky tacky."

Nicole had a sudden memory of herself at barely seventeen years old. Thanks to her skipping fifth grade, she had been a full year younger than the other seniors ready to graduate, but still years beyond them academically. She had gotten into every school she applied to: Harvard, Princeton, Stanford, all of them. But her parents had been trapped in an income bubble — too rich for financial aid, too poor for private tuition. The plan had been for Nicole to attend UC Berkeley, but then the letter came in the mail: on-campus housing was full. She would need to find an apartment.

She remembered pleading with her father, the letter from Berkeley unfolded in front of him like a pink slip on the kitchen table. "I can do it, Dad. I'll spend all my time in classes and the library anyway, so it's only a matter of walking to and from campus once a day. Just a few blocks. They even have safety monitors to walk you home after dark."

He had avoided eye contact with her as he endlessly twirled spaghetti around his fork. "You're too young, Nicky. You're just a girl. And it's *Berkeley*." He said it like it was a war-torn country on the opposite side of the world, instead of a six-hour drive from their home in Irvine.

"Mom, please. Tell him. I've never gotten into any trouble. Ask any teachers at school. I do everything I'm supposed to do, all the time. I follow every rule. I can be trusted."

Her mother was banging dishes around in the sink, but even in profile, Nicole could see her pursed lips. "We know all that, Nicky. But we won't be there. Your teachers won't be there. No one will be there to set the rules for you."

It was only when Nicole started to cry that her mother finally turned off the running water, joined them at the table, and grasped both of Nicole's hands in hers. "We know you, Nicole. I know you better than I even know myself, because you're my baby. We can't let you get *lost.*"

Nicole remembered looking to her father for some explanation, but he just nodded once at the certitude of her mother's statement and continued to twirl his pasta.

Nicole had no idea what her parents meant at the time, but it would soon become apparent that her parents had indeed known their only daughter. Just like her family's income bubble, young Nicole had been in a bubble of her own — her intelligence robust, but her personality still . . . inchoate. They had feared that she would be lost in the crowd. Unfortunately, her fate was worse.

The sound of a car horn brought her back to the present. Noticing the short stretch of open road in front of her, she gave a friendly wave to the honking driver behind her and pulled forward.

According to the GPS, she had twenty-nine more miles to go. Nicole hadn't seen Dwight Cook since college, but she had read about him in the newspaper. Everyone in America had.

A full hour later, Nicole pulled into the crowded parking lot of an office park. The sleek glass buildings were surrounded by grass so green it looked spray painted. Above the entrance of the main building, giant purple letters spelled out the company name: REACH.

The young woman behind the high-gloss white desk in the lobby had piercings on the left side of her nose and through her right eyebrow. Nicole resisted the temptation to ask if her face felt crooked.

"Nicole Hunter, here to see Mr. Cook. I have an appointment." For the first time in nearly eighteen years, she had used her maiden name when she had called. Even then, she hadn't been certain that Dwight would remember her.

Nicole knew other people who still kept up with their college friends. Her neighbor Jenny had gone to school in New York but organized Bay Area mini-reunions once a year. And she knew from other friends that their Facebook pages were filled with shared photographs and remember-whens.

Of course, Nicole couldn't even have a Facebook page. It would undermine the very purpose of having a clean slate with a new last name in a new city.

But even without her special circumstances, Nicole wouldn't have stayed in touch with her college crowd. She never really had friends at UCLA, other than Susan. How lucky she had been to get paired with someone like her — someone who looked after her. She had won the roommate lottery.

It had been just the two of them freshman year. Then sophomore year, Susan had brought in Madison — a fellow actress from the theater department — because they could get a better suite if they took a triple.

It was also through Susan that Nicole had first met Dwight Cook, who would go on to launch REACH the summer after his sophomore year in college.

"Nicole!"

She looked up at the sound of her name. The lobby was designed as an atrium, open from the floor to the glass ceiling three floors up. Dwight was looking down at her from the top of a circular staircase.

Once he had descended to the ground floor, he smiled awkwardly. "You look the same."

"As do you," she said, even though it stretched the truth. His face was different

— paler, fuller. His hairline was beginning to recede.

But his attire seemed like a retread of her memories: high-waisted blue jeans and an ill-fitting Atari T-shirt that had already been retro when they were college freshmen. Even more startlingly familiar were his mannerisms. The jittery gaze and excessive blinking had been noticeable in an awkward teenager but were even more so in a grown man who was probably close to being a billionaire.

He led the way past the pierced receptionist, down a long hallway of offices. Most of the workers appeared to be in their twenties, many of them perched on top of giant fitness balls instead of traditional office chairs. At the end of the hall, he opened a door, and they walked into a courtyard behind the building. Four people were shooting hoops on a nearby court.

He didn't wait for her to sit before taking a spot on a cushioned chaise. She did the same, knowing he hadn't meant to be rude.

"You said you wanted to talk about Susan."

Again, she wasn't offended by the lack of small talk. He might have been considered a king of Silicon Valley, but she could already tell he was still the same uncomfortable kid who had worked in the campus computer-science lab with Susan.

He sat affectless as Nicole told him about the show, *Under Suspicion,* and the possibility that they would be featuring Susan's case. "Did you get a letter from the producer?" she asked.

He shook his head. "Once Susan's murder became a story about Hollywood, no one seemed to care that she was also a brilliant programmer. I doubt the producer even realizes we knew each other."

Back in college, it had taken Nicole a few outings as a trio — her, Susan, Dwight — to realize that Susan had been hoping to play Cupid between her lab partner and freshman dorm-mate. On one level, the pairing made sense: both Dwight and Nicole were off the charts in raw intelligence. And now that Nicole saw it for what it was, they were both — let's face it — peculiar. They were both projects for Susan, who tried her best to coax them from their shells. Dwight found comfort in computers. Nicole eventually found it in — well, she didn't like to think about that part of her past.

But after only two dates, Nicole had realized the fundamental difference between Dwight and her. Her oddness was short-lived. She had been young, sheltered, and so busy succeeding that she'd never learned how to exercise independent thought. She just had to find her way. Dwight's "issues" ran deeper. Nowadays, they'd probably say he was somewhere "on the spectrum."

At the time, Nicole thought that made her the better catch. But she hadn't learned the hard way — not yet — how dangerous a young, brilliant woman's desire to find her own way could be.

"Well, that's why I came here, Dwight. I'd like to tell the show about your friendship with Susan. How she had another side to her."

Dwight was looking in the direction of her face, as he had probably learned people expected him to do during a conversation, but he wasn't really connecting to her. "Of course. Susan was always so kind to me. She looked after me. I was lucky we happened to work for the same professor, or I never would have met her."

In other words, he felt the way she did about winning the roommate lottery.

"So I can tell Laurie Moran you'll help with the show? Appear on camera?"

He nodded again. "Anything to help. Anything for Susan. Should I ask Hathaway, too?"

"Hathaway?"

"Richard Hathaway. Our professor. That's how Susan and I met."

"Oh, I hadn't thought of him. Is he still at UCLA? Have you kept in touch?"

"He's retired from the university, but we're definitely in touch. He works right here at REACH."

"How funny to have your former professor in your employ."

"More like a partner, really. He's helped me from day one. I'm sure he'd be willing to help with the show, too."

Nicole wondered whether Dwight found comfort in keeping his college mentor close, someone who knew him before he was a twenty-year-old millionaire on the cover of *Wired* magazine. "Sure," she said. "That would be great."

She almost felt guilty for pulling Dwight Cook into this. He was the head of REACH, a tech company that had become a household name in the 1990s by changing the way people searched for information on the Internet. She had no idea what they worked on now, but from the looks of these grounds, Dwight was still a major player in the tech world.

But that was exactly why Nicole had come to Palo Alto. Frank Parker had become a famous director, but Dwight was a kind of celebrity in his own right. The more high-profile people who were involved in the production, the less screen time the show would devote to the roommate who dropped out after her sophomore year, changed her name, and never went back to Los Angeles again.

Once Nicole was in her car, she pulled Laurie Moran's letter from her purse and dialed her office number on her cell phone.

"Ms. Moran, it's Nicole Melling. You contacted me about my college roommate, Susan Dempsey?"

"Yes." Nicole heard the rustling of a plastic bag in the background and wondered if she had caught the producer midlunch. "Please, call me Laurie. I'm so happy to hear from you. Are you familiar with *Under Suspicion*?"

"I am," Nicole confirmed.

"As you probably know, the name of our show indicates that we go back and talk to the people who have remained literally under suspicion in cold cases. Obviously you don't fit that bill, but you and Susan's mother will remind viewers that Susan was a real person. She wasn't just the pretty girl with an aspiring actress's headshot. She wasn't Cinderella."

Nicole understood why Susan's mother put so much stock into this producer.

"If you think your show can help bring attention back to Susan's case, I'm happy to help."

"That's fantastic."

"And I hope you don't mind, but I took the liberty of contacting another college friend of Susan." She briefly described Dwight Cook's working relationship with Susan in the computer lab, followed by the news that Dwight was willing to participate in the show. The producer sounded thrilled, just as Nicole expected.

As Nicole pulled out of the office park's lot, she looked in the rearview mirror and felt incredibly proud of Dwight Cook. Susan's death had presented a gigantic challenge to the lives of everyone she knew. Both Nicole and Keith Ratner had quit college. Rosemary had told her she barely left her bed for a full year.

But somehow Dwight had managed to create something transformative in the aftermath. She wondered if whatever made him different from other people had enabled him to channel his grief in a way the rest of them could not.

She was so wrapped up in her own

thoughts that she never saw the off-white pickup truck pull out of the parking lot behind her.

15

Dwight Cook closed and locked the door to his office, located far from most of REACH's employees. That was the way he liked it.

Dwight constantly felt all these kids looking at him, wanting to know the tall, lanky billionaire who still dressed like a teenage nerd but was nevertheless pursued by several well-known supermodels. His employees assumed that Dwight's office was isolated because he did not want to be disturbed. The truth was that Dwight could not possibly run this business the way it needed to be run if he made too many connections to the people who worked for him.

Dwight had realized in middle school that he wasn't like other people. It wasn't that his own behavior was so unusual, at least not that he could determine. Instead, he was different in his *reactions* to other people. It was as if he heard voices more loudly, perceived movements to be bigger and faster, and felt every single handshake and hug more intensely. Some people — too many of them — were simply too *much* for him.

For one year, in ninth grade, his school placed him on a "special" education track, suspecting that he suffered from some form of "autism-related disorder," despite the absence of an official diagnosis. He remained in regular classes and still dominated the grading curves. But the teachers treated him differently. They stood a little farther from him, spoke more slowly. He had been labeled.

On the last day of school, he told his parents that he would run away unless he could start tenth grade in a new school. No special treatment, no labels. Because although Dwight was different from other people, he'd read enough books about autism, Asperger's, ADD, and ADHD to know that those labels didn't apply to him. Each of those conditions was supposedly accompanied by a lack of emotional connection. Dwight, in his view, was the opposite. He had the ability to feel so connected to a person that the sensation was overwhelming.

Take today's reunion with Nicole, for

example. He had forced himself to sit still in his seat across from her, to not touch her. He had a hard time maintaining eye contact because to hold her gaze too long would have brought him to tears. She was a living, breathing, vivid memory of Susan. He couldn't look at her without remembering the searing pain he had felt at Susan's kindhearted attempts to play matchmaker between him and Nicole. How could Susan have been blind to the fact that he loved her?

He hit the space bar of his computer's keyboard to wake up the screen. Every once in a while, misperceptions about him came in handy. Right now, for instance, the physical separation between him and his employees would ensure that nothing interrupted his activities.

He opened the Internet browser and Googled "Cinderella Murder Susan Dempsey." He suppressed a bite of anger at the fact that even *he* used Google most of the time as his search engine. REACH was a pioneer in changing the way people searched for information on the Internet. But then Google came along, extended the idea a step or two, and added some cool graphics and a name that was fun to say. The rest was high-tech history.

Still, Dwight couldn't complain about his success. He'd made enough money to live comfortably for ten lifetimes.

He clicked through the search results. He found nothing new since the last time — probably a year ago — that he had checked for any developments about his friend's unsolved murder.

He remembered sitting at his computer twenty years earlier, knowing that he was probably among the top twenty people in the world when it came to maneuvering his way around the quickly changing online world. Back then, people still used telephones and in-person conversations to convey information. The police department produced hard copies of reports and faxed them to prosecutors. He had wanted to know the truth about the investigation into Susan's death so desperately — who knew what? What did the police know? — but his skills could only get him so far at the time. The information simply wasn't digitized.

Now every private thought had a way of casting a technological footprint that he could track. But he was the founder, chairman, and CEO of a Fortune 500 company, and hacking into private servers and e-mail accounts was a serious crime.

He closed his eyes and pictured Susan.

How many times had he sat outside her dorm, hoping to catch a glimpse of her as she led an entirely separate life from the one they had together at the lab? This television show would be a onetime opportunity — every suspect on camera, questioned anew. Frank Parker, the man who seemed to care more about the success of his movie than Susan's death. Madison Meyer, who always seemed resentful of Nicole and Susan. Keith Ratner, who never realized how lucky he was to have a girl like Susan.

Being on this television show would be a small price to pay. He would know far more than even the show's producers. Dwight spun his office chair in a circle and cracked his knuckles.

It was time to get to work.

Laurie checked the time on her computer screen once again. Two forty-five P.M. Surely Brett Young was back from lunch by now. She had called him yesterday from Los Angeles and left a voice mail with an update. This morning, she had e-mailed him a more complete summary of the Susan Dempsey case. Still no response.

She closed her office door and allowed herself to kick off her pumps and lie down on the white sofa beneath her windows. Flying out to Los Angeles, just to catch Madison Meyer unguarded, had taken its toll. The coast-to-coast red-eye was unbearable, but not so much as being away from Timmy any longer than necessary. She was feeling the sleep deprivation now. She shut her eyes and took a deep breath. She just needed a little rest.

Before she knew it, she was no longer in her office above Rockefeller Center. She was in another place, in a different time. She recognized the playground on Fifteenth Street, back when they still lived downtown.

Timmy is so tiny, only three years old. His legs are straight in front of him, like pins, as he squeals from the swing. "Whheeeee! Higher, Daddy, higher!"

She knows precisely what day this is. She knows what will happen next, even though she was not there to see it with her own eyes. She has replayed this scene countless times.

As Greg pushes his son once more on the swing, he lets out a grunt, feigning physical exertion, even as he is careful not to let his toddler sail too high. As an emergency room doctor, he has seen more than his fair share of children injured during overly exuberant play. "This is the last one," he announces. "Time to go home and see Mommy. One-minute warning."

"Doctor!" a voice calls out.

In the last of countless selfless demonstrations of his love for his son, Greg sees the gun and steps away from Timmy in an attempt to pull this stranger's attention from the boy.

A gunshot.

"DADDY!!!"

Laurie bolted upright at the sound of her son's scream.

Grace was staring at her from the doorway, her hand still on the office doorknob.

"I'm sorry. I didn't mean to surprise you. I knocked but you didn't answer."

"It's okay," Laurie assured her, even though she knew she wasn't really okay. Would the nightmares ever end? "I must have dozed off. That red-eye was a killer." She felt a pang in her chest as the last word left her mouth.

"Really? I slept the whole way and feel fine," she said.

Laurie resisted the temptation to throw a pillow at Grace's sky-high upsweep. "And that's the difference between being twenty-six and thirty-seven. Anyway, what's up?"

"Brett called. He wants to see you in his office."

Laurie ran her fingers through her hair. Nothing like seeing your boss for an important meeting straight from a nap.

"You look fine," Grace said. "Good luck, Laurie. I know how much you want this."

17

Brett's secretary, Jennifer, waved Laurie past her guard station into the inner sanctum. But when Laurie opened Brett's office door, she didn't find Brett alone. A second man was in one of his guest chairs, his back to the door.

"Excellent timing," Brett declared, rising from his desk. "Look who we have here."

The second man also stood, and then turned to greet her. It was Alex Buckley. A former college basketball player, he rose at least four inches taller than Brett. She hadn't seen him for at least a month, but he was as gorgeous as she remembered. No wonder juries and television cameras loved him. She took in his dark, wavy hair; firm chin; and blue-green eyes behind black-rimmed glasses. Everything about his appearance made him seem strong and trustworthy.

She was glad that Brett was now positioned behind Alex so her boss could not see the way Alex was looking at her. It was the way he always looked at her when she walked into a room. Though he was clearly happy to see her, there was a tinge of sadness — almost longing — in his eyes. That look made her feel like she needed to apologize — both to Greg for somehow making another man feel that way about her, and to Alex for not being able to return the feelings he so obviously had for her (at least, not yet).

She looked away before either Alex or Brett could sense her thoughts. "What a nice surprise," she said with a smile. She held out her hand for a shake, and he leaned in for a quick hug.

She pulled her pencil skirt to her knees before taking the unoccupied chair across from Brett's desk.

"I know I've kept you on pins and needles all day, Laurie. But I wanted to make sure I had all the facts on your pitch for the Cinderella Murder. Your summary was helpful. But it also made it clear that your budget's going to skyrocket."

"Our costs are low compared to what we can bring in in ad revenue —"

Brett held up a palm to silence her. "I don't need you to explain the economics of television to me. You're planning to interview people who are sprawled all over the state of California, one of the most expensive places to film, by the way. Not to mention that last-minute trip you already made yesterday, just to get Madison Meyer on board."

She opened her mouth to speak, but up went his palm again.

"I get it. The trick worked, so good job. My point is that this isn't like talking to a dead guy's wife, mistress, and business partner, who all live in Westchester. You're going to be hopping from UCLA to the Hollywood Hills to Silicon Valley to who knows where. You're not going to keep some guy like Frank Parker on board if you're shooting from some dingy hotel conference room with tuna fish sandwiches from room service. You'll need a nice place to film, complete with the kinds of luxuries the Hollywood crowd is used to. You're going to be spending some serious dough."

This time, he held up the palm before she even got her mouth open.

"And that's why I wanted to talk to Alex. Every critic, every focus group said his hosting was the key to our first special."

"I understand that, Brett. But Alex has a law practice to run. He might not have that kind of time."

"The *he* you're speaking about in the third person," Brett said impatiently, "is sitting right next to you, and — great news! — he already agreed."

Alex cleared his throat. "Well, yes. But *he* was told that you specifically asked for me."

Typical Brett. Anything to get what he wanted.

"It's perfect timing," Brett announced. "He was just explaining that he had a major case that was supposed to be a one-month trial suddenly disappear. How did you explain it again?"

She could tell that Alex wanted to speak to her privately, but there was no way to extract themselves from Brett's office. "I convinced the prosecutor my guy had a legitimate alibi. I found security camera footage placing him in the VIP lounge at a club in Chelsea when he was supposedly shooting a rival gang member in Brooklyn. Not to mention the cell phone pings that placed their supposed eyewitness on the Lower East Side when the crime was happening."

"There you have it," Brett said, slapping his desk for emphasis. "No wonder this guy gets the big bucks. I can't *wait* to see him lay into Frank Parker. I'm hoping he's the one who did it. I can already see the ratings. You could end up with a Pulitzer!"

Laurie was pretty sure that no one gave Pulitzer Prizes to reality television shows.

Alex started to rise from his chair again. "I think I should let you two talk about this. If Laurie would prefer someone else —"

"Don't be ridiculous," Brett said, waving Alex back into his chair. "Laurie's *thrilled.*"

"Of course," she added. "I'm absolutely thrilled."

And she was. He truly was a skilled interrogator. She knew her father would be happy too, for his own reasons. He was always trying to get her to spend more time with Alex.

"Very good then," Brett said. "Now, take the rest of the day off to celebrate the good news while Alex and I continue with our March Madness talk. We were having a heated debate about who'll make the Final Four. And, no offense, but you might want to brush your hair or something. That trip out to Los Angeles took a toll on you."

Right. No offense.

18

Steve Roman knew that Martin preferred to receive any bad news quickly, the proverbial bandage being pulled from the wound. After parking his pickup truck at the discount monthly parking space he paid for south of Market, he pulled up AG's number.

"Yes?" That high-pitched yet assertive voice.

"Nothing essential to report," Steve began. Yesterday's check-in had been easy: the target had left the house only for trips to Costco, a fish market, and a strip mall for something called Pilates. Now he had to keep Martin calm. "But she did hit the road, a straight shot from her home to a company in Palo Alto. Something called REACH. It looks . . . I don't know, modern."

"It's a computer company," Martin said. "Good to know. Keep watching her."

Steve felt a churning heat working its way up from his stomach. "Before, when you called me, you said something about sending a message? When the time was right. Is that something I should be doing now?" No, Steve thought to himself, please don't make me hurt anyone. I might not be able to stop.

"Nothing yet. Just watch her. And, as you did today, tell me where she goes. And, this is important — find out to whom she speaks."

Steve was always impressed by Martin's proper grammar. He swallowed, knowing how much Martin despised being questioned. For every loyal follower, the church seemed to have ten critics doubting AG's mission of advocating for God's goodness through service to the poor. While Steve had been so inspired by AG, cynics assumed the worst about the church's fund-raising efforts. As a result of all the scrutiny, Martin could be secretive. And just as *he* had fully devoted himself to the word of God, Martin expected his followers to devote themselves to him.

"Is she someone I should be worried about?" Steve finally asked. He had practiced the wording of his query.

"No," Martin said definitively. "She was — in the past. Just between me and you . . ."

Steve now felt a different kind of warmth encompassing him. Martin was letting him further into the AG circle.

"Between me and you," Martin continued, "I was younger then. I trusted Nicole too quickly, before I should have. But now she's an impediment to our advocacy of God's goodness, to say the least."

"Got it," Steve said.

It wasn't a complete explanation for why he was driving all over the Bay Area, but it was more knowledge than he had before. Steve merged onto I-280, reinvigorated.

19

Laurie was just packing up her briefcase when she heard a triple tap on her office door, followed by the appearance of Grace's head.

"Do you have time for a visitor?" Grace's voice was tremulous as she asked the question.

A visitor was the last thing Laurie needed. Though she could have done without Brett's comment about her appearance, her boss had a point when he suggested that she leave early. She'd been working nonstop since Rosemary Dempsey agreed to participate in the show. All she needed to do today was call Rosemary to tell her the good news about the studio's official approval, and then she was hoping to get home in time to greet Timmy when he and Dad got home from school.

"I'm sorry, Grace. Do I have an appointment I forgot about?"

She heard a man's voice behind Grace. "I can come back another time."

Alex.

"Of course." Trying to keep her tone even, Laurie said, "Please, come in, Alex."

When Alex safely passed Grace to enter the office, Grace batted her eyelashes and pretended to fan her face with her hands. It was her *What a hunk* expression, and she made it a lot around Alex Buckley. During the filming of the first installment of *Under Suspicion,* when Blue Eyes had been killed by a policeman before he was able to kill Laurie, Alex had run immediately to her and Timmy and swept them into his arms. Grace and everyone else may have seen the moment as a brave man's natural reaction to a dangerous situation, but Laurie had felt his desire to connect to her, like heat from a lightbulb, ever since.

She waited for Grace to close the office door before speaking. "I swear, Grace's IQ drops fifteen points when you're around."

"If only I could replicate that effect with jurors."

She gestured for him to sit in the gray swivel chair facing the windows and then positioned herself on the sofa across from him. "How have you been?" she asked.

"Good. Busy. I've tried calling a couple of times."

She nodded and smiled. "I'm sorry. Time gets away from me. Between work and Timmy . . ." Her voice trailed off. "You wouldn't believe this kid's activities. I feel like I need an appointment to see my own son. He's taking karate lessons now. Plus, of course, soccer. And now he says he wants to take up the trumpet, ever since he accompanied his grandpa to a police benevolent association party and saw a brass band in action. Now Dad has him watching YouTube videos of Louis Armstrong, Miles Davis, Wynton Marsalis, and Dizzy Gillespie. Timmy just stares at the screen, mimics the movements with his hands, and puffs out his cheeks like a blowfish. Who knew there was such thing as air trumpet?"

She was rambling, and they both knew it.

"Leo told me about the trumpet obsession. Rangers game last week."

"Right, of course."

Her father had reminded her afterward to return the messages Alex had left her about trying to get together for dinner.

"So," he said, clasping his hands together, "that Brett Young's a little crafty, isn't he? He told me before you came into the office that you were the one saying the Susan

124

Dempsey case would only work if I agreed to be the host."

" 'Crafty' is a word that suits him well. But, to his credit, you *are* the right person for the job. I don't think Frank Parker will exactly be forthcoming."

"I saw your expression when you saw me in Brett's office. He sprang this on you. The last thing I want is to be around if you don't want me there."

"No, I —" She forced herself to slow down and choose her words carefully. "I had been waiting to hear from Brett all day. So if I looked surprised when I walked in, it was only because I expected to find him alone. But of course I'm delighted you're available. I care about this case. Susan Dempsey was only nineteen years old when she was murdered. And now her mother has gone twenty years without any resolution. Can you imagine what that must be like for her? Her only child? Two full decades?"

It would be an even bigger hell than the five years Laurie had experienced without knowing who killed her husband. The loss of a child would devastate her.

"How can you do it, Laurie?" Alex asked. "You are drawn to these horrible, haunting stories. Aren't you ever tempted to — I don't know — produce a fluffy show about dating or models?"

"I guess some women know romance and fashion. I know people like Rosemary Dempsey." She gave him a sad smile. "I honestly feel like this show can help people, Alex. Sometimes I wonder what would have happened if —" She stopped herself from completing the thought.

"If someone had done for you what *Under Suspicion* has done for others."

She nodded.

"And you're really okay with me helping?"

"I want you to," she said. For Rosemary, she thought to herself. She had originally asked for Alex as a host for the launch of *Under Suspicion* because of his uncanny ability to get witnesses in the courtroom to blurt out information they had vowed to keep secret. He was a present-day Perry Mason, but much better looking.

"Then I'll do it. Tell me what I need to know."

Susan could have handed him the files and gone home. Instead, she gave him the rundown on every person she'd lined up for the show and answered his follow-up questions the best she could. How certain were police about the time of Susan's death? Could anyone confirm Frank Parker's whereabouts besides Madison Meyer? How solid was Keith Ratner's alibi?

She was impressed all over again by the laserlike precision of his questions. It was this kind of interaction that had led to the attraction between them in the first place when they reinvestigated the case of "The Graduation Gala."

Without the show to work on together, they had fallen into a comfort zone where they might share an occasional meal, or Alex might take her family to sports events. But now he'd be back in her life on a daily basis, and together they'd pore over motivations like love, envy, and rage.

She took a deep breath to keep her thoughts from racing forward. "Well, now that it's all official, it's time to get ready for pre-production. I think I blacked out how much work it is. How did Brett get you to sign on again?"

"You know Brett. His main focus was explaining why I was so much better than anyone he could possibly imagine. The man must think the way to my heart is through my ego."

"We were successful enough last time that the studio has upped my budget. The aesthetics of the show will be a little better, but I've put most of the money into information gathering. Instead of putting each person in front of a camera, we're doing more research beforehand. We're trying to do preliminary interviews with everyone, mostly off-camera. Hopefully the process will get them comfortable. Maybe even produce leads."

"The way lawyers sometimes use depositions. Do your fishing expedition outside of the courtroom. Go in for the kill in front of the jury."

She smiled, flattered, and then looked at her watch. "I've got to get home to Timmy. And as Brett said, that red-eye took its toll on me. I feel like a wreck."

"Well, you don't look it."

She forced herself to break eye contact and then rose from the sofa to walk him out. Her focus right now was on her family and on telling Susan Dempsey's story. There was no room for anything — or anyone — else. Not yet.

20

"What are you going to have?" Lydia asked, perusing the menu. "Probably something healthy, I bet. I still can't get over that wholesome selection of groceries you brought home the other day."

Rosemary wished her neighbor hadn't brought up the contents of her shopping bags. It reminded her how annoyed she had been at the woman's nosiness. She pushed away the moment of irritation and reminded herself why she was having lunch with Lydia in the first place: because she was a neighbor, and her act of assistance that day had been generous, and Rosemary had not made any new friends since she had moved to Castle Crossings nearly a year and a half ago.

Rosemary's first attempt to return the gesture had come yesterday morning, when she'd brought Lydia a jar of jelly beans, which she had mentioned as her favorite vice. Now they were having their first real outing together, a lunch at Rustic Tavern. It was a gorgeous day, so they had agreed on a quiet table on the restaurant's garden patio.

"I'm not nearly as virtuous as my groceries would suggest," Rosemary said, closing her menu. "And to prove it, I'll have a bacon cheeseburger with french fries."

"Oh, that sounds delicious. I'm doing it, too. And a salad to start, just so we can say we ate a vegetable?"

"Sounds like a plan."

They had finished their salads and ordered refills on their glasses of cabernet when Rosemary asked Lydia how she had ended up living in their shared neighborhood.

"Don was the one who wanted the extra security," she explained. "It seemed weird to me, since the kids were out of the house by then. But we take the grandkids one weekend a month, and you see all these horrible stories about kids snatched when the adults aren't watching. Oh, Rosemary, I'm so sorry. I didn't mean —"

Rosemary shook her head. "No, please, go on."

"Anyway, Don said it would be safer for the kids in a gated community. Like he says, he can't crack heads like he used to."

Rosemary was silent, wondering if she'd misheard, but Lydia obviously saw the confusion register on her face.

"Right, no reason why that would make any sense to you. Don — that's my husband — his background is in security management. The hands-on variety. He ran body service, as they call it, for all kinds of professional athletes and musicians. That's how we met."

"You had a secret life as a professional athlete?"

"Oh, no. Sorry. My kids tell me all the time, I'm a horrible storyteller. I'm not *linear*, is what they say. *Drip, drip, drip with the information*, according to them. No, I met Don in 1968 when we were still young'ns. Well, he was a young'n: only twenty years old, working security on Jimmy O'Hare's first world tour." Rosemary vaguely recalled the name as that of a southern rock singer from around that era. "I was twenty-five but lied and told everyone I was twenty-one. Musicians back then didn't like us much older than that."

"So you were a — backup singer or something?"

"Oh, gosh no. I can't carry a note to save my life. We had a karaoke contest at the home association party a few years ago, and my friends threatened to evict me from Castle Crossings if I ever sang in front of them again. Trust me, you don't want to hear me sing. No, I lied about my age because I was a road companion. A *groupie* is the more common vernacular."

Rosemary nearly spit out her wine across the table. Never judge a book by its cover, especially when the book is a person, was the lesson.

The ice — and Rosemary's expectations — fully broken, their conversation fell into an easy rhythm. They had lived very different lives but found unpredictable parallels between Lydia's life on the road and young Rosemary's own adventure of leaving Wisconsin for California.

"And how did you decide to move across the street?" Lydia asked. "You didn't want to stay in your old house?"

Rosemary found herself picking at her french fries.

"I'm sorry. Did I say something wrong again?"

"No, of course not. It's just — well, the answer is complicated. I raised Susan in that house. I mourned her there. I lived more years in that house with Jack than anywhere or with anyone else. But when he passed, the place was just too big for me to live in alone. It was hard to walk away from all those memories, but it was time."

"Oh, Rosemary. I didn't mean to bring up something so upsetting."

"It's okay. Really."

Lydia reached over and patted her wrist. The moment was interrupted by the buzz of Rosemary's phone against the table.

"Sorry," she said, inspecting the screen. "I need to take this."

"Rosemary," the voice on the phone said, "it's Laurie Moran. I have good news."

Rosemary was muttering the requisite acknowledgments — "Yes, I see, uh-huh" — but was having a hard time ignoring Lydia's expectant looks.

When she finally hung up, Lydia said, "Whatever that was about, you seemed very happy about it."

"Yes, you could say that. That was a television producer in New York. The show *Under Suspicion* has picked my daughter's case for their next feature. The producer can't make any promises, but I have to pray that something new comes out of this. It's been twenty years."

"I can't imagine."

Rosemary realized that it was the first time she had spoken about Susan to anyone who hadn't known her or been investigating her death. She had officially made a new friend.

21

Dwight Cook wished he could gut the interior of REACH's headquarters and start over. The design concept had sounded great when the architect first pitched it. The three-level building had plenty of open space, some of it with forty-foot ceilings, but was also filled with nooks and brightly painted crannies with couches and bistro tables for people to gather in small groups. The idea, according to the architect, was to create the illusion of one large, continuous, "mazelike" space.

Well, the maze effect had worked.

Was it only he who craved monochromatic symmetry?

He blocked out all the horrible visual distractions and thought about the work that was taking place within these ridiculously shaped walls. REACH had been around for nearly twenty years and still managed to hire some of the brightest, most innovative tech workers in the country.

He reached the end of the hall and turned right toward Hathaway's office. His former professor had been at REACH from the beginning in every possible way. But regardless of their work together, he would always think of Hathaway as his professor, the man responsible for building REACH into an empire.

Hathaway's door was open, as was the norm in REACH's "corporate culture."

Richard Hathaway was well into his fifties by now but still looked essentially the same as when UCLA coeds had dubbed him the school's "most crush-worthy" teacher. He was of average height with an athletic build. He had thick, wavy brown hair and a year-round tan, and always dressed like he was about to tee off at a golf course. As Dwight approached, he could see that Hathaway was reading a magazine article called "Work Out Smarter, Not Longer."

Dwight took a seat across from Hathaway, unsure how to raise the subject that brought him there. He decided to ease into it, the way he had noticed people did when they were trying to avoid a topic. "Sometimes when I walk around the building, it reminds me of your lab back at UCLA."

"Except we were working with computers

the size of economy cars. And the furniture wasn't as nice, either." Hathaway was always quick with a good line. How many times had he saved the day by "tagging along" to a meeting with a potential investor? Dwight had surpassed Hathaway in programming talent, but without Hathaway, Dwight would have always worked for someone else.

"The walls were straight, though," Dwight said, making his own attempt at the same kind of humor.

Hathaway smiled, but Dwight could tell that his self-deprecating one-liner had fallen flat.

"What I meant," Dwight continued, "was that we have all these kids — smart, idealistic, probably a little weird." Now Hathaway laughed. "They all believe they can change the world with the right piece of code. I remember your lab feeling like that."

"You sound like a proud parent."

"Yes, I suppose I am proud." Dwight tried so hard not to feel his emotions that he had never learned to describe them.

"It's fine to be proud," Hathaway said, "but REACH has investors with expectations. It would be nice to be relevant again."

"We're more than relevant, Hathaway." Dwight had called him "Dr. Hathaway" long after they both left UCLA. Despite the professor's insistence that Dwight refer to him as Richard, Dwight just couldn't do it. "Hathaway" had been the compromise.

"I mean front-page-of-the-*Journal* relevant. Our stock price is holding steady, Dwight, but others' are going up."

Even as a professor, Hathaway was never the tweed-jacket-and-practical-shoes type. He made it clear to his students that technology could not only help people and change the world, it could also make you rich. The first time an investment banker wrote them a seven-figure check, enabling REACH to set up shop in Palo Alto, Hathaway had gone directly to the car dealer for a new Maserati.

"But you're not here to relive the old days," Hathaway said.

Dwight trusted Hathaway. They'd had a special connection from the moment Hathaway had asked Dwight, after freshman midterms, to work in the lab. Dwight had always felt like his own father was trying to either change him or avoid him. But Hathaway had all the same interests as Dwight and never tried to tell him to act like anyone other than himself. When they worked together, combining Dwight's code-writing skills with Hathaway's business savvy, it was a perfect match.

So why couldn't he tell his friend and mentor of twenty years that he was hacking the e-mail accounts of everyone who might be connected to Susan's murder?

Oh, how desperately he wanted to tell him what he'd learned. He knew, for example, that Frank Parker's wife, Talia, wrote her sister to say she was "dead set against Frank ever speaking that girl's name again." Was Talia opposed to the show because she suspected her husband was involved?

And then there was Madison Meyer's e-mail to her agent, insisting that once she was in a room alone with Frank Parker again, she was "sure to land a true *comeback* role." That one definitely made it sound like Madison had something to hang over Frank's head.

And yet, Dwight could not bring himself to tell Hathaway what he'd been up to. He knew Hathaway would worry about the corporate implications if Dwight were caught hacking into private accounts. No one would ever trust REACH with information again. Their stock price would plummet. This would have to be one secret he kept from his oldest friend.

But Hathaway was looking at him expectantly. "What's up, Dwight?"

"I think I actually forgot. That walk down

the maze must have made me dizzy." He was pleased when Hathaway smiled. The line had worked.

"I do that all the time," Hathaway said. "But, hey, since you're here: I got a call from a Laurie Moran? A TV special about Susan Dempsey? They said you gave them my name. I thought everyone sort of knew Frank Parker did it but the police could never prove it."

Dwight wanted to scream, *But I might be able to!* Instead, he said, "I just want people to know that Susan was more than her headshot. She wasn't some wannabe actress. She was . . . truly phenomenal." Dwight heard his own voice crack like a middle schooler's. Once he was on camera, would everyone watching know how obsessed he had been with his fellow lab assistant? "And, let's face it," he added, "you'd be better on TV than me."

"Are you sure this is a good idea? They'll be asking about the work in the lab. You know I don't like anything that calls attention to how this company got launched."

It had been nearly twenty years since they started REACH. Sometimes Dwight actually forgot how the idea had originated, but Hathaway never did.

"It won't be like that," Dwight insisted.

"Shows don't get ratings by delving into the details of web-search optimization. They just want to hear about Susan."

"Very well, then. If you're in, I'm in."

As Dwight returned to REACH's colorful labyrinth, he felt completely alone. He couldn't remember any time when he'd kept information from Hathaway. But he realized the real reason he had not shared his activities with his professor. He didn't want Hathaway to be disappointed in him.

He had to find out more, though. The reason I want to do the show, he thought, is because once I have physical proximity to the others, I can clone their phones and finally prove who killed Susan. But, no, he couldn't say any of that.

He had to do this. For Susan.

22

Without the rearview camera on the dash of her Volvo, Rosemary Dempsey might have clipped the edge of the newspaper recycling bin that had been thrown a bit too haphazardly to her curb after weekly pickup.

She loved the new technology that surrounded her every day, but it always made her wonder what Susan and Jack would have said about it.

As she shifted out of reverse, she caught sight of Lydia in her peripheral vision, watering her hydrangeas with a gardening hose. She wore bright orange rubber shoes and matching gloves, one of which waved in Susan's direction. Rosemary returned the wave and added a friendly beep of the car horn. She made it a point to watch her speedometer as she rolled down the street. Knowing Lydia, any excessive speed could threaten their budding friendship.

Rosemary smiled as she navigated the

turns through Castle Crossings, trying to imagine Lydia Levitt forty years ago, with bell-bottoms and platform shoes instead of gardening gear.

She was still smiling when the GPS told her that her destination was on the right. The navigation system's estimate of the drive time had been nearly perfect: forty-two minutes to San Anselmo.

As Rosemary passed driveways filled with Porsches, Mercedes, even a Bentley, she started to wonder if her Volvo would be the worst car on the block. She saw one cream-colored pickup truck two houses down from Nicole's, in front of a McMansion that overfilled its lot, but that car obviously belonged to a landscaper.

"You have arrived at your destination," her car announced.

Rosemary had been to Nicole's home before but still took a moment to register its beauty. A perfectly restored five-bedroom Tudor in San Anselmo with sweeping views of Ross Valley, it was, in Rosemary's view, far too large for a couple with no children. But as Rosemary understood it, Nicole's husband, Gavin, could afford it, plus he frequently worked at home rather than commute to San Francisco's financial district.

The forty-minute drive was a small price to pay to deliver this news in person.

Nicole greeted her at the door before she had a chance to ring the bell. She gave Rosemary a quick hug before saying, "Is everything okay? You were so secretive on the phone."

"Everything is just fine. I didn't mean to alarm you." Rosemary was so aware of her own loss as a mother, sometimes she forgot how Susan's death must have affected others. When one of your best friends dies when you are only a teenager, do you spend the rest of your life on high alert?

"Oh, thank goodness," Nicole said. "Come on in. Can I get you anything?"

The house was silent.

"Is Gavin home?" Rosemary asked.

"No, he has a dinner meeting with clients tonight, so he's working at the office today."

Rosemary had grown up one of five children and had always wanted to have a large family. But it was more than ten years before joyfully, happily, Susan had come along.

She was a social bee, always attracting the neighbor kids and then her schoolmates. Even when she'd gone to college, the house wasn't silent. It still somehow buzzed from her energy — her phone calls, miscellaneous pieces of laundry left strewn around the house, her CDs blasting from the stereo when Rosemary flipped the switch.

Rosemary had never asked Nicole why she and Gavin had opted for a silent house, but she couldn't help but feel sorry for them over the choice.

She followed Nicole into a den lined floor-to-ceiling with books. One wall was dominated by business books and historical nonfiction. The other wall popped with every kind of novel — romance, suspense, sci-fi, what some people called more "literary" fare. She felt a pang as she remembered Susan's calling her from UCLA two days after the big move: "You'd love my roommate. She has amazing taste in books." The novels had to be Nicole's.

Once they were seated, Nicole looked at her expectantly.

"So you haven't heard yet?" Rosemary asked.

"No," Nicole said. "At least, I don't think so. I have no idea what you're talking about, and the anticipation is going to give me a premature heart attack."

"It's really happening. Laurie Moran called me. The head of the studio approved Susan's case as *Under Suspicion*'s next feature. And everyone has signed on: me, you, Madison, Frank Parker, and — color me shocked — Keith Ratner. She even got people who knew Susan from the computer lab."

"That is wonderful news," Nicole said, reaching over and briefly clasping Rosemary's hands in hers.

"Yes, I think so, too. I feel like I pressured you into it, so I wanted to thank you personally."

"No, no pressure at all. I couldn't be happier."

Rosemary had been on an emotional roller coaster ever since she opened Laurie Moran's letter, but she still felt like Nicole was responding strangely.

"Laurie said they'll do pre-production interviews with all of us. No cameras, for the most part. Just hearing our side of things so they know what to ask us once they yell 'action.' "

"Sure, no problem."

Did Rosemary imagine it, or had Nicole's eyes just moved toward the staircase of her empty house? "You're happy about this, aren't you, Nicole? I mean, you and Madison were the only people my daughter ever lived with besides her parents. And, well, Madison was always sort of the add-on. Whether you wanted to be or not, you were the closest thing to a sister that Susan ever knew."

Whatever distance Rosemary sensed in Nicole immediately vanished as her eyes began to water. "And for me, too. She was my friend, and she was . . . amazing. I promise you, Rosemary. I will help. Me, you, this show. If there's any way to find out what happened to Susan, we're going to do it."

Now Rosemary was crying, too, but she smiled through the tears. "We'll show Frank Parker and Keith Ratner what a couple of determined women can do. It has to be one of them, right?"

When Rosemary was ready to leave, Nicole led the way to the front door, and then wrapped her arm around Rosemary's shoulder as she escorted her down the steep walkway from her front porch to the street.

Rosemary paused to take in the breathtaking view of the valley, all green trees backed by blue hills. "I don't know whether I've ever told you this, Nicole, but I was so worried about you when you decided to leave school. I wondered whether you were, in some way, another victim of what happened to Susan. I'm so happy that things have worked out well for you."

Nicole gave her a big hug and then patted

147

her on the back. "You drive safe, okay? We have big things to look forward to."

As Rosemary climbed into the driver's seat, strapped on her seat belt, and pulled away from the curb, neither woman noticed the person watching them from the cream-colored pickup truck, two houses down.

The truck pulled away from the curb and followed Rosemary south.

23

Martin Collins worked his way down the aisles of his megachurch, conveniently located right off I-110 in the heart of South Los Angeles, shaking hands and offering quick hellos and blessings. He had delivered a rousing sermon to a packed house of four thousand, on their feet, their hands raised to God — and to him. Most could barely make rent or put food on the table, but he saw bills flying when the baskets were passed.

The early days of recruiting new members in tattoo parlors, bike shops, and sketchy bars and painstakingly converting them, reinventing them, were long over.

To see thousands of worshippers enthralled by his every word was exhilarating, but he enjoyed this moment — after the sermons, after the crowd dwindled — even more. This was his chance to speak in person to the church members who were so devoted to him personally that they would wait, sometimes hours, to shake his hand.

He circled back around to the front of the church, saving for last a woman who waited in the front pew. Her name was Shelly. She had first arrived here eighteen months ago, a walk-in who had found a flyer for Advocates for God in the bus station. She was a single mother. Her daughter, Amanda, sat next to her, twelve years old with milky skin and light brown eyes fit for an angel.

Martin reached out to hug Shelly. She rose from the pew and clung to him. "Thank you so much for your words of worship," she said. "And for the apartment," she whispered. "We finally have a home of our own."

Martin barely listened to Shelly's words. Sweet little Amanda was looking up at him in awe.

Martin had found a way to bring substantial funds into Advocates for God. Because they were now a government-recognized religion, donations were tax-free. And the dollar bills thrown from wallets in a post-sermon fervor were nothing compared to the big money. Martin had mastered a feel-good blend of religious and charitable language that was like a magic recipe for scoring high-dollar philanthropic contributions. He'd found a way to make religion cool, even in Hollywood. Not to mention the huge federal grants he landed with the help of a few like-minded congressmen.

The money allowed the group to back its mission of advocating God's goodness by helping the poor, including supporting members who needed a safety net. Shelly had whispered her gratitude for a reason. Martin could not provide a roof for every struggling follower — just the special ones, like Shelly and Amanda.

"Still no contact with your sister?" Martin confirmed.

"Absolutely none."

It had been two months since Martin had convinced Shelly that her sister — the last member of her biological family with whom she had contact, the one who told her she was spending too much time at this new church — was preventing her from having a personal relationship with God.

"And how about you?" he asked little Amanda. "Are you are enjoying the toys we sent over?"

The child nodded shyly, then smiled. Oh, how he loved that expression — filled with trust and joy. "Can I get a hug from you, too?" Another nod, followed by a hug. She was still nervous with him. That was okay.

These things took time. Now that she and her mother were in an apartment that he paid for, he would increase the amount of time he spent with both mother and daughter.

Martin knew how to lure people in. He had been a psychology major in college. One course had an entire section of the syllabus devoted to battered woman syndrome: the isolation, the power and control, the belief that the batterer is all-powerful and all-knowing.

Martin had earned an A+ on that part of the course. He didn't need the textbooks and expert explanations. He had seen those characteristics in his own mother, so incapable of stopping his father from hurting her . . . and young Martin. He had understood the connection between fear and dependency so well that at the age of ten, he had vowed that when he was older, he would be the controller. He would never *be* controlled.

And then one day he was flipping channels in the middle of the night and saw a minister of a megachurch on television, a 900 number scrolling at the bottom of the screen for donations. He made everything sound so black-and-white. Ignore the word of the Lord and burn, or listen — and donate money — to the nice-looking man on the television and earn a place with God. Talk about power.

He started watching that preacher every night, practicing the words and the cadence. He researched the IRS rules for religions. He learned about faith-based grants, which allowed churches to get government money by administering charitable programs. He whitened his teeth, joined a tanning center, and printed glossy brochures promising people closeness to God by helping the poor.

The only problem had been the police. They didn't have any proof yet, but Martin's predilections had come to the attention of Nebraska law enforcement, and he was tired of their slowing down when they passed his house or saw him near a playground. Off he went to Southern California, filled with lots of sunshine, money, and people searching for a way to feel good about themselves. Advocates for God was born.

And though he clothed himself in religiosity, he knew that the keys to his power had been learned in his own household, watching the way his father controlled his mother.

Ingredient number one: fear. This part was easy. Martin didn't have to hurt anyone. A nondenominational yet fervently religious church like Advocates for God tended to attract people who were already afraid of the world as they knew it. They wanted easy answers, and he would happily oblige.

Number two: power and control. Martin was the "supreme" Advocate for God, a direct vessel for the voice of God. He, in short, was their god. When he spoke, they listened. That aspect of the church had earned AG more than its share of detractors, but Martin didn't need everyone in the world to believe. He had sixteen thousand church members and counting, and a track record of raising more than four hundred dollars per year per follower. The math worked.

Number three: isolation. No friends, family members, or other people to interfere with AG's hold. Early on, this had been Martin's biggest challenge, and he had learned his lesson with Nicole. Now he was more selective, forcing church members to earn their way into AG's inner circle with years of loyalty. Until they knew too much about AG's finances, he could afford to let people walk away.

His cell phone buzzed in his front pocket. He retrieved it and looked at the screen. It was Steve reporting from up north.

"I have to get this," he explained to Shelly. "But I'll check in on you tomorrow."

"That would be nice," the woman said, giving him another hug. Martin patted little Amanda on the head. Her hair was soft and warm. If he timed his visit right the next day, she would be home from school, before Shelly left the janitorial job he had found for her at an office building.

He answered as he made his way to the room's rear exit. "Yes?"

"Nicole had a visitor to her house today, the first in the time I've been watching. A woman, must have been seventysomething, driving a Volvo. I followed her to a neighborhood called Castle Crossings, outside of Oakland. Looks pretty nice. Maybe it's her mother?"

"No, her mother died in Irvine a few years ago." Martin slipped through a fire door into the stairwell for privacy. "Did you get a name?"

"Not yet. It's a gated community. Not to worry — Keepsafe has plenty of alarms here, so I can get past the entrance. I know the car and the license plate. I'll find her house tomorrow and get an ID."

Sometimes Martin thought about how easy it would be to collect dirt on his potential enemies if he had a police officer or two in his inner circle. A cop could run the plate in seconds. But cops weren't wired to succumb to Martin's formula. He had considered simply bribing someone to be on his payroll, but he figured any cop who would take a bribe would sell him out in a heartbeat.

Once *Under Suspicion* started filming, Martin could rely on Keith Ratner to find out what, if anything, Nicole planned to say about Advocates for God. But until then, all Martin could do was wait and take whatever drops of information Steve could gather.

"Very well," he said. "Thank you, Steve."

Once Steve hung up, Martin threw his phone so hard that the sound of the screen shattering echoed through the vacant stairwell.

24

When Laurie's eyes blinked open the next morning, she took a moment to realize that she was back in her own bed, not on a plane or catnapping in her office. The digital clock read 5:58. She couldn't remember the last time she woke up before the sound of her alarm. Crashing at 8:30 the previous night had certainly helped.

As she turned the alarm to OFF, she heard the clinking sounds of dishes in the kitchen. Timmy, as usual, was already awake. He was so much like his father that way, up and at 'em first thing in the morning. She recognized the smell of toast. She still couldn't believe her little boy could make his own breakfast.

A crack of light broke the darkness of her bedroom, and she saw Timmy backlit in the doorway, holding a tray. "Mommy," he whispered. "Are you awake?"

"Indeed, I am." She turned on the lamp

on her nightstand.

"Look what I have for you." He walked slowly, his gaze fixed on the rim of a glass filled with orange juice, then rested the tray gently on the bed. The toast was crispy, just as she liked it, already slathered with butter and strawberry jam. The tray was one of two that had been her fifth-anniversary gift to Greg — made of wood, as tradition called for. They never had the chance to use them together.

She patted the empty spot on the bed next to her, and Timmy crawled in. She pulled him in tight for a hug. "What did I do to deserve breakfast in bed?"

"I could tell you were sleepy last night. You were hardly awake when you tucked me in."

"I can't get much past you, can I?" She took a bite of toast, and he giggled as she used her tongue to catch a wayward drip of jam.

"Mommy?"

"Hmm-hmm?"

"Are you going to keep flying to California for work?"

She felt her heart sink. The first *Under Suspicion* had featured a case in Westchester County. She'd been home every night. But this show required a change in geography. She hadn't even thought about explaining all of this to the son who was apparently already feeling the impact of her travel.

She returned her toast to her plate and pulled Timmy close again. "You know my show tries to help people who've lost loved ones, like we lost your daddy, right?"

He nodded. "So bad guys like Blue Eyes might get caught. Like how Grandpa used to be a police officer."

"Well, I'm not quite as heroic as that, but we do our best. This time, we are helping a woman in California. Someone took her daughter, Susan, from her twenty years ago. Susan is the focus of our next show. And, yes, I'll need to be in California for a little while."

"Twenty years is a long time ago. More than twice as old as me." He was looking at his toes, wriggling out from beneath the sheets.

"Grandpa will be here with you full-time."

"Except Grandpa said you couldn't even call the other night because of time zones. And then when you got home, you were so sleepy, you almost fell asleep at dinner."

She'd spent all these years since Greg's death terrified for their safety, convinced that Blue Eyes would carry out his threat against them. Her son's anxiety over having his mother spend time away from the house for her career wasn't even on her radar. She had lived so long in warrior-widow mode that she'd never processed the guilt of being a regular working, single mother. She felt tears pooling in her eyes but blinked them away before he could see them.

"I always take care of us, don't I?"

"You, me, and Grandpa. We take care of each other," Timmy answered matter-of-factly.

"Then trust me. I'm going to figure this out. I can work and be your mom, all at one time, okay? And you always come first. No matter what." This time, she couldn't stop the tears. She laughed and kissed him on the cheek. "Look what happens when this sweet boy makes breakfast in bed. Mom gets all sappy."

He laughed and handed her the glass of juice. "Time to brush my teeth," he announced. "Can't be late."

He sounded like her now. All the pieces of the Cinderella Murder show were in place and she couldn't help thinking about what her father said about putting herself in the company of a killer. An involuntary shudder went through her. A working mother's guilt was the least of her worries.

25

The host at Le Bernardin greeted Laurie with a warm handshake. "Ms. Moran. I saw your name in the book. What a pleasure to welcome you again."

There was a time when this had been a regular stop for her and Greg on their weekly babysitter nights. Now that she was the sole breadwinner and her usual date for dinner was a fourth grader, the Morans were more likely to opt for hamburgers or pizza than three-star Michelin fare.

But today's decadent meal was meant to celebrate Brett Young's official approval for the Susan Dempsey production. And Grace and Jerry were Laurie's honored lunch guests.

"Three of you today?" the host confirmed.

"Yes, thank you very much."

"Oh, and here I was hoping I'd get a chance to see that adorable Alex Buckley," Grace said. "Jerry told me that he agreed to host again."

"Yes, but just the three of us for lunch, I'm afraid."

Jerry fit right into their elegant surroundings with his coiffed hair and dark blue suit. But as they were getting seated, Laurie noticed a woman at the next table glaring judgmentally at Grace. It could have been for the poofed-up hair, the heavy makeup, the three pounds of costume jewelry, the micromini hemline, or the five-inch stilettos. Regardless of the reasons, Laurie didn't like it. She stared straight at the woman until she looked away.

"In any event," Laurie teased, "don't you think Alex is a little old for you, Grace? He's got a dozen years on you."

"And from what I can tell," Grace said, "each one has made him better-looking."

Jerry smiled and shook his head, used to Grace's boy-crazy talk. "We have bigger fish to fry than your fascination with our host," he said. "I know you call the shots, Laurie, but I don't know how plausible it is for us to be flying back and forth to California constantly."

She thought about Timmy's wide eyes that morning in bed as he asked her how often she would be going to California. Now that she had convinced Brett Young to approve the Cinderella Murder, there was no turning back.

"I'm with you," she said. "If you could think of a way to produce the entire show from New York, you'd be my hero for life."

Grace registered her opinion with a *tsk*. "Sun. The ocean. Hollywood. Feel free to send me out to do as much work as you need."

"I've started a punch list." Jerry was the most organized person Laurie had ever met. The key to success, he liked to say, was to plan your work and work your plan. "We can hire an actress who looks like Susan to re-create — probably blurred — the foot chase in the Hollywood Hills."

"If we do that, we need to be careful not to add any ideas or inferences to what we absolutely *know* to a certainty," Laurie said.

"Of course," Jerry said. "Like, obviously, we wouldn't show the actress running out of Frank Parker's house. But we know her body was found, strangled, in Laurel Canyon Park. And based on the discovery of her missing shoe, abrasions to her foot, and the path of flattened grass leading to her body, police believed her killer chased her from the roadway of the park entrance into the park's interior. That was the part I thought we could re-create, the sprint from the park sign to the place her body was found."

She nodded her approval.

"The real question," Grace said, "is how she got to that roadway. Her car was parked on campus."

"We'll highlight that, too," Jerry said. "Photographs from the investigation will suffice, I think. And I've already got a forensic pathologist lined up to talk about the physical evidence. A woman named Janice Lane, on the medical school faculty at Stanford. She's a frequent expert witness and presents well on camera."

"Excellent," Laurie said. "Make sure she knows that we don't include any prurient details. Susan Dempsey's mother doesn't need grisly descriptions of her daughter's death on national television. Dr. Lane's primary role should be a discussion of the timeline. It was the estimate of the time of death that helped Frank Parker establish an alibi."

Jerry began to explain. "Based on temperature, lividity, and rigor mortis —"

"Someone's been brushing up on his science," Grace said.

"Trust me," he said, "it's all Dr. Lane. She makes this stuff sound easy. Anyway, based on the science, the medical examiner estimated that Susan was killed between seven and eleven P.M. on that Saturday night. She was scheduled to arrive at Frank Parker's house at seven thirty. When she hadn't arrived by seven forty-five, he called Madison Meyer, who jumped in her car and arrived at the house around eight thirty. According to both Parker and Meyer, she stayed until close to midnight."

"What were they doing all that time?" Grace asked. From the look of her arched brow, she had her theories.

"I'm not sure that's our business," Jerry said, "unless it has something to do with Susan Dempsey's death."

"You're no fun."

Laurie made a time-out sign with her hands. "Focus on the facts, guys. According to Frank and Madison, he made the decision to cast her within an hour. He was so excited about it that he wanted to show her the short film that was the basis for *Beauty Land* and talk more about the project. He hadn't eaten yet so he ordered takeout; a pizza delivery record from nine thirty P.M. backed that up."

Grace whispered a thank-you to the waiter who refilled her water glass. "But if Susan could have died any time between seven and eleven, and Madison didn't get to Frank's until eight thirty, she's not really a full alibi. Where was he between seven and eight thirty?"

"Except you've got to take all the evidence into account," Jerry reminded her. "Susan was due to arrive at Frank's at seven thirty. The idea is that there's no way Frank could have gotten into a chase with Susan, killed her, taken Susan's car back to the UCLA campus, and returned to his house, all before Madison arrived an hour later. Not to mention, placing a phone call to Susan's cell and then to Madison at the dorm room in the middle of it all. If Madison's telling the truth, Frank's in the clear."

"Still," Laurie said, "the whole alibi seems fishy to me: it seems hard to believe that Frank called another actress fifteen minutes after Susan was supposed to arrive, and that she just hopped in her car immediately."

"Ah, but it does make sense," Jerry said, "when Frank Parker is notoriously obsessed with punctuality. He has fired people for showing up five minutes late. And we saw how obsessed Madison is with being famous. If someone dangled a studio film in front of her and said jump, she'd ask how high."

Grace still wasn't fully sold on the theory. "But you also saw how she fixed her lipstick just to answer the door at her ratty house. I can only imagine the work she'd put into looking good for Frank Parker."

"See?" Laurie said. "These are all the things we have to establish in our initial interviews with them. We go first for a gentle retelling of whatever version of the story they gave back then. See if we can catch them in an inconsistency."

"When do we bring Alex in?" Grace asked, smiling.

"You are singular in your focus today, aren't you?" Laurie asked. "Brett Young has approved a budget to cover screening interviews with every participant, followed by what we'll call our summit session: back-to-back interviews, all in the same location. That's when Alex swoops in for the tough questions, after we've done our groundwork."

"For that part," Jerry said, "I thought we'd rent a house near campus, something big enough for the whole production team. That will save us money on lodging, and then we can use the house as the location for the interviews with Alex."

Laurie wasn't sure how she felt about living with all her coworkers, but from a financial perspective, she couldn't argue with Jerry's logic. "Sounds like a plan," she said. "If nothing else, I'd say we've already earned this delicious lunch."

As the waiter recited elaborate food descriptions from memory, Laurie nodded along politely, but her thoughts were spinning as she envisioned all the work they had in front of them. She had guaranteed Brett Young the best *Under Suspicion* possible. And, just this morning, she had given her word to her nine-year-old son that she would do it all while being a full-time mother.

How could she possibly keep both promises?

26

Lydia Levitt sat cross-legged on the sofa in her living room, her laptop perched across her knees. She typed a final period and then proofread her online review of Rustic Tavern, the restaurant she and Rosemary had selected for lunch the previous day. She deleted the last period and replaced it with an exclamation point. *I will definitely be back — five stars!* She hit the ENTER key, satisfied.

The website thanked her for her review. It was her seventy-eighth entry. Lydia believed in giving businesses feedback, for good or for bad. How else could they know what consumers valued and be able to improve? Not to mention, writing the reviews gave her something to do. Lydia loved to stay busy.

It wasn't just the delicious food and beautiful patio that had made yesterday so enjoyable. She was excited to have found a new friend in Rosemary Dempsey. Lydia had lived at Castle Crossings for twelve years now, and the entire time, she had been older than almost everyone else in the neighborhood. These kinds of planned communities tended to attract young couples, eager for a safe, predictable, homogeneous place to raise their children.

For the most part, Lydia had found company among the self-named "Castle Crossings grandparents," the parents of the young couples, living nearby to either help with child care or facilitate grandparent time.

But Lydia hadn't met anyone quite like Rosemary at Castle Crossings. Rosemary struck her as adventurous. Interesting. And, maybe because of the terrible loss she'd suffered, she seemed a bit haunted.

Even so, Lydia could tell that Rosemary had been shocked at lunch when Lydia mentioned her wild-child days in the late sixties. If their meal had not been cut short by the phone call Rosemary had received from that television producer, Lydia might have found a way to fully explain the connection between that part of her life and her current identity as the rule-follower of Castle Crossings. Lydia had seen what life was like when everybody did whatever he or she felt like doing, willy-nilly. After she saw friends overdose, or lose their families to alcoholism, or get their hearts broken because one person's idea of live-and-let-live is another person's definition of betrayal, she saw the value in playing by the rules.

Lydia set her laptop on the coffee table and walked to the front window, parting the gray linen drapes with her fingertips. Rosemary's driveway was empty. Shoot. She was looking forward to another visit.

She was just about to let the drapes close when she noticed a cream-colored pickup truck parked in front of the house next door to Rosemary's. The driver exited, wearing cargo pants and a black windbreaker. He was probably close to forty years old, with a shaved head. He looked tough and lean, like a boxer.

He was walking toward Rosemary's yard.

She let the drapes fall but kept a tiny slit open to peer out. Oh, how Don teased her when she did this. They both knew that everyone called her "the nosy neighbor."

"What else am I supposed to do with myself all day?" she would ask Don. "I'm bored, bored, bored." Spying on the Castle Crossings crowd, like posting online reviews of restaurants, kept her busy. She found such pleasure in conjuring up imaginary tales from the humdrum comings and goings around these quiet cul-de-sacs. In her alternate version of this neighborhood, Trevor Wolf's band of teenage after-school buddies was plotting a series of bank robberies. Mr. and Mrs. Miller were cooking methamphetamine in the basement. Ally Simpson's new rescue dog was actually a trained drug K9, working undercover to expose the Millers' nefarious activities. And, of course, affairs abounded.

"You've got such an imagination," Don liked to say. "You should write a mystery novel one day."

Well, Don was at the health club, so he wasn't around to catch her spying today.

She peered through the crack in the drapes as the pickup-truck man first knocked on Rosemary's door, then leaned over to check out the view through her living room window. When he turned away and began retracing his steps through the yard, she assumed he was returning to his car. Instead, he turned left, facing away from her, and headed toward the side of Rosemary's house.

Now, that was interesting. She began conjuring explanations: a burglar who had somehow slipped past security at the front gate; someone affiliated with that television show Rosemary had mentioned yesterday; a door-to-door proselytizer, out to introduce Rosemary to a new religion.

That's it! Her church. She remembered Rosemary mentioning an upcoming flea market at Saint Patrick's. She said she was grateful that she didn't have to lug all of her giveaways to the church herself. A volunteer was supposed to come by to haul them for her. A pickup truck would be just the right vehicle for the job. Maybe Rosemary had arranged to leave the donations behind her house in the event she wasn't home to meet him.

Lydia pulled on a fleece from the coatrack by the front door. She could help load the truck, or at least say hello on Rosemary's behalf.

She crossed the street and then followed the same path the man had taken, walking to the right side of Rosemary's house to her backyard. She found him trying the sliding glass door, unsuccessfully. She remembered how Rosemary had unlocked her front door when Lydia helped her with the groceries earlier that week.

"I told her she really doesn't need to keep her doors locked," Lydia called out. "That's basically the reason most people live here."

When the man turned, his face was expressionless.

"I'm Lydia," she said, waving as she approached. "The neighbor across the street. You're from Rosemary's church?"

No change in expression. Only silence. Maybe he was deaf?

She stepped closer and noticed now that he was wearing black gloves. It didn't seem quite that cold to her, but she always seemed to run a little warmer than other people. He finally spoke, only one word. "Church?"

"Yes, I thought you were from Saint Patrick's. For the flea market? Did she tell you where she left everything? I got the impression she had a bunch."

"A bunch of what?" he asked.

Now that she was right next to him, she noticed the insignia on the breast of his windbreaker.

"Oh, you're from Keepsafe?" She knew about the company from Don's days in the security industry. They were one of the most common providers of home alarms in the country.

At the mention of the company, the man appeared to wake from his daze. His smile was somehow even stranger than his previously blank expression. "Yes, I'm from Keepsafe. Your neighbor's alarm sent an alert to our local station. She hasn't cleared it and didn't answer when we called. We automatically do a home visit to be sure. Probably just a misunderstanding — a dog knocking over a vase, that kind of thing."

"Rosemary doesn't have a dog."

Another weird smile. "I meant that as an example," he said. "These things happen all the time. Nothing to worry about."

"Are you sure you even have the right house? Rosemary doesn't have an alarm system." That was the kind of thing Lydia would have immediately noticed when she walked into Rosemary's house.

The man said nothing, but the smile was still there. For the first time in her life, Lydia believed that the danger she sensed was anything but imaginary.

27

After a ritualistic postdinner game of Clue and a nighttime snack of peanut butter on apple slices, Laurie tucked Timmy into bed to the sounds of running water and clanking dishes from the kitchen.

She found her father loading the dishwasher.

"Dad, you don't need to do that. You already do so much for Timmy when I'm at work."

"Used to be that cleaning up after dinner was an hour-long chore. I think I can handle throwing away takeout containers and tossing a few plates into a machine. I know how hard you've been working."

She took a sponge from the sink and began to wipe down the granite counters. "Unfortunately, I'm not even done for the day."

"It's nine o'clock, Laurie. You're going to burn yourself out."

"I'm fine, Dad. Just one more phone call." Producing the show in California was going to be a bear, but at least the time zone differences made it easier for her to contact the West Coast long after normal people would have stopped working. "Jerry is scheduling interviews with the other participants, but I owe it to Susan's mother to contact her personally."

Rosemary Dempsey picked up after two rings. "Ms. Moran?"

"Hi again. And, please, call me Laurie. I was calling to confirm some dates. We'd like to come next week for some one-on-one time with you. And then the following week, we'd like to have each person do a sit-down with Alex Buckley. That will be down in Southern California. Is that going to be possible for you?"

"Um, sure. Whatever you need."

Rosemary's voice sounded different — soft and hesitant. "Is everything all right?" Laurie asked. "If you're having second thoughts —"

"No, not at all. It's just . . ."

Laurie thought she heard a sniffle on the other end of the line. "I think I've caught you at a bad time. It can wait until tomorrow."

Rosemary cleared her throat. "Now is fine.

I could use the distraction. Something awful has happened here. One of my neighbors was found murdered. Police think she was beaten to death."

Laurie didn't know what to say. "Oh, Rosemary. That's terrible. I'm so sorry." She realized the words were as unhelpful as any that were spoken to her when people learned about Greg's death.

"Her name was Lydia. She was very nice. She was — well, she was my friend. And they found her in my backyard."

"In *your* yard?"

"Yes. I don't know why she would have been there. They think it's possible she interrupted someone trying to break in."

"That's absolutely terrifying. This just happened today?"

"A few hours ago," Rosemary confirmed. "Police only just now let me back in my house, but my yard is still off-limits."

"So it was in broad daylight?" *Just like Greg,* she couldn't help thinking.

"The whole neighborhood is in shock. Things like this never happen here. So, honestly, getting out of the house for the show will be good for me."

It did not take them long to mark off a full day to film in the Bay Area, and for Rosemary to clear the three days they had planned to gather everyone in Southern California. Laurie promised to be in touch about location details for the latter once Jerry had located a rental house for what they were calling the "summit session."

"Again, I'm so sorry about your friend," Laurie said once more before wishing her good night. When she hung up, her father was lingering in the doorway.

"Something bad happened?" he asked.

"I'd certainly say so. One of Rosemary's friends, a neighbor, was killed in Rosemary's backyard. Police think she may have interrupted a burglar."

"Was Rosemary's house broken into? Anything missing?"

"I don't know," Laurie said. "The police had just let her back in. It sounded like she was still processing it all."

Her father was working his hands, thumbs against index fingers, the way he always did when something was bothering him. "Someone tries to break into her house and kills her neighbor, just as you're looking into her daughter's murder?"

"Dad, that's a stretch. You know as well as anyone that good people get hurt for all kinds of absurd reasons that only a sociopath could understand. And the victim here wasn't Rosemary Dempsey. It was a neighbor. This isn't even the same neighborhood that Susan grew up in. There's no connection."

"I don't like coincidences."

"Please don't worry about this, okay?"

She walked him to the front door as he pulled on his coat. He gave her a hug and kiss before leaving, but as she watched him walk to the elevator, she could still see him deep in thought, working those hands.

28

Leo's short walk to his apartment, a mere block from Laurie's, was filled with troubled thoughts. First he saw a woman hunched in the open door of a Mercedes — her back to the sidewalk, keys dangling from the driver's-side lock, completely focused on reaching for something in the passenger seat. One quick shove — maybe a blow to the back of the shoulder — and a carjacker could make off with her car before she could yell for help. Twenty feet later was a bag of garbage at the curb, a discarded bank statement clearly visible through the thin plastic. A half-decent identity thief could clean out the account before morning.

Then, right in front of his own building, a man was picking up scattered pills from the sidewalk and placing them into a prescription pill container. The guy was probably twenty-five years old. A tattoo on the back of his shaved head read FEARLESS.

Anyone else would assume the man had been a little clumsy, but not Leo. He'd bet the contents of his own wallet that the pills were aspirin, and that Mr. Tattoo Head had just scammed some poor pedestrian and was now reloading for the next round.

It was one of the oldest sidewalk shakedowns around. Sometimes the "dropped" item was an already-broken bottle. Sometimes a pair of preshattered sunglasses. Tonight, it was an open prescription container filled with baby aspirin. The con was to bump into a patsy, "drop" the item to the sidewalk, and then pretend it was the other person's fault. *I can't afford to replace it.* Generous people offered compensation.

Where other people would look down this block and see a woman at her car, a bag of garbage, and a guy picking up his dropped package, Leo saw the potential for crime. The response was completely involuntary, like seeing letters on a page and reading them automatically. Like hearing two plus two and thinking four. He thought like a cop at a basic cellular level.

Inside his apartment, he fired up the computer in the room that doubled as a home office and bedroom for Timmy. It wasn't as fast or sleek as the equipment Laurie had, but it was good enough for Leo.

He started by Googling Rosemary Dempsey. He skimmed the blog entry that had originally drawn his daughter to the Cinderella Murder case. Laurie had shown it to him when she was first considering the case. The author mentioned that Rosemary had moved out of the home where she'd lived with Susan and her husband before their deaths. Rosemary now lived in a gated community outside of Oakland. Bingo.

He Googled "Oakland murder gated community" and then limited his search to the last twenty-four hours. He found two news entries, both posted in the last hour by local media outlets in Northern California. Lydia Levitt, seventy-one years old, killed that afternoon in her neighborhood of Castle Crossings.

He searched for Castle Crossings and located the zip code for the area, and then entered it into the website CrimeReports. Only thirteen reported incidents in the last thirty days, almost all of them shoplifting. In the map function, he zoomed into the area directly around the gated community where the victim had lived. Zero incidents. He expanded the search to the last year. Ten incidents, nothing violent. Only one residential burglary in an entire year.

And yet today, just as *Under Suspicion* was

getting ready to feature Susan Dempsey's murder, a seventy-one-year-old woman was murdered outside the home of Susan Dempsey's mother.

Leo knew that he had a tendency to worry about his daughter, not just as any father would, but as a cop. And the buzzing he felt right now was coming from the cop part of his brain. It was as primal as a lizard on an algae-covered rock, sensing the impending crack of a sledgehammer.

Leo wasn't being a paranoid parent. He was certain that Lydia Levitt's murder had something to do with *Under Suspicion.*

When sunlight broke through his bedroom blinds the next morning, Leo realized that he had not slept, but he had made a decision. He reached for the phone on his nightstand and called Laurie.

"Dad? Is everything okay?"

It was always the first thing she asked if he called too late at night, too early in the morning, or too many times in a row.

"You said you were worried about Timmy given the production schedule in California."

"Of course I'm worried. I'll figure something out, though. I always do. I can fly home on weekends. Maybe we can set up a

Skype schedule, though I know that video-conferencing isn't the same as really being together."

He could tell he was not the only one who had spent the night worrying.

"That won't be necessary," he said. "We'll go with you. Timmy and me, both."

"Dad —"

"Don't argue with me on this. We're a family. I'll talk to his school. It's only a couple of weeks. We'll hire a tutor if necessary. He needs to be close to his mother."

"Okay," Laurie said after a small pause. Leo could hear the gratitude in his daughter's voice. "That's amazing. Thank you, Dad."

He felt a pang of guilt for not mentioning an ulterior motive for tagging along to California, but there was nothing to gain from discussing his worries. Laurie was not going to pull the plug on the Cinderella Murder at this point. At least he would be there to protect her if something went wrong.

He prayed that, for once, the cop part of his brain was misfiring.

29

Laurie and Grace pulled into the lot in front
of REACH's Palo Alto headquarters shortly
after ten A.M. The drive from their hotel in
San Francisco had made New York City
traffic seem hypersonic by comparison.
They had only arrived in California yesterday, but Laurie was already homesick.

Today's interview with Susan's former
classmate at the UCLA computer lab was
the first of the preparatory interviews prior
to next week's summit session in Los Angeles. It had made sense for them to start in
the Bay Area, gathering background information before moving closer to both the
scene of the crime and the likely suspects.
While Laurie and Grace were meeting with
Dwight Cook, Jerry would be scouting
locations in Susan's old neighborhood. The
plan was to open the episode with a mon-
tage of photographs of Susan, interspersed
with footage of her high school and child-

hood home.

Laurie shivered as she stepped from the passenger seat of their rental car. She was wearing a lightweight cashmere sweater and black pants, with no jacket. "I always forget how chilly the Bay Area can be."

"How do you think I feel?" Grace wore a jade-green silk blouse with a deep V-neck and a black skirt that was short even for her. "I was picturing Los Angeles sunshine and mojitos when I packed."

"We're only here three days. Then you'll get your time in Hollywood."

Dwight Cook greeted them in the lobby, dressed in an expensive suit and solid red tie. Based on the photographs Laurie had seen, she had expected his uniform of jeans, T-shirts, zip-up hoodies, and canvas sneakers. She might ask Jerry to suggest that he wear whatever made him "most comfortable" to the summit taping. Looking at him today, he came across as an older version of a child in his first suit at confirmation.

Dwight led the way through the building, a labyrinth of brightly colored hallways and oddly shaped nooks and crannies. When they finally reached his office, it was absolutely serene by comparison, with cool gray walls, slate floors, and clean, modern furniture. The only personal touch in the office was a single photograph of him in a wet suit and flippers, preparing to scuba dive from the edge of a yacht into sparkling turquoise water.

"You're a diver?" she asked.

"It's probably the only thing I enjoy more than work," he said. "Can I offer you something to drink? Water? Coffee?"

She declined, but Grace took him up on the offer of water. Laurie was surprised when Dwight retrieved a bottle from a mini-fridge with a Nespresso coffeemaker on top of it.

"I half expected a remote-controlled robot to roll in," Laurie said with a smile.

"You have no idea how many times my own mother asked me to invent Rosie the Maid from *The Jetsons.* These days, Silicon Valley's all about phones and tablets. We've got data-compression projects, social net-working apps, location interfacing technol-ogy, you name it — if it interacts with a gadget, I've probably got someone in this building working on it. The least I can do is grab my own water and coffee. Nicole tells me that your show has been successful in solving cold cases."

The abrupt change in subject was jarring, but Laurie could understand that someone as successful as Dwight Cook operated at maximum efficiency at all times.

"No guarantees," she said cautiously, "but *Under Suspicion*'s primary purpose is to revive investigations, shedding new light on old facts."

"Laurie's being too modest," Grace said, flipping a long lock of black hair behind her shoulder. "Our first episode led to the case being solved while we were still filming."

Laurie interrupted Grace's hard sell. "I think what Grace is saying is that we're devoted to doing our very best for Susan's case."

"Is it hard for you, Laurie, to work on these cases given that you lost your own husband to a violent crime?"

Laurie found herself blinking. Nicole had warned her that Dwight could be socially "awkward." However, she could not recall anyone ever asking her so directly about the personal impact of Greg's murder.

"No," she finally said. "If anything, I hope my experience makes me the right person to tell these stories. I think of our show as a voice for victims who would otherwise be forgotten."

He looked away from her direct gaze. "I'm sorry. I've been told that I can be overly blunt."

"If we're being blunt, Dwight, I may as well tell you that there are rumors that you and Susan were rivals at the lab. You were competitors for Professor Hathaway's approval."

"Someone suggested that I would have hurt Susan? Because of Hathaway?"

She saw no need to tell him that it was Keith Ratner who mentioned the theory during a phone call in which he also condemned Susan's mother for her long-standing suspicion of him and named everyone Susan had ever met as an equally viable suspect, including Dwight Cook. While Ratner's theories had all sounded pretty desperate to Laurie, these initial interviews were her opportunity to float every possible theory when cameras weren't rolling. It was good practice for when Alex Buckley grilled them more closely.

"It wasn't just about your mentor," she explained, "but your actual work. You were working at the school's lab and then formed REACH just two months after Susan died, quickly raising millions of dollars in investment capital to support your search-capacity innovation. That kind of money could be a powerful motive to get her out of the picture."

"You don't understand at all," Dwight

said wistfully. Laurie had expected him to be defensive, to lash out at her with facts to demonstrate his superiority in programming skills over Susan. But instead, he sounded genuinely hurt. "I, of all people, would never have hurt Susan. I would never hurt anyone over money or anything else, but certainly not Susan. She was . . . she was my friend."

Laurie could hear the change in Dwight's voice every time he spoke Susan's name. "It seems like you were fond of her."

"Very."

"Did you know her boyfriend, Keith Ratner?"

"Unfortunately," he said. "He never took much of an interest in me, but he'd drop by the lab to meet Susan — when he wasn't late or standing her up. Let me guess: he was the one who suggested that I stole REACH from Susan?"

"I can't say."

"You don't need to. It's further proof that he never paid attention to Susan's work. He was clueless as to what she was doing at the lab. Susan never worked on search functioning, which is all REACH was when it started. She was developing voice-to-text software."

It took Laurie a moment to understand

the phrase. "Like automated dictation?" she asked. "I use that on my phone to dictate e-mails."

"Exactly. If you have any doubts, we can clear them up right now." He picked up his telephone and dialed a number. "The *Under Suspicion* folks are here. Can you pop up?"

A minute later, a handsome man in his late fifties walked into Dwight's office. He was dressed casually in a lightweight madras shirt and khaki pants, but the look suited him well, with his tan and a full head of dark waves. He introduced himself as Richard Hathaway.

"We were just talking about Susan's work with you at UCLA," Laurie said.

"Such a waste. That sounds cold, I know. Any loss of a young life is a waste. But Susan was bright. She wasn't twenty-four/seven at the keyboard, the way some programmers are." He gave Dwight a smile. "But she was creative. Her ability to connect socially — in a way some of us computer types struggle with — helped her connect technology to real life."

"I'll step out for a moment," Dwight offered. "Mrs. Moran has something she needs to ask you."

Once she was alone with the former professor, Laurie asked if Susan had been working on a particular project.

"It might help to understand how I ran my lab. Computer work can be solitary, so my research assistants acted primarily as teaching assistants for my intro classes. They might also help on isolated portions of my own work, which at the time was in software pipelining — a technique for overlapping loop iterations. And of course you have no idea what any of that means, right?"

"Nope."

"Nor should you. It's a method of program optimization, interesting only to people who write code. Anyway, I selected students whose own independent projects during freshman year showed promise. Susan's was speech-to-text, what most of us would call dictation. It was all pretty rudimentary in the nineties, but Steve Jobs could never have given us Siri without basic speech-recognition function. If she had lived — well, who knows?"

"Did she work with Dwight on REACH?"

"REACH didn't exist yet. But she and Dwight worked in proximity to each other, if that's what you mean. But Dwight's work was quite different. As you probably know, REACH launched a new way to locate information on the Internet, back when people were still calling it the World Wide

Web. No, that wasn't anything like Susan's area of interest."

"Professor —"

"Please, 'Richard' is fine. I retired from the academy long ago, and even then, I didn't particularly care for the titles."

"You seem young to be retired."

"And I've been retired a long time. I left UCLA to help Dwight build REACH. Imagine being a sophomore in college and having captains of industry fighting to get a meeting with you. I recognize brilliance when I see it, and I was willing to support him full-time while he insisted on finishing up at UCLA — to make his parents proud, if you can believe it. I thought it would be a pit stop for me as I transitioned to the private sector, and yet here I am, twenty years later."

"That's nice that the two of you are so close."

"It may sound corny, but I don't have any kids of my own. Dwight — well, yes, we are indeed close."

"I get the impression that Dwight might be more comfortable speaking with our host, Alex Buckley, if he has an old friend like you around." What she meant was that Hathaway would present far better on television than the unpolished Dwight

Cook. "Is it possible you could join us for filming in Los Angeles? The current plan is to locate a house somewhere near the university."

"Absolutely," he said. "Whatever you need."

Keith Ratner's accusation of a professional rivalry between Susan and Dwight seemed far-fetched when first offered. Now both Dwight and Professor Hathaway had debunked it. Laurie would confirm with Rosemary and Nicole that Susan had never had run-ins with Dwight, because it was essential that she follow every possible lead.

But every fiber of Laurie's being told her that the real answers to Susan's death could only be found in Los Angeles.

30

Dwight was alone again in his office once Hathaway offered to escort the TV people out of their maze of a building.

He could tell from the look Hathaway gave him as he walked out that he wasn't pleased with the producer's questions about REACH, but at least they hadn't wandered into thorny territory. The notion that Susan had anything to do with the technology was completely off base.

Still, he wished he could rewind the clock and start the morning over again. He planned to bring up the subject of Laurie's late husband as a way to make his contact with her more personal. But the overture had gone over like a ton of bricks. When Dwight and Hathaway first started meeting with venture capitalists, Hathaway had told him, *You're just so* blunt! *I'm talking blunt like a ten-pound mallet. That's fine when you're talking to me, but when it comes to money, you've got to learn some nuance.*

Their relationship was blunt by design. Dwight's mind wandered to that Friday night of his sophomore year when Hathaway had stumbled upon him in the lab, catching Dwight hacking into the registrar's office's database. Though he wasn't cheating or changing grades, Dwight wanted to prove to himself that he could slip through the virtual walls of his own university. It was illegal, and a violation of the school's code of conduct, plus Dwight had been stupid enough to do it on the computer lab's equipment, which the university often monitored. Hathaway said he believed that Dwight had no ill motives and would defend him to the university, but he felt obligated to notify the administration to protect his own lab.

Dwight was so upset about disappointing his mentor that he came to the lab late the following night, intending to clean out his workstation and leave a letter of resignation. Instead of finding the lab empty, Dwight found a female student he recognized from the Intro to Computer Science class for which he was a teaching assistant. She was leaving Hathaway's office. Dwight couldn't help but think of the campus whispers about the most "crush-worthy" teacher.

He might have slipped out of the lab, resigning as intended, if the soles of his tennis shoes hadn't squeaked against the tile floors. Hathaway emerged from his office and explained that he saw no reason to report Dwight's hacking to the university after all. The administration would only blow the activities out of proportion, failing to understand the natural curiosity of someone with Dwight's blossoming talents. He forced Dwight to promise, however, that he would channel those skills into legitimate work — the kind that could earn a young man a fortune in Silicon Valley.

That conversation eventually gave rise to a strange kind of friendship. The student-teacher, mentor-mentee relationship became more peer-to-peer, marked by utter mutual honesty. Hathaway was the first adult to ever treat Dwight like a real person, not like a broken child who needed to be fixed or isolated. In return, Dwight accepted Hathaway, even if he was a little shady. How else would REACH have ever started if he and Hathaway had not trusted each other completely?

If only Dwight had Hathaway's knack for schmoozing. Maybe he could have mentioned Laurie's husband without sticking his foot in his mouth. He hoped he hadn't offended her so much that she would cut him from the production.

Once everyone was gathered in Los Angeles, all he'd need was a few seconds of access to each person's cell phone, and all their texts, e-mails, and phone calls would be downloaded automatically to Dwight's computer. The problem was, he didn't know whether they'd all show up for filming at once or if their appointments would be back-to-back.

Thinking about the Los Angeles shoot gave him an idea. He pulled up the last e-mail he had received from Jerry, the assistant producer who Laurie mentioned was scouting locations near campus. He opened a new message and began to type.

After hitting the SEND key, he leaned back in his chair and looked at the photograph next to his computer. Hathaway had snapped it three years ago on a dive trip during REACH's annual corporate retreat to Anguilla. The company had flown every single employee — down to the student interns — for a four-day stay at the luxurious Viceroy. Everyone had gushed over the sprawling resort property and the pillow-soft white sand of Meads Bay, but for

Dwight, those trips were always about traveling beneath the water. The picture on his desk was from a wall dive at the keys of Dog Island with a sheer one-hundred-foot drop. He swam with tuna, turtles, yellowtail snapper, even a reef shark and two southern stingrays. Deep in the sea is where his thoughts found calm.

He stared into the water in the photograph, wishing he could jump through the frame. He needed calm right now. This television show had him feeling all the pain of losing Susan again. And when he wasn't reliving the pain, he was wired with anticipation about the possibility of finally learning who had killed the only woman he had ever loved.

31

Rosemary Dempsey ran her fingertips along the dark gray granite countertop as she paced the length of the kitchen. "It feels so strange to be back here. I cooked in this room almost every day for nearly forty years."

Rosemary had put together a collection of her daughter's childhood photographs and mementos — a blue ribbon won in a science fair, the banner she'd worn as her high school's homecoming queen. She had even given Laurie and her crew the guest book from Susan's memorial service.

Now they were inside the Dempsey family's former home, where Jerry had arranged for them to shoot today's interview. This was the kitchen where Rosemary first learned that her daughter's body had been found in Laurel Canyon Park.

"I thought it would be traumatic to come back here," Rosemary said. "But after what happened in my backyard last week, it's nice to get away from my 'new' neighborhood."

"Have the police made any progress in your friend's investigation?"

"Apparently not. You might have found another case for your show," she said with a sad smile.

Laurie could tell that Rosemary needed to ease into a conversation about that horrible morning when she learned of Susan's death. Laurie shot a look to Jerry, who was lingering next to the cameramen stationed near the sliding glass doors at the edge of the kitchen. He gave her an *okay* sign. Though they were keeping their distance, they could capture what they needed to get on video.

"Has the house changed much since you lived here?" Laurie asked.

Rosemary stopped pacing and looked around her. "No, not in any obvious way. But it feels completely different. Their furniture — it's much more modern than ours. And our art is gone. The photographs. All of the things that made this house our home are either with me at the new place or in storage."

"If it wouldn't be too painful," Laurie said, "maybe you can point out a few details in the house that were significant to your daughter. Perhaps we can start with her room?"

Laurie wouldn't need footage from other parts of the house, but a tour through the home was a way to get Rosemary to loosen up and start talking about Susan. The show only worked when they could portray the victim not as a piece of evidence in a mystery to be solved but as a living human being.

Rosemary led the way up the mission-style staircase to a bedroom at the end of the upstairs hallway. Her hand trembled as she turned the doorknob. The room was set up now as a nursery, with lavender-colored walls hand-stenciled with yellow tulips.

She walked to the window and fingered the latch. "See how the overhang above the front porch is just beneath the window here? I used to check this lock every single night because I had a fear that someone would sneak in and grab my baby."

Next she walked to the closet and ran her fingers along the inside of the door frame. "This is where we used to chart her growth, drawing a new line for every birthday. They've painted it over since then, but I swear, you can still seem them. See? Faint little lines."

Laurie looked over Rosemary's shoulder

and smiled, even though all she saw was clean white paint.

When they were back in the kitchen and in front of the cameras, Laurie felt like Rosemary was ready. "Please," Laurie encouraged gently, "tell us how you learned about your daughter's murder."

Rosemary nodded slowly. "It was the weekend of Jack's sixtieth birthday. We had a big party here on Saturday, outside. It was a beautiful night. Everything was so perfect, except Susan couldn't be there. She called that afternoon to wish Jack a happy birthday, but he was at the club for a round of golf. He worked *so* hard. Always. She was in good spirits, excited about school, and very excited about the audition she had that night."

"The one with Frank Parker?"

"Yes. She told me his name, but I hadn't heard of him. She said he was a real up-and-comer. She said . . . she said she felt 'lucky,' like it was 'too good to be true.' " Her voice caught as she repeated her daughter's words. "Then we got the call from the police the next morning. The funny thing is, I had a terrible feeling all day that something was wrong, like this vague but terrifying foreboding."

"About Susan?"

"No, not initially. More this floating anxiety. But that all changed once the police called. It was the LAPD. They had found a body. You know the rest — one of her shoes had fallen off, presumably as she was chased through Laurel Canyon Park. Her cell phone was nearby too. Her lucky necklace had been pulled from her throat. They wanted to know why she might have been at the park. I told them she was meeting that night with Frank Parker. It was only later that we learned that his house was only a mile or so from the location where they found her body."

Laurie could see the grief gripping Rosemary, all these years later. She knew full well it would never disappear. "Going back to Frank Parker, did that strike you as peculiar, for him to meet with Susan at night?" Laurie asked gently.

"No, but she didn't tell me she was going to his house. And I assumed that her agent would be there. Trust me, if I could turn back time, I'd stop her from ever going to that audition."

"Why? Because you think Frank Parker is the one who hurt your daughter?"

Rosemary looked down at her hands and shook her head. "No. I wish I could have stopped her from going up to the Hollywood

Hills that night, because at least she would have been closer to campus, where she knew her way around. She wouldn't have been wearing silver shoes that she couldn't run in. At the very least, even if she couldn't escape, she wouldn't have been called Cinderella, as if my daughter were some pretty little girl trying to win a prince for the night. That nickname and the Hollywood setting wouldn't have been such a painful distraction."

"A distraction from what, Rosemary?"

Rosemary paused, pressing her lips together as she chose her next words. When she finally spoke, any nerves she'd had about the cameras were gone. She looked directly into the lens like a trained TV star. "A distraction from the truth, which is that the most dangerous person in Susan's life was much closer to home: her boyfriend, Keith Ratner. He was a cheater and a liar, and he knew my Susan was going places he could only dream of. I will go to my grave believing he is the one who killed my baby."

32

The next morning, Laurie hopped out of the van in front of Nicole Melling's house. It was ten degrees warmer on this side of the Golden Gate Bridge than it had been when they'd left their hotel in downtown San Francisco half an hour earlier.

Jerry let out a whistle as he took in the view. "I may never go back to New York City."

The house was situated at the top of a ridge above town, at the edge of Sorich Ranch Park. They were looking out across Ross Valley to two tree-covered mountains in the distance, the green of the leaves broken only by the early blooming of dogwoods.

Laurie heard the van's rear door slide open and watched as Grace managed to climb out in form-fitting leggings and thigh-high leather stiletto boots. "Wow," she said, following the direction of their gaze. "That's almost enough to make me appreciate nature."

"It's hard to believe we're only twenty miles away from the city," Laurie said.

Jerry nudged Grace, who was fiddling with her iPhone. "Your love of nature didn't last long," he joked.

"Not true. I was doing research," she said indignantly. She held up the screen and showed an image close to the view in front of them. "Those are Bald Hill and Mount Tamalpais," she said, stumbling over the pronunciation. "And in case you're wondering, according to Zillow, this house is worth —"

Jerry admonished her with a scolding index finger. "No! It's bad enough that you cyberstalk everyone you meet, but I do *not* want to be a part of it. Yesterday, Laurie, she found a website called Who's Dated Who. The grammar's wrong, first of all. It should be Who's Dated *Whom.* But thanks to that nonsense, I spent the entire delay at baggage claim hearing about the various ingénues linked to Frank Parker before he finally got married."

"Oh, Jerry, if you only knew. That list was so long, it could have kept us occupied through hotel check-in."

Jerry wasn't done complaining. "And

speaking of baggage claim, do you think you brought enough luggage, Grace? I managed to make the trip with only a carry-on."

"Don't blame the bags on me!" Grace protested. "It was your father, Laurie. He insisted on packing heat. Transporting a gun from New York to California means checking luggage. So, yes, Jerry, I figured if I had to go through the process, I might as well bring all my favorite shoes."

Laurie shook her head and laughed. Jerry and Grace worked incredibly well together, but sometimes she felt like they warranted their own reality show with their Mutt-and-Jeff personality differences.

"My father doesn't *pack heat,* Grace. But once a cop, always a cop: the man can't sleep if he doesn't have that gun in his nightstand. Now, let's focus on Susan's former roommate. And what she might be hiding."

The interior of Nicole Melling's home was as picture-perfect as its surroundings. Nicole greeted them in a light-filled foyer lined with brightly colored contemporary art. Laurie had done some cyber research of her own and had been unable to find a single photograph of Nicole online. All she had were a couple of high school yearbook

209

photos Jerry had tracked down from Nicole's hometown of Irvine, and her freshman class photo at UCLA. Even in her college photograph, Nicole hadn't looked much older than fourteen.

The woman standing in front of Laurie today looked nothing like Laurie had expected. It's not that Nicole had aged poorly. The adult version was far more attractive than the plain-looking, freckle-faced girl from those photographs. But she had changed her appearance drastically. The strawberry-blond hair that had hung well past her shoulders was now dyed and cropped into a dark brown, chin-length bob. Perhaps it was only for the cameras, but at least for today, she wore dramatic makeup, her eyes lined with charcoal. Perhaps more striking than any identifiable physical change, there was a confidence in the way she carried herself that had been lacking in those early photographs.

"Nicole," Laurie said, offering a handshake, "thank you so much for being a part of *Under Suspicion*. Rosemary told me how close you and Susan became in college."

"She was very caring toward me," Nicole said quietly. She led them through the foyer into a large living room with open views of the valley outside.

They were interrupted by the appearance of a man wearing a loose oxford-cloth shirt and khakis. He had a bit of a paunch and was beginning to bald but had an inviting smile. Laurie thought she detected the faint smell of soap.

"Hey there. I thought I should at least say hello. I'm the husband, Gavin."

Laurie rose from her chair to shake his hand. "You certainly didn't have to take the day off for us," she said.

"Oh, I didn't. I work upstairs." He pointed to the staircase off the foyer.

"Gavin's in finance," Nicole explained. "His firm is in the city, but he works here unless he has meetings."

"Lucky you," Laurie said. "Did you also go to UCLA? Is that how you met?"

"Oh no. I was out of Harvard and working at a start-up in San Francisco — one of the first companies that let regular people buy and sell stock online without a broker. I met Nicole in a bar."

His wife rolled her eyes in frustration. "I hate it when you tell people that. It makes me sound cheap."

"What's worse is that she fell for my completely cheesy pickup line. I asked her if she had a Band-Aid, because I skinned my knee falling for her."

Laurie feigned a groan. "Oh, that is *awful.*"

"True," Gavin said, "but it was intentionally awful. There's a difference."

"To be clear," Nicole said, "that's just how we *met.* I felt sorry enough to give him my phone number, but we began to date properly after that."

"And what brought you up to San Francisco after UCLA?" Laurie asked. She knew that Nicole quit school after her sophomore year and assumed it was because of what happened to Susan. She was always amazed to learn how the death of one person rippled out to change the course of so many other lives.

"I had originally wanted to go to Stanford or Berkeley, so I guess I felt a pull from Northern California. I mean, look at that view."

The story sounded polite but superficial. "So, did you continue school up here?" Laurie asked.

"Nope." Nicole shook her head and said nothing more.

"It's just, I couldn't help but notice that many of the people closest to Susan seem to have left school. You, Madison Meyer, Keith Ratner."

"You'd have to ask them. I assume it's not

uncommon for actors to leave school if they start getting regular work. And of course Madison got that role in *Beauty Land.* As for me, I think Susan's death made me realize life was short."

"Are you still in touch with Madison or Keith?"

Nicole shook her head.

Laurie got the impression that this subject was making Nicole uncomfortable and decided to approach the questioning from a different angle. "So, when Mr. Pickup Man here threw you his clever line, you were still new to the area?"

Gavin was the one who laughed. "Like, just-off-the-train new. And nervous. She admitted giving me her number, but what she didn't tell you was that she gave me a fake name."

"No, really?" Laurie asked. "Why in the world?"

Nicole shifted in her seat. "Wow, I did *not* think we'd be talking about this. Truth be told, I was in that bar with a fake ID. I didn't want the bartender to hear me using a name that didn't match the license I'd just shown him. Besides, I can't be the first woman who made up a fake name with a stranger trying to talk her up at a bar."

"Certainly not," Laurie said. But usually

the fake name would come with a fake number, too. How many times had a younger Laurie, borrowing the lyrics of an old pop song, scribbled *Jenny, 867-5309,* on the inside of some drunk playboy's matchbook?

"Anyway," Gavin said, "it was love at almost-first-sight. We got married exactly six months after we met."

Nicole smiled and patted her husband's forearm. "Like I said, life is short."

"I never realized that Susan was the reason you were willing to jump in so fast," Gavin said. "In fact, Nicole never even talked about being Susan's roommate until we happened to bump into Susan's mother, Rosemary, at one of those huge dim sum places in Chinatown. Remember that, honey?"

Nicole raised her eyebrows but said nothing.

"You remember," her husband prompted. "Over all that noise from the tables and the food carts, I heard some woman yelling, 'Nicole. Nicole Hunter?' That's her maiden name. And then Rosemary runs over and gives my wife this huge hug. So, of course, I ask her, 'Who's that?' And then she tells me she was roommates with the Cinderella Murder victim."

"It wasn't something I liked to talk about," Nicole said. "Even now."

"Anyway, I was the one who went back to Rosemary's table and insisted that she give us a call."

Laurie had gotten the impression from Rosemary that Susan and Nicole had been best friends, but now she was learning that Nicole initially did not mention Susan's murder to her own husband and had no relationship with Susan's mother until Gavin suggested it.

She had been warned by Rosemary that Nicole could be shy and might even come off as aloof. But sitting here in Nicole's living room, watching the woman continue that polite smile, Laurie was certain that Susan's supposed best friend was lying to her.

33

Jerry snapped his seat belt closed and started the engine of the van. "Take one more look at that amazing view," he said, "because I think that was the only reason to drive up here."

"No kidding," Grace said, leaning forward from the backseat. "That was a total bust. Talk about a cold fish."

So Laurie was not the only one who had noticed that Nicole hadn't exactly been forthcoming with her memories of Susan Dempsey.

Jerry used his turn signal, despite the absence of any oncoming traffic, and pulled away from the curb. "It's like she wasn't even there."

"I agree," Laurie said. "She did seem a bit distracted."

"No, I mean, like she wasn't even there at UCLA," Jerry said. "She didn't stay in touch with her friends. She didn't offer any stories about Susan other than how nice she was to her. All she wanted to do was talk about everyone else: how strange it was that Frank Parker wanted to meet Susan at his home, how hungry Madison was for fame, how Susan had caught her boyfriend flirting with other girls multiple times. It's like she wanted us to focus on everyone else except her."

Laurie was trying to figure out why Nicole might have held back with them when her thoughts were interrupted by her cell phone. It was her father.

"Is everything okay, Dad?"

"All good. I think we've got Timmy on a decent schedule after the flight west. He slept until seven thirty, had a big breakfast at the hotel restaurant, then we went down to Fisherman's Wharf for lunch and had a whole platter of fish and chips."

"You know you're not supposed to eat that stuff." Only last year, her father had been rushed to Mount Sinai Hospital with cardiac fibrillation. Two stents in his right ventricle later, he was now supposed to keep a heart-healthy diet.

"No worries, Dr. Laurie. I got grilled halibut and salad. And — in full disclosure — four french fries."

"I suppose we can let that slide. We're on

our way back to the hotel now. Dinner at Mama Torini's?" Laurie had visited San Francisco with her parents when she was considering applying to Stanford twenty years ago. Her best memories of the trip were of Leo locking Laurie's mother in a cell at Alcatraz and dinner at Mama Torini's, with its red-and-white-checked tablecloths and heaping portions of fettuccine Alfredo prepared tableside. "I think Timmy would love it."

"Great minds think alike. That's why I was calling. I made a reservation at seven. Figured that was as late as we could push it with Timmy but knew you were working."

Even with Timmy and her father here, she was having a hard time juggling her schedule to see them. She assured her father she'd be back to the hotel within the hour and hung up.

Grace was leaning forward from the backseat again, fiddling with her phone. "Remember that site Who's Dated Who?" she asked.

"Whom," Jerry corrected. "Who's Dated *Whom.* I'm going to write them an e-mail, demanding that they add an 'm.' "

"Well, I looked up Susan's high school sweetheart, Keith Ratner. Get a load of this." She began rattling off a long list of names of women who had been linked to the B-list actor over the years.

"I think I've only heard of two of those people," Laurie said. They were both actresses a good ten years younger than Keith.

"Oh, he's in no position to land anyone famous anymore," Grace said. "But my point is that the list is long. Rosemary and Nicole both said he cheated on Susan. Guess a player's always a player."

"But cheating's not the same as killing someone," Jerry said.

"No," Grace said, "but if she caught him? I could picture it. Keith could've been driving her up to the audition either hoping to get a part for himself or making sure Frank didn't try to get handsy with his girl. If Susan confronted him about cheating, they could have gotten into a fight. She gets mad and storms out of the car. I know I've done it. He starts chasing her. They fight, and things get out of control."

It wasn't a bad theory. It would explain how Susan had wound up near Laurel Canyon Park while her car was found on campus.

Jerry stopped at a red light. "Too bad Keith has an alibi, and we don't have any evidence."

"It's like that old game Clue," Laurie said,

thinking about playing the game with her son at home. "We look at every possible theory and try to poke holes in each one. When there's only one theory standing, we might actually have some answers."

"And that's where our dreamy host, Alex Buckley, comes in," Grace said. "Speaking of which, let's type his name in here and see what we find. Ooh, he's no Keith Ratner, but he's not exactly a monk." Grace began reading names from Who's Dated Who. Laurie recognized more than a few: a model, an actress, an opera singer, a morning news anchor.

The light turned green, and Jerry took a right turn. Laurie was so distracted by Grace's babble that she did not notice that the cream-colored pickup truck that had been parked on Nicole's street was now taking the same turn behind them.

34

Martin Collins rested in a rattan lounger on the back deck of his 8,700-square-foot Sunset Strip home. He looked out beyond his infinity pool to the sun beginning to set on the city below. He had purchased this house four years ago for more money than he had ever dreamed of earning. It was a far cry from the fleabag apartment where he'd grown up in Nebraska. He was born to live here.

He returned his attention to the folder of documents on his lap. They were mock-ups of the latest brochures for Advocates for God, complete with photographs of smiling church members handing out canned goods to the needy, family picnics, and Martin throwing a Frisbee for a yellow Labrador retriever. Market research showed that, more than any breed, people associated Labradors with strength and trust. Martin nodded approvingly. These were the kinds of images that new followers could pass on to friends and family members to expand Advocates for God's numbers. More members meant more contributions.

The moment of optimism was cut short as he remembered that he needed to call Steve Roman for an update on Nicole. He pulled up the number on his cell and hit ENTER.

"Good timing," Steve said by way of a greeting. "I just left Nicole's house. The TV crew was there."

"Any chance you know what she told them?"

He felt his frustration rise when Steve answered in the negative. For the past week, Steve's reports had been abnormally terse. It might be time to send another minion to replace him.

"Is there something you're not telling me?" Martin asked.

"Of course not," Steve assured him.

Martin was aware of Steve's violent past — the robberies, the bar fights, the unpredictable attacks of anger he used to have before finding the church. Still, Steve had never given him cause for worry. More than perhaps any other devotee of Advocates for God, Steve had truly changed. And he was loyal.

"I stayed in the truck while the crew went in the house," Steve was saying. "It's a big place. She must have done pretty well for herself — money-wise, I mean."

"So that's all you have?"

"For now, but I'm tailing the TV crew. They just dropped off two guys and a bunch of equipment at a warehouse and are weaving through downtown San Francisco now. I figure if I stay on them, I might be able to overhear something. What specifically should I be listening for?"

"You know how we talk about people who don't understand Advocates for God? Who try to say the worst about our good works? Well, Nicole might be the worst enemy this church has. Given a platform on a national TV show, she may be tempted to attack our beliefs. To make up lies about either AG or me personally. I need to know what, if anything, Nicole reveals about her time at UCLA."

Though Martin typically gave away no secrets, it had been impossible to rely on Steve as his eyes and ears without trusting him with at least some background information. So Steve knew that Nicole had been an early member of Advocates for God who left on bad terms. He knew that Nicole's college roommate Susan Dempsey had been murdered, and that her death was the focus of this television show that had Martin concerned about unfavorable news coverage.

Martin had no plans to reveal anything more. After all, that had been his mistake with Nicole — letting her know a side of him that she was not ready to see. At first, when she quit school and left town, he kept waiting for the other shoe to drop, questioning whether he had done enough to ensure her silence. But then months became years, and years became close to two decades.

And now this stupid show. He had watched the first special and knew how thorough they were in their reporting. Would Nicole be able to get through this without her association with AG coming to light?

"But the show is about Nicole's roommate," Steve said. "What does Susan Dempsey's murder have to do with AG?"

"You are asking more questions than you should, Steve."

Martin spoke with his usual chilly confidence.

"My apologies," Steve said cautiously. "I'll keep watching. Wait, they're stopping now at some high-rise hotel. Yeah, they're getting out. I can tell which one's in charge by the way she's giving orders — a woman in the front passenger seat. I'll park and get a bead on her on foot. See what I can find out."

"You do that, Steve."

35

It was barely seven o'clock in the evening, but Nicole was already at her bathroom vanity, washing off the heavy layer of makeup she'd worn for the cameras today. Gone, too, was her tailored black sheath dress, replaced with her usual ensemble of yoga pants and a hoodie.

When she was done patting her face dry, she opened her eyes to find Gavin's image behind hers in the mirror.

"That's my wife," he said, wrapping his arms around her waist and giving her a kiss on her freshly scrubbed cheek. "You looked beautiful today, but I always prefer you like this."

She turned to face him and returned his embrace. "I've never been beautiful. The makeup certainly helps, but I don't understand how anyone can put up with all of that work every day."

"You've always been beautiful to me."

"Please, when you met me, I still looked like a dorky teenager. I guess I should be grateful now that I've always looked young for my age."

Gavin was smiling to himself.

"What's so funny?" she asked.

"Telling that TV producer about how we met. It's been a long time since I thought about that. We owe our marriage to that fake ID of yours."

"I had that ID because of Madison. She got them for Susan and me so we could go celebrity-watching on the club scene."

"I can't even picture you doing that."

That, Nicole thought, is because you never knew me when I was a follower. A lemming. The girl whose own parents knew she would get "lost" on her own. The one who started spending more time with the crooks at Advocates for God than with her own best friend.

"Are you done with your work?" she asked.

"Just a couple e-mails, and I'll be yours for the night."

"Sounds good. I'll start dinner. Lasagna sound good?"

"Delicious," he said, giving her another buss on the cheek.

He padded down the hall to his office,

while she made her way downstairs to the kitchen. As she chopped some fresh basil for the pasta sauce, she replayed her conversation today with the television crew. Nicole thought that she'd done a good job talking about Madison, Keith, and Frank Parker, the three people who were truly under suspicion. But before they'd even spoken about the investigation, Laurie had launched all those questions about why Nicole had left college and moved to the Bay Area. She even seemed a little too curious about the fact that Nicole had given Gavin a fake name when they first met.

Did she know that Nicole had been using that fake identification for more than wine purchases after she fled Los Angeles? Did she already know about Advocates for God?

No, it was impossible. Nicole had never even spoken the words "Advocates for God" or "Martin Collins" since she left L.A. She was too terrified.

Maybe Keith Ratner had told the producers about Nicole's association with AG. After all, she was the one who first introduced him to the racket. No one in Advocates for God would refer to it as a racket, of course. They called it a religion. They said they were committed to "good works."

That was so long ago that sometimes Nicole had a hard time remembering when exactly Susan had started to feel so much animosity about Advocates for God. At first, Susan was supportive. Just like Susan had her theater activities and computer work without Nicole, Nicole was finding a new network of friends in what she had initially described to Susan as a "volunteer group" focused on "serving the poor." But when Nicole began to advance farther into the circle — and began soliciting donations from wealthier students like Susan — Susan questioned the church's ongoing demands for money.

It was the very beginning of spring semester, sophomore year, when Nicole told Susan that she had started seeing Martin Collins over the holiday break, not just as part of the group, but as his girlfriend. She expected Susan to be worried about the age difference: Nicole, having graduated early from high school, was only eighteen, and Martin was twenty-nine. But Susan's concerns ran deeper. She said Advocates for God was a fraud. That Martin was lining his pockets with money meant for the poor. That he was enlisting vulnerable people to treat him like God. She said she felt like Nicole was slipping into "another world." That she was "brainwashed." She asked why a twenty-nine-year-old man would be interested in a college sophomore in the first place.

"How can you know anything about Martin when you've never met him? How can you judge AG when you refuse to learn anything about it? No wonder Martin says you're trying to corrupt me!" Nicole had yelled. It was their very first argument.

But it wasn't until Nicole invited Keith to join Martin and her at a revival that Susan truly became angry. Nicole had never seen her like that. Susan was always so calm, smiling like she was telling herself a secret joke or listening to her own private soundtrack. But that day, she was screaming at Nicole with such fervor that her pale face turned bright red, makeup streaking her cheeks. *Keith needs attention from every girl he meets. First it was Madison. Now it's you. But you're worse than Madison. She's a harmless flirt, but you had to take my boyfriend to your ridiculous Bible-thumping cult! What is* happening *to you, Nicole? It's like I don't even know you anymore.*

Even now, Nicole could not actually remember picking up her political science textbook and throwing it at Susan's head. She just saw Susan freeze, her mouth open in shock. She remembered trying to apologize, but Susan wouldn't calm down. "That's it, Nicole," she had screamed from the doorway. "I love you, but you either quit that cult or you're moving out!"

It was the last conversation they ever had.

Nicole had fled the dorm, too, walking to Martin's house, and then into his bedroom unannounced. He wasn't alone. In that moment, Nicole realized why Martin had liked her in the first place. She had always looked younger than her age. But as it turned out, she was not quite young enough for Martin Collins.

36

Mama Torini's looked exactly as Leo remembered it: red-and-white-checked tablecloths, dark wood molding, bright yellow walls barely visible beneath decades of Italian movie posters and signed celebrity photographs. He couldn't believe it had been twenty-two years since he was here with Laurie and Eileen. He wished his wife were here to share the experience with her grandson, but he had lost her ten years earlier to a heart attack, before she'd even had a chance to meet Timmy. He wished Laurie's husband, Greg, were here, too. But like the song said, you can't always get what you want. He was lucky to have Timmy and Laurie in his life.

Leo noticed a well-dressed man at the next table admiring Laurie's appearance as she took her seat. As usual, his daughter was completely unaware of the attention. Her focus was entirely on Timmy as she pointed out an autographed picture of Wynton Marsalis with two of the restaurant's waiters.

"So what did you and Grandpa do today?" she asked once they were settled in.

"We walked and walked," Timmy said, "like probably a hundred miles. We walked even more than we do in New York. And you can feel it more because of all the hills. I was like . . ." He stopped talking long enough to pant like a tired dog. "I told Grandpa when we got back to the hotel room that if we took one more step, my feet would fall off."

She feigned a look beneath the table. "We just walked here, and you've still got your feet. Did you actually see anything while you did all this walking and panting?"

"It was awesome! We saw everything," he said excitedly. "Chinatown; the piers; a place called Exploratorium, which was totally cool. And, Grandpa, what was that super-steep, twisty street?"

"Lombard. And the kid here walked it bottom to top like a champ."

"That certainly does sound like a busy day," Laurie said.

Timmy's rendition made it sound as if sightseeing had consumed their entire day. But Leo had found time to do some work on his own. His primary job here was to watch his grandson while Laurie was working, but if he was truly going to keep them both safe, he couldn't turn off the part of his brain that had brought him to California — the cop part.

NYPD inspector Leo Farley had spent twenty minutes of Timmy's television time on the phone with Detective Alan O'Brien, the lead investigator in the murder of Lydia Levitt. Somebody else calling the Alameda County sheriff's department about an unsolved homicide the previous week might have gotten the brush-off, but more than thirty years on the job came in handy, despite retirement and being on a different coast.

He knew from Detective O'Brien that the police had no suspects in Lydia's murder, even unofficially. The sad reality was that domestic violence was usually to blame when women were killed. But police had found absolutely no evidence to suggest any discord, let alone physical violence, in the Levitt marriage. By all accounts, Lydia's husband, Don, was a stand-up citizen with an ironclad alibi at the time of his wife's murder, thanks to surveillance cameras at his gym.

The next theory was some kind of secret

life that might have put Lydia in danger. But a thorough search of the family's home and computers had turned up no reason to believe that Lydia was anything other than she appeared to be: a seventy-one-year-old wife, mother, and grandmother who liked to garden, eat out at restaurants, and talk to her neighbors.

According to Detective O'Brien, the most likely explanation was that Lydia interrupted a burglary attempt at Rosemary's house. The police were chasing down the local thieves in hopes of a tip.

"Did Rosemary tell you that her daughter was murdered twenty years ago?" Leo had asked the detective.

"She did," Detective O'Brien had said. "She was understandably upset about her neighbor and then mentioned it brought back memories of Susan. The Cinderella Murder. Gotta wonder whether that one will ever be solved."

"That's actually why I'm in California." Leo explained Laurie's decision to feature Susan Dempsey's case in *Under Suspicion*. "I've got to admit that I didn't feel too right when I heard there was a murder at the home of one of the show participants right when production was starting."

"You think Lydia Levitt's murder is somehow related to *Under Suspicion*?"

"I thought I should at least throw the possibility out there. And if you happen to pick up on anything that indicates a connection, I'd sure appreciate a call."

Leo had to hope Detective O'Brien would keep his word. He sounded trustworthy over the phone. Until Leo could prove to Laurie that Rosemary's neighbor was killed because of the show, he would never be able to convince her she was in danger.

There'd been one other phone call during Timmy's nap, from Alex Buckley. That one he could share with his daughter.

"Alex called today," he said.

"He called me too but didn't leave a message. What's he up to?"

Leo could never tell whether Laurie was actually interested in Leo's Alex updates or was just following along, as she would with any other story.

"He's looking forward to the trip out."

"Great. Once we get to the summit session, he can go into cross-examination mode."

"That's why he was calling. He's heading to Los Angeles tomorrow."

Leo saw the confusion on his daughter's face.

"I think you misheard, Dad. We're laying

236

the groundwork for now, getting some first-person narratives. Alex isn't needed until the summit."

"I know that was the plan. But I guess Brett decided he wanted Alex to have as much contact as possible with the suspects, or the players, or whatever you call them. Alex said something about Brett having sprung news on you before, so he was trying to make sure you knew he was flying out early."

Timmy's summary of the day's activities had finally gotten Laurie out of work mode, but now Leo could see the tension immediately return to his daughter's face. "No, I didn't know that. Typical Brett."

"Are you upset? Alex is our friend. He's a good man."

"I want him to come. Of course I do. But I had intended to get my own fix on the people he'll be interviewing first."

"It sounds like you are trying to come up with reasons to keep him away —"

"Dad. Please."

Leo knew it was time to change the subject. "So you met Susan's roommate today? Nicole?"

She nodded. "She was nothing like I expected. I got a very peculiar vibe off of her. I know it sounds crazy, but I've got to wonder if the police even looked into her as a suspect. They may have had their hands too full with the others to have even asked where Susan's supposed best friend was."

"Sometimes I really do think you inherited my cop brain."

"This is more my reporter brain. *Under Suspicion* may be reality TV, but I haven't forgotten my journalistic roots. Just as we don't want to skew the facts to make people look guilty if they are not, I don't want to present Nicole as the angelic best friend if there's another side to the story."

"So what are you going to do?"

"I'm going to find out the truth about who Nicole Melling really was back at UCLA — back when she was known as Nicole Hunter."

Steve Roman's thoughts were halted by the appearance of the bartender, his dark hair slicked back into a ponytail, his tight black T-shirt accentuating his biceps.

"Another club soda, sir?"

Steve snuck a glance at the woman, older gentleman, and child. The woman was signaling for the check. "I'm good," he said. "Thanks."

Steve tried to avoid any temptation to imbibe alcohol, but tonight, his presence at the bar in Mama Torini's was unavoidable. This stool, just fifteen feet from the television woman's table, allowed him to overhear her conversation with ease.

From what he could gather, Nicole Melling, née Hunter, was keeping her mouth shut about whatever beef she had with Advocates for God. If that were the only news to report, Martin would be relieved. Maybe he would even cut Steve loose from this assignment, and Steve could return to his former routine.

But now Steve had learned they had a new problem. From this bar stool, he had Googled "production of Under Suspicion." He had immediately found a photograph of the woman he'd identified as the boss of the production team. Her name was Laurie Moran. She was the show's creator and producer. He had also learned that Laurie was a crime victim herself, and the daughter of a cop. One more search had confirmed that the older man at the dinner table was her father.

And now the woman had announced that her curiosity about Nicole was piqued and that she'd be taking a close look at her background. *I'm going to find out the truth about who Nicole Melling really was.*

Martin would not be happy.

37

Alex Buckley looked down at the suitcase
and garment bag, packed up and still open
on his bed. He had traveled long distances
before for cases, and he was accustomed to
appearing on television, but this was the
first time he had combined the two. He had
managed to accommodate six suits and a
variety of more casual options in his luggage.

When Brett Young had called him this
afternoon to ask him to move up his plans
to fly to Los Angeles, Alex had wanted to
check with Laurie. He had seen the way
Young had surprised Laurie by calling
without telling her. So he bought himself
time by telling Brett he needed to check his
trial schedule. In reality, he had used the
borrowed moments to call Laurie, but she
hadn't answered. He had phoned Leo instead, who assured Alex that Laurie would
value his early input. But now that his bags

were packed, he had to wonder whether Leo might have his own reasons for wanting to bring Alex to California. When he got there, would he cramp Laurie's rhythm with her production team? This would be the first time they'd worked together since developing a friendship outside of the show.

When he was invited to host *Under Suspicion*'s inaugural episode about the Graduation Gala Murder, he couldn't resist. He had followed the case closely when he was a sophomore at Fordham and had always been convinced that one of the guests celebrating at the gala was the killer. As it turned out, his suspicions were incorrect. The lasting mark of his participation in the show wasn't the discovery of the true killer's identity but his devotion to Laurie Moran.

"Do you need a car service for tomorrow, Mr. Alex?"

"How many times do I need to tell you to drop the 'Mr.,' Ramon? Alex is fine. Heck, you can even call me Al, as the song says."

"That is not how Ramon rolls, sir."

Alex shook his head and laughed. Occasionally he looked at his own life and could not believe it. Ramon was sixty years old, born in the Philippines. Divorced, with one adult daughter in Syracuse, he was Alex's "assistant." Alex preferred that term to "butler," which had been Ramon's title in his previous employment for a family that had relocated to the West Coast. The decorator who had ensured that Alex's apartment was finished tastefully had recommended hiring Ramon when she saw that Alex was so busy at work that he frequently bought new undershirts because the laundry was backed up.

Alex's apartment on Beekman Place, with views of the East River, had six rooms, plus servant's quarters, much too large for a bachelor. But it had enough space for a dining room to entertain friends, a home office, Ramon, and Alex's younger brother, Andrew, a corporate lawyer who visited frequently from Washington, D.C. In Alex's mind, his home reflected his commitment to friends, family, and loyalty. And yet, he understood how it all probably looked to someone who didn't truly know him.

What he really meant was how it probably looked to Laurie.

Last December, he thought it was all going to be easy. The man Timmy called Blue Eyes had tried to kill the boy and his mother. On instinct, Alex ran in and swept both Laurie and Timmy into his arms. For that brief moment, they almost felt like a family.

But, just as quickly, Leo had appeared, and Laurie and Timmy had pulled away from Alex's embrace. Leo, Laurie, and Timmy were the family. Alex was a friend. A coworker. A buddy. Not family. Not, most important, Greg.

At first, Alex reasoned that Laurie simply wasn't ready for another relationship. Certainly he could understand the possible reasons. She had a demanding career and a child to juggle. She had lost her husband. She wasn't over Greg yet. Maybe she never would be.

But now, the night before he was supposed to fly to Los Angeles to work with Laurie again, he wondered if her reluctance was specific to him personally. In addition to an apartment that might have seemed too large and a butlerlike assistant who called him "Mr. Alex," he had somehow been saddled with a public persona fit for the tabloids.

How many times had he seen his own photograph in the society pages with a woman on his arm, the caption hinting at a growing romance? But because his part-time job as a trial commentator had made him something of a pseudocelebrity, these pairings always seemed to be blown out of proportion. Andrew had even told him about a website that purported to list every single person Alex had ever supposedly dated. Most were names Alex didn't recognize.

Why would a woman as smart and confident as Laurie trust someone like him? She had a career and child to worry about. There was no room for some six-foot-four, airbrushed, blow-dried lothario. Could she allow Timmy to become attached to another man who, as she perceived it, might fall out of his life?

Alex looked down once again at his bags and then replaced a flashy purple paisley tie with conservative navy stripes, knowing the swap wouldn't make one bit of difference.

38

"Wow, Mom. This is almost like that big breakfast they had at the hotel when we went to Aruba."

The Aruba vacation last winter had celebrated the success of the first episode of *Under Suspicion*. Laurie felt like she'd been working nonstop ever since.

Laurie placed a hand on Timmy's shoulder as she took in the breakfast options spread across the gigantic island in the middle of the kitchen. Laurie had been skeptical about the idea of their all camping out under one roof in Los Angeles, but with Brett already complaining about the show's budget, she'd been in no position to challenge Jerry's logic about using one house for both lodging and the summit-session filming.

Of course, she hadn't anticipated the house in Bel Air would look like a Normandy estate. Nor that each of them —

Jerry, Grace, Laurie, Timmy, Leo, and Alex — would have a separate room, complete with en suite bathroom and king bed topped with the smoothest sheets Laurie had ever felt. Now she and Timmy had woken up to find a fully catered meal waiting for them in the kitchen, courtesy of Jerry's careful planning.

"Can I have a bagel?" Timmy said, starting to flip through the assortment on the tray.

"Please don't touch every single one, okay?" Nine-year-old boys had no concept of germs. "And of course you *may* have one."

"And *may* I have butter and cream cheese and lox and fruit salad?"

"You may. Just make sure you leave enough of everything for everyone else."

"You mean, no hogging."

"Exactly." Where did he learn this stuff?

She was watching Timmy smear cream cheese on a poppy-seed bagel when Jerry walked in. He was dressed as casually as she'd ever seen him, in a yellow polo shirt and navy chinos. His hair was still damp from the shower. "Oh, excellent. Craft services has already been here."

"You know we're not filming here today, right?" Laurie clarified. "We're doing our preinterview with Keith Ratner."

"I know. But having them provide the food is really not much more expensive than going out to eat, plus it saves time. They'll be here for all three meals with cleanup at night unless I call them off. And I figured, why not indulge on our first morning? Besides, we saved so much money on this house that we could afford to have the extra catering."

She gestured for him to look at their surroundings. Next to the open kitchen was an enormous living room, complete with a fireplace and three separate seating areas. The dining room could easily accommodate sixteen people. Outside, a swimming pool fit for a resort sparkled in the sun.

"I find it hard to believe that this house fits within a budget set by Brett Young."

"It does for us," Jerry said, beaming with pride, "because we got it for free."

"Excuse me?"

"That's right. When I called Dwight Cook to set an interview schedule, I told him that the location for the summit session was to-be-announced and that we'd be finding a house near campus. Turns out he bought this place for his parents when REACH first hit it big. His parents decided a couple of years ago that they needed a smaller place, all on one floor. I guess he won't sell it because of capital gains taxes or something I'm not rich enough to understand. He has a property manager handle it as a high-end rental for movie shoots and whatnot. But we got it for free. Are you mad?"

"That the house came from Susan's co-worker at the computer lab?"

He nodded. "I probably should have run it by you, but I figured you were busy enough without having to micromanage those kinds of details."

She had been swamped, but it would have been nice to know that they were receiving a subsidy from Dwight Cook. It certainly was not the first time they had received assistance from someone involved in a case. For "The Graduation Gala," they filmed the entire show at the home of the victim's husband. He had even paid participants additional compensation out of his own pocket to guarantee their presence. Still, the journalist in her cringed a little.

Jerry helped Timmy pour a glass of orange juice. "I figured it was okay since Dwight's not even a suspect. He was a friend of Susan, and let's face it, he's so successful that crashing in his empty house isn't exactly a deep reach into his wallet. Plus in the Graduation Gala case —"

"It's okay, Jerry. You don't need to explain. I would have made the same decision. We just need to disclose it during the show."

Laurie's own job would be easier if she started trusting Jerry more to make autonomous decisions.

"The house is really pretty," Timmy said, setting down his orange juice glass. "Thank you for finding this place for us, Jerry."

"My goodness. If you could bottle up that sweetness and sell it in a can, Dwight Cook wouldn't be the only one who was rich."

Laurie turned at the sound of footsteps and saw her father and Alex Buckley walking into the kitchen.

"What's all this?" Leo boomed.

"Jerry got us breakfast!" Timmy exclaimed.

"Even better," Jerry said. "Jerry hired someone to get us breakfast."

Alex gave her a quick good-morning peck on the cheek and headed straight for the coffee. He had an iPad in hand, which she knew he would use to peruse the *New York Times.* He had arrived so late the previous evening that they'd barely had a chance to say hello to each other.

She watched as Timmy leapt out of his seat to give Alex and his grandfather an overview of the buffet. Looking at the three of them, she realized she was smiling and still felt the warmth of Alex's kiss on her cheek.

She deliberately glanced away at the empty place setting at the table. "So we're all here except for Grace," she said. "She's probably still working on her hair and makeup."

"Actually," Jerry said, "I told her she could sleep in."

"We're supposed to see Keith Ratner today." She looked at her watch. They should be leaving before too long. "We can review strategy on the ride there. Rosemary has always been convinced Keith was involved."

"I know, the boyfriend's important. But he's almost as celebrity-conscious as Madison Meyer. That's why I thought you should bring Alex instead of me and Grace. Assuming, of course, that's okay with you, Alex."

Alex looked up from his coffee. "I wouldn't say I'm a celebrity, but I'm happy to do whatever Laurie would like."

Another point for Jerry. He was right. Alex would likely snow Keith Ratner — she might as well take advantage of his expertise. "Alex, if Keith has been holding on to information about Susan's murder all these years, I can't imagine anyone who might have a better chance of getting him to talk."

"I don't know, Jerry," Leo said cheerfully. "It sounds to me like you're playing Alex and Laurie to get yourself a day off."

"Absolutely not, Mr. Farley," he said, waving his punch list. "Grace and I have a long to-do list ahead of the summit session next week."

Laurie smiled. "Dad, I can assure you that Jerry is always working. Speaking of work, Alex, you and I should be heading out. And, Jerry, you can scratch one phone call off your list. We'll make sure Keith knows where to come next week for the big shoot."

39

Three hundred sixty miles north, Dwight Cook was just waking up in his Palo Alto mansion. Though the home had more than nine thousand square feet, he spent most of his time in this enormous master suite with sweeping views of the foothills. But this morning, he was more interested in another one of his real estate holdings. He immediately reached for the laptop on his nightstand and opened the viewer for the surveillance cameras in the Bel Air house.

The first camera to appear overlooked the entryway. Laurie Moran was walking toward the front door. He recognized the man behind her as Alex Buckley, the show's host.

Dwight used the right-arrow key to flip through the cameras situated around the house.

The assistant, Grace, was coming out of one of the bedrooms on the second floor, singing an old disco song. The others were all finishing breakfast in the kitchen, the child asking whether they'd have time for a trip to Disneyland. The surveillance equipment — built into the walls, completely undetectable — was working flawlessly. Dwight had had the system installed in all his properties for extra security, but now it would be serving another role.

Dwight wouldn't be going to Los Angeles until this weekend, but for all practical purposes, he was right there with the production team. And once the summit sessions began, he'd be able to see and hear everything.

40

Laurie led the way to the their black SUV. In addition to the Land Cruiser, they had also rented a full-size van for production use, and a separate sedan for Leo and Timmy to tool around in. She dangled the keys as she walked. "Would you care to drive, or should I?"

"Your choice."

"I've never driven in Los Angeles before. I suppose I should at least try it. If I feel like I'm putting our lives in danger, I'll pull over and we can switch."

"Sounds like a plan," Alex said, "though I'd be more worried about the life of any driver stupid enough to upset you."

"I'll admit, I can be a tough customer," Laurie laughed. "I'll try to avoid any road-rage incidents."

She had already entered their destination into the GPS. Once they were both belted in, she started the engine for the short drive to Westwood.

"I'm surprised you don't have a driver," Alex said.

"Says the man with the butler," she said wryly. "Seriously, have you not *met* Brett Young? He has been all over me about the budget for this episode. It's not cheap to shoot in California. I think we can manage our own driving."

"That house certainly doesn't look like budget-friendly lodging."

"Funny you should mention that. Jerry just told me this morning that it belongs to Dwight Cook. We're using it free of charge."

"You sound irritated."

"It's fine. I just know that Jerry had a hundred opportunities to mention that detail a little earlier."

"But then you might have said no, and he'd be back to trying to find a space big enough to house us all, and suitable for filming, all on the studio budget. As they say, better to ask for forgiveness than permission."

"You're right. I think it's hard for me sometimes to see Jerry as someone other than the skinny intern who used to fetch coffee."

"It's not my business, but from what I've seen, he's a far cry from that. He's very good at his job."

"I know. Sending you to meet with Keith today is a perfect example. He and Madison are status conscious. They live in a world where their worth is measured daily by how fast the valet at the Ivy fetches their car. He's not exactly A-list, but he'd run right over Jerry and Grace."

"No one runs over Grace," Alex said.

"True."

"Where are we meeting him?"

"A little bookstore in Westwood. From what I read online, it seems like an alternative kind of place — counterculture stuff."

"Why there? I thought he said he was at some church thing the night Susan was murdered."

She should have known that Alex would have fully reviewed all the case materials. "Yes, at least *allegedly*. But the church wasn't exactly a church yet. It was fledgling. A bit fringy, if you ask me. At the time, Keith told police he was at a discussion group at the bookstore. Once the police investigated further, they learned that it was a meeting for some group called Advocates for God."

Several group members vouched for Keith's whereabouts at the time of Susan's murder, but, based on what Laurie knew

256

about the church, she wondered if they might be so insular as to cover for one another.

"They've come a long way since holding recruiting meetings at indie bookstores," Alex said. "Isn't it a big West Coast megachurch now?"

"And how do you think they got there?" she asked. "Money. They say they 'advocate for God's goodness' " — she added air quotes for good measure — "but they're all about raising money. Supposedly it all goes to serving the poor, but you've got to wonder. Meanwhile, the church's members seem to follow along blindly."

"And that's why you said Keith *allegedly* has an alibi for Susan's murder."

"Exactly. Admittedly, at the time, Ratner was a starving actor and was only just beginning with AG. If he was involved in Susan's murder, I don't see why the church would stick its neck out to cover for him."

"In the lawyering world, we call what you're doing arguing with yourself."

"I know. I can look at every suspect and think they're completely innocent, then, in the blink of an eye, picture them chasing poor Susan into that park. Even her friend Nicole was acting completely out of sorts when we spoke to her, like she was hiding something. I can see why the police were never able to solve the case."

"Hey, don't get frustrated yet. We're just getting started."

The tiny store was crammed floor to ceiling with books, many of them used. A whiteboard behind the cash register listed upcoming events. That night, an author would be signing copies of his book *Legalize Everything.*

The sole employee sported a bushy beard that made it difficult to estimate his age. "You guys looking for a coffee shop or something?"

So she wasn't alone in thinking that she and Alex looked out of place here. Fortunately, the jingle of the bell on the front door interrupted the moment. Laurie could tell from Keith Ratner's expression that he immediately recognized Alex from television.

"I didn't think we were shooting today." He ran his fingers through his tousled dark hair.

"We're not," she explained. "But Alex wanted the opportunity to meet you before the cameras are on."

Alex offered a handshake. "Hey, Keith, good to meet you. I was a huge fan of *Judg-*

ment Calls." Keith Ratner had played a young prosecutor in the short-lived courtroom drama.

"Thanks for meeting us," Laurie said. "And before I forget, we have the location for next week's summit session. It's a house not too far from here." She handed him a piece of paper with the Bel Air address on it.

"No problem," he said, slipping the address into the front pocket of his jeans. "Wow. This store hasn't changed at all. Talk about a blast from the past."

"You haven't been here for a while?" Laurie asked.

"I only came here twice, I think, both for events."

"Advocates for God events, you mean."

"Sure. Does that matter?"

"Only if your church members were backing you up because you share the same religion."

"So much for a little friendly conversation." He looked to Alex for help, but Alex pretended to browse a shelf labeled HAIKU AND TANKA. "The only reason I was ever *under suspicion* in the first place was because Rosemary never liked me. I had six different people confirm to the police I was with them all night — first here at the store,

259

then we went out for coffee. But because we were part of a new church people didn't understand, it's like our word didn't count."

"Sorry, Keith, this isn't about oppressing you for your belief system. You have to admit, when we spoke on the phone, you tried to deflect attention onto anyone but you."

"Human nature." Keith looked to Alex again. "The criminal defense lawyer here must understand that. Someone killed Susan, and it wasn't me — so, yeah, I guess you could say I suspect everyone else. People seem to forget that she was my girlfriend. For four years. I loved that girl."

"Yet you cheated on her," Alex said. He wasn't going to play good cop.

"I never said I was perfect. Why do you think I went looking for a religion? Something to believe in? I was a bad boyfriend, but that doesn't make me a murderer. Did you even look into the stuff I told you about Dwight Cook? Pretty convenient that he happened to *invent* something so valuable within months of Susan's murder."

"Actually," Laurie said, "I did look into your theory. And what I learned was that you knew so little about your own girlfriend that you had no idea what she was working on. Her professor even confirmed that

Susan's research had nothing to do with the idea that became REACH."

"Professors don't know anything about who their students *really* are. Dwight followed Susan around like a lapdog. It seemed like every time I'd come by her dorm, he'd be lingering nearby. I don't care how much money he's made. I'm telling you: something was off about that kid."

"You sound desperate, Keith."

He shook his head. "Check it out if you don't believe me. You know, when I said I'd do this, you told me you'd be objective, that you were a reporter at heart. But it's obvious that Rosemary's infected your brain about me. I'm out of here."

"We're just asking questions," she said. "And you signed a contract."

"Then sue me."

The jingle of the bell as he exited felt like a buzzer ending a boxing round that Laurie knew she had lost.

41

Keith could feel his cell phone shake in his hand. It had been years since he'd lost control. He certainly could not recall ever speaking to Martin Collins so firmly. "I can't do it. You should have heard the way they were running down AG. I couldn't control my anger. I had to leave to keep myself from saying more than I should."

"Of all people, Keith, don't you think I know what it is like to have our beliefs belittled by people who can never understand our good works?"

Keith should have known that Martin would not accept his decision, but Martin didn't understand his frustration. Keith had heard the ridicule in Laurie Moran's voice when she mentioned Advocates for God. She could never begin to understand how AG had saved him after Susan died.

Service to others and guidance from Martin as to the certainty of God's goodness had kept Keith from taking out his grief through booze and girls. And then there were the group sessions. Keith began to examine his guilt at treating Susan poorly when she was alive. He realized that all his betrayals were little acts of revenge. As much as he loved Susan, she made him feel small. He remembered how other couples in high school would talk about being treated like honorary family by one another's parents. His friend Brian even got birthday and Christmas presents from his girlfriend Becky's family.

But Keith had never gotten the slightest sign of approval — let alone affection — from Rosemary or Jack Dempsey. Jack worked so hard, he probably wouldn't have been able to pick Keith from a lineup. And Rosemary? She treated Keith like dirt, with her constant sighs of disappointment and barbed comments insulting his dream of being a star.

Susan always told him to ignore it. She said her mother was just protective and would have had the same response if Susan were to date a prince who was also a Rhodes scholar. But, after Susan's murder, Keith realized that he had absorbed the criticism. Hurting Susan — having power over her —

had been a way to keep her from hurting him.

Now Keith felt like Rosemary Dempsey was calling the shots all over again. He tried once more to explain it all to Martin.

"The way that television producer spoke to me brought back all my old insecurities. And the way they talked about AG reminded me of how Susan would call it a scam when Nicole first became involved."

"You didn't give them any indication that it was Nicole who introduced you to the church, did you?"

"Of course not."

"Remember, if they ask, you were handed a flyer on campus and were curious. With all the pamphleting I did back then, it's perfectly believable. Do not say *anything* to link Nicole with AG."

"I won't be saying anything at all. I don't want to be part of that show."

"You know better than this. Sometimes it's not about you, Keith. How are you best positioned to serve the work of God?"

"How can it be God's work to be in a house full of people who make fun of everything our church stands for?"

"A house?"

"Yes, they have a house for filming. They're also going to be staying there." He retrieved the address from his pocket and read it to Martin.

"Listen to me: you will call the producer and confirm your participation. Advocates for God is a *group* serving God, and Nicole's participation in this show is a direct threat to that group. I have reason to believe that Nicole isn't saying anything about us for now, but the television show may be digging into Nicole's background."

" 'Reason to believe'?"

"I'm relying on you to update me about her involvement and to steer the investigation away from anything that might lead to AG. Do you understand?"

Sometimes Keith wondered whether he should be more questioning of Martin's commands. But without Advocates for God, what would he have?

42

Determined to stick to her family's post-dinner board game ritual, Laurie gathered the crew in the den of the Bel Air house to play Bananagrams, which was like Scrabble on speed. Timmy's favorite moments of the game were the banana-related puns: "split" to start playing and "peel" to pull new tiles. Grace had won the last three games in a row, each time telling Timmy that she might not have been the smartest person in the room, but that she was the most competitive person in the entire world, "and that matters more in the long run."

Laurie could tell that both Timmy and Leo approved.

Everyone was playing except for Jerry, who was hunkered in a chair by the fireplace, working on plans for next week's summit sessions.

"Take a little break," Leo said. "Your eyes are going to cross."

"Can't take a break when you live with your boss." Jerry looked up from his notes and winked at Timmy, who laughed at the joke.

Laurie thought that if anyone should have been working late tonight, it was her. She had blown the meeting with Keith Ratner today. The man was arrogant, but he had a point. Rosemary was so convinced that Keith was involved in Susan's death, but was her suspicion based in fact or on her belief that Susan never would have gone to Los Angeles in the first place if not for her boyfriend? And would anyone have even questioned his alibi if it had come from six members of a book club or established group, instead of Advocates for God?

She was supposed to be spelling out words with her tiles, but she kept hearing Keith's voice: *You told me you'd be objective.* Objective reporting meant checking his alibi.

She excused herself to make a phone call. She looked up the phone number for the church of Advocates for God and received a message system. "This is Laurie Moran, calling for Reverend Collins." She had read that Martin Collins was the founder and minister of Advocates for God. Though the alibi witnesses who had spoken to police were all individual church members, she had to believe that Collins would have been aware of the situation given the group's relatively small size at the time and the high-profile nature of the investigation. "It's about a church member named Keith Ratner and a police investigation from 1994. If he could return my call, I'd appreciate it."

Laurie was heading back to the makeshift game room when Jerry waved her over to his corner.

"You really should hang it up for the night," she said. "I'm starting to feel guilty."

"Then you have no idea how late I usually work in New York. Besides, this is fun. I was just going through old copies of the UCLA newspaper that I downloaded onto my computer. I thought it might be worth exploring the aftermath of Susan's killing on the campus. Were students afraid? Did the university add security? That kind of thing."

"Good thinking."

"Thanks. And then I saw this."

He rotated his laptop so she could see the screen. The headline read TECH PROFESSOR LEAVES FOR PRIVATE SECTOR, FIRST JOB IS FOR UCLA STUDENT.

The article was published in September 1994, the first edition in the school year following Susan's death, reporting the university's loss of Richard Hathaway, a popular and prolific computer science professor, to a booming, Internet-fueled private sector job.

According to the article, a university policy requiring ownership of all faculty research and development could have played a role in Hathaway's departure. The author hinted that the policy could make it difficult to hire and retain professors in the most innovative and profitable fields. It also reported that Professor Hathaway's first private-sector gig was as a consultant to UCLA junior Dwight Cook, who was currently seeking financing for his Internet-search technology.

The caption beneath Professor Hathaway's photograph read, "Professor could earn his annual UCLA income in a day's work for a successful start-up."

But it was the last paragraph of the article that Jerry highlighted for Laurie on his screen:

Professor Hathaway may be familiar to students beyond the computer science department as the male professor named "most crush-worthy" by this publication for three of the last five years. Though that award is one of many tongue-in-cheek honors bestowed by the paper's editorial board, not everyone always saw the humor. Last year, a student filed a complaint with the university, repeating campus rumors that Professor Hathaway had dated female students and alleging that he showed favor to attractive female students on that basis. The student withdrew the complaint when she was unwilling to provide the names of any students who may have been involved with the popular teacher, and no other students came forward to confirm her allegation.

Jerry looked at Laurie to make sure she had finished reading. "We know Susan was one of his favorite students. And she was definitely attractive."

Laurie looked again at the photograph accompanying the article. Hathaway would have been in his late thirties at the time. When she met him in Dwight Cook's office, she had noticed he was handsome, but his face was fuller and his hair thinner than in this photograph. As she looked at the younger version, it dawned on her that Hathaway's features were similar to Keith Ratner's. Dark hair, strong cheekbones, and a killer smile. She could imagine that a woman might be attracted to them both.

Susan and her professor? It was a theory that the police had never even considered.

"I'll check with her roommates, see if there were any signals that Susan and Professor Hathaway might have been an item. If they were, Dwight Cook certainly didn't know about it. I could tell when I first spoke to him that he'd been carrying a torch for Susan himself, and then Keith made it sound like Dwight was pretty obsessed with her. No way would he have kept Hathaway as his right-hand man at REACH if the teacher crossed that line with Susan. But the article calls him a consultant. We know that Hathaway was instrumental to REACH from the very beginning. That means he got stock options and big money. I know you told me that Hathaway confirmed that the idea for REACH was Dwight's and not Susan's, but —"

"You're thinking Dwight Cook might have murdered Susan?"

"I don't know, Jerry. If I've learned anything, it's that it's often the least likely suspect."

She thought of her husband's murder. Because Greg was an emergency room doctor, the police thought he might have crossed paths with a deranged patient who became fixated on him. It never dawned on anyone that Greg was targeted by a socio-path consumed by hatred of her own father, NYPD inspector Leo Farley.

Laurie was reminded of her conversation with Alex that morning; Jerry really had moved on since his intern days. He was now close to a partner for her on the show, and she needed to treat him that way. "I'll call Rosemary again so we aren't just taking Hathaway and Dwight's word for it about Susan's lab work. She'll know what Susan was working on."

Laurie had hoped to narrow the field of people under suspicion before the summit session, but her list of suspects seemed to be growing.

43

By the time Dwight Cook slipped his key into the lock of his Westwood bungalow, it was nearly midnight. He and Hathaway had taken REACH's jet to Los Angeles, but the flight had been delayed by fog in the Bay Area.

Hathaway teased him for hanging on to this modest little house, which Dwight had bought at the end of his junior year, once REACH appeared solid enough as a start-up for him to get a small mortgage. In fact, Hathaway teased him for returning to college at all. Hathaway was so confident in REACH's potential to pull in major cash that he'd retired from his tenured position.

But Hathaway had always been more financially motivated than Dwight. It sounded overly simple, but Dwight really did enjoy college — not the parties or hanging out in the quad, but the learning. So even after REACH launched, he found a way to finish college. Besides, he had Hathaway to oversee the corporation.

As soon as he locked the door behind him, he opened his laptop and logged in to the surveillance cameras at the Bel Air house. He had not been able to check updates while he was with Hathaway.

He fast-forwarded through hours of tape for a quick overview. The house was empty most of the day. The little boy and his grandpa came home first, followed by some television for the boy and phone calls for Grandpa. Then Jerry and Grace, followed by Laurie and Alex Buckley. It looked like they were wrapping up the night with some kind of game in the den.

He hit PAUSE. Jerry was in the corner by himself while everyone else was playing the game. Laurie seemed to stop and talk to Jerry alone. He rewound to the beginning of their conversation and hit PLAY.

By the time he watched Laurie resume her seat at the game table, Dwight wanted to throw his laptop across the room. When he set out to monitor the activity at the house, he thought it would give him some semblance of control, but this was maddening. What he really wanted was to be in the room with them. If they would only ask him the right questions, he could set them straight.

Susan and Hathaway? The thought made him physically ill. It was also ridiculous. Susan was too blinded by her devotion to that abominable Keith Ratner to notice anyone else.

And the idea that Susan had been the one to develop REACH? The technology that had launched REACH wasn't Susan's idea; it wasn't even Dwight's — not really. As Hathaway had pointed out, he and Dwight were two halves of a whole. On his own, Dwight might never have conceived such a grand idea. But without Dwight's programming talent, Hathaway might have gotten bogged down and someone else would have caught up and surpassed him before REACH was off the ground.

It had nothing to do with Susan.

He wanted Susan's murder solved, but now the people at *Under Suspicion* were on the completely wrong track, and he couldn't correct their misconceptions without revealing the fact that he was monitoring their conversations. He was stuck. All he could do was watch and listen and hope. Oh, Susan, he thought wistfully.

He switched his screen over to the We Dive SoCal website. He hoped someone might have tips about new sites for him to explore while he was in Los Angeles, but it looked like he was going to stick with his usual dives: Farnsworth Bank, on the windward side of Catalina, and the oil rigs off of Long Beach.

It was probably good he'd completed these tens of times before. Dwight was at his best when he kept a routine. Eight A.M. wake-up. Coffee. Three-mile jog. Cereal with fruit. Work. The occasional dinner with Hathaway. Reading. Sleep. Repeat.

Ever since Nicole had appeared at REACH with the news that *Under Suspicion* would be featuring Susan's case, that routine had been disrupted. Once he found out who killed Susan, his life could return to normal.

And in the meantime, he needed a reprieve in the water. Just three more days before he could dive.

44

Madison Meyer pushed open the door marked 2F. "I can*not* . . . believe . . . that this dorm is still here. It was new at the time, but, wow, is it dated now."

The building was three stories of blond brick, divided into efficient suites. Every campus in America had similar dormitories from the same era. This was the triple room that Susan, Nicole, and Madison had shared sophomore year.

"Hey, guy in the black baseball cap." Madison was pointing to one of the cameramen. "I'm turned this way for a reason. Please don't move around to my right side. I told you it's not a good angle for me."

"We have *all* your requests from your agent," Grace said flatly.

Laurie could tell that Grace wanted to put Madison the diva in her place, New York City style. Jerry would have had more patience but had stayed at the house in Bel

Air to stage the upcoming summit sessions. "I think what Grace is trying to say," Laurie gently offered, "is that we take care of all of that during editing. Besides, most of your camera time will be at the summit session."

"And, yes," Grace added, "we'll have someone there for hair and makeup. And vegetarian options for all meals. And the brand of bottled water you requested."

Alex Buckley placed a hand gently on Grace's shoulder. "And now I think Grace is trying to say that your agent did a very good job by you."

Grace and Madison both laughed at the line. Laurie would never stop marveling at the way attention from a good-looking man could make some women forget everything else.

Temporarily assuaged, Madison continued with her tour of the dorm room. Laurie would have preferred to have both Nicole and Madison here, but Nicole had been reluctant to extend her trip down to Los Angeles before the summit session. The one upside to Nicole's absence was that they might be able to get Madison to open up about what Nicole had been like when they were dormmates. Laurie was determined to uncover whatever Nicole had been holding back.

Once they were finished with the walk-through, Laurie asked Madison how she came to live with Susan and Nicole as sophomores, after the two others were assigned as roommates freshman year.

"Let's just say they were luckier on the freshman-roommate draw than I had been. The woman I roomed with first year was a real piece of work. Her own family called her Taz. As in, the Tasmanian Devil. All she had to do was walk in a room, and it was as if a tornado had blown in. She was loud and obnoxious and would borrow my clothes without asking. A nightmare in every way. So, no, we were not going to be one of those pairs, like Susan and Nicole, who would stick together like glue going forward. When the housing lottery opened for the next year, I let everyone who would listen know that I wanted to pair up. Susan asked if I wanted in with her and Nicole."

"How did you know Susan?" Laurie asked.

"From the theater department."

"I've heard that the two of you were rivals of sorts. You ended up competing for the same parts, given your physical resemblance."

"You know what they say. Sometimes you need a competitor to bring out your best."

279

"Was that odd for you, to live with your rival? Plus, I assume by then they had their own rhythm as a twosome. Did you ever feel like a third wheel?"

"Forgive me if this sounds cocky," Madison said, looking directly at Alex, "but I have never felt redundant. It's just not how I'm programmed. But, sure, if you're asking if sometimes I felt like I was the odd woman out, there were certainly times. Little things, like teasing me about being too flirtatious. We all have a little mean girl in us, and Susan and Nicole weren't above giving me the occasional cold shoulder."

Laurie could sense resentment beneath Madison's otherwise cautious words, but the petty feuds that arose among friends weren't usually grounds for murder. It was time to move on to issues that had been raised during other interviews.

"Do you happen to recall what Susan was working on in the computer lab?" Laurie asked.

Madison answered without a pause. "A dictation program. She got the idea because her father would often work at home on the weekend, using a dictation machine to draft motions and briefs. But then he'd have to wait until Monday for a secretary to do the typing."

In addition to Dwight and Professor Hathaway, Nicole and Rosemary had also confirmed the nature of Susan's work. It was clear that Dwight Cook had not stolen the idea for REACH from Susan, as Keith Ratner had suggested.

But then there were also the rumors about Professor Hathaway being romantically involved with students. Laurie had spent last night trawling the Internet for more information about Hathaway. From what she could tell, even though he initially left UCLA to pursue opportunities in the private sector, his only work since then had been for REACH and had been extremely lucrative. She had even found some trade journals speculating that Hathaway was the real brains behind the operation, while Dwight provided the kind of young, quirky persona that investors were looking for in the early dot-com years. But she had found nothing more about allegations of on-campus dalliances.

"How about Susan's relationship with her boyfriend?" Laurie asked.

"Oh yeah," Madison said offhandedly, "that guy. What was his name again?"

"Keith Ratner." It struck Laurie as peculiar that Madison wouldn't remember Keith, especially since both of them had gone on to have some success as actors.

"Right. The two of them were high school sweethearts. Totally devoted to each other."

"Really?" Alex said. "Because we've been told that Keith may have had an eye for other girls."

"Not that I ever noticed."

"Do you think it's possible that Susan could have been seeing someone else besides Keith?" Laurie asked.

On this point, Madison was more emphatic. "Absolutely not. She wasn't like that. Besides, she just wasn't that into dating. I mean, she had a boyfriend, but even Keith wasn't really a top priority. She was into school and her work and theater. It's like Keith was her fourth priority, like they were some old married couple."

Laurie noticed that Madison was looking directly at Alex again. Why didn't she come right out and say it: *I would never be boring. I make men my priority.* She was so obvious.

"And what about Nicole?" Laurie asked.

"What about her?"

"Rosemary tells me what a good friend Nicole was to her daughter, but sometimes mothers don't know every detail of a child's life while she's away for college. Like you said, we all have a little mean girl in us. Were

Nicole and Susan ever mean with each other?"

"Funny. I can't remember anyone asking about Nicole after Susan was killed. The whole focus was on Frank and me. I'll be honest. I didn't like Nicole very much, and I assume the feeling was mutual. But if she was going to kill someone, it would've been me, not her beloved Susan. That was a joke, by the way. She wouldn't kill anyone. And neither would I, and neither would Frank Parker."

"So who does that leave as a suspect?" Alex asked.

"I've always thought the key to finding her killer was figuring out how she got up to Laurel Canyon. Her car was still on campus." She looked out the window and pointed to a parking lot behind the dorm. "Just back there."

Alex paused to follow her gaze out the window but already had the follow-up question locked and loaded. "People have suggested —"

"That Frank did it, I covered up for him, and one or both of us drove her car back to campus afterward. But I am one of two people in the very unique position to know that didn't happen. Susan's car had been giving her trouble, so I've always wondered

283

if she accepted a ride with somebody to avoid the risk of a breakdown."

Laurie didn't remember seeing anything in the police reports about car problems. "Was her car not working?"

"It was — what was the word she'd use? One of those SAT words for being moody. 'Mercurial'! She loved that word."

As Laurie thought through the possibilities, she realized that this tiny detail about Susan's car could be significant. The reconstruction of Susan's timeline on the day of her death had been built around the assumption that she would have driven herself from campus to Frank Parker's for the audition. Based on that assumption, the likely killer was either Frank or someone she might have been with prior to her audition. But what if she had gotten into someone else's car on her way to Frank's?

As if reading her mind, Alex asked, "Do you think Susan would take a ride from a stranger?"

Madison shrugged. "I can't see it, unless she was late and really desperate. But sometimes we don't think of strangers as strangers, you know? Maybe someone she recognized from campus offered her a lift? And then she didn't realize he was a creep until it was too late."

Or, Laurie thought, the *someone* was her boyfriend, Keith Ratner, just as her mother thought from the very beginning.

Alex was shifting gears to another topic. "You mentioned being one of only two people who knew for certain where you and Frank Parker were that night," he said. "How has it felt for you all of these years, to have people question your credibility?"

"Obviously, it's horrible, and frustrating, and infuriating. It's not that complicated: I got a call from a critically acclaimed director saying that another UCLA student stood him up and would I be willing to read on short notice. I knew the other student was Susan and figured she must have chickened out or something. So I thought, Her loss, my gain. I hopped in my car and went straight there. I stayed until close to midnight. You know the police checked his phone records, right? And we had pizza delivered around nine thirty, and that was confirmed too. And yet people who have never met me are essentially calling me a liar, based on absolutely no evidence."

It was true that the police investigation confirmed the pizza delivery, but the delivery boy had no idea whether the man who paid for the pizza at the door was alone or with company. Phone records also con-

285

firmed the fact that Frank placed a call to the phone in Madison's dorm room, but, as Madison had noted, only the two of them knew what was said during the call or what transpired afterward.

"You just happened to be home on a Saturday night?" Laurie interjected. She had thought from the very beginning that something was odd about Madison's account of the evening. Just last week, Madison had made them wait on her porch while she freshened her lipstick. Would she really hop into her car on no notice for an audition?

But now that Laurie had a better sense of who Madison was, she saw the wrinkle that had bothered her. "I got the impression you had a busy social life back then. It's hard to imagine that you'd be in your dorm, standing around, when the phone rang at seven forty-five on a Saturday night."

"I wasn't feeling well that night."

"And yet you were well enough to get in your car for an audition? I can't imagine you went to Frank Parker's house wearing sweats and no makeup."

Madison smiled, again directly at Alex even though Laurie was firing the questions. "Of course not. And I was never sitting around my dorm on Friday and Saturday nights. That particular Saturday? I was supposed to go to a Sigma Alpha Epsilon party, so, yes, I was looking my best. But then I wasn't feeling well — as I said — so I thought I might stay home. Then Frank called, and I just happened to be dolled up and ready to go. I hopped in my car and got a fantastic role. I mean, I won a Spirit Award, but people still want to believe I only got that role because I vouched for Frank. But I *earned* it."

"But the role might have gone to Susan if she hadn't been killed."

"You don't think that put a huge cloud over the entire experience for me? Susan and I were competitors, but we were also friends. Everyone seems to forget that. How many times do I have to say this? I got Frank's call at seven forty-five, I went straight to his place, I was with him from eight thirty to midnight, we got pizza around nine thirty, and then I came home. I had nothing to do with Susan's death."

45

Laurie let Grace do the driving back to Bel Air. She never got the chance to drive in New York City and was enjoying the experience, despite the hideous Los Angeles traffic.

"So what do you think?" Laurie asked once they were on the road. Alex had climbed into the SUV's backseat before Laurie could protest.

Grace was the first to offer an opinion. "Uh-uh, I'm not buying it. That line about her and Susan being friends? Maybe so, but just as quickly, she was all, *I won a Spirit Award, and I earned it.* I'm sorry, but that's cold." She was waving one finger around in the air for emphasis, and Laurie felt the car swerve within the lane.

"Grace, two hands on the wheel, please."

"Sorry, I just get a little worked up by that woman. And that timeline? Whoa, did that sound rehearsed. *Seven forty-five, eight thirty, nine thirty, midnight,* like a little wind-up doll."

Laurie agreed on both points. Madison had stood by her alibi of Frank Parker, but it was almost too good. Every detail of her recollection of that night was absolutely consistent with the version she had given police twenty years ago. That was not how real memories worked. They evolved over time, some pieces deteriorating while others crystallized. Details got muddled and mutated. But Madison had nailed every line, as if she were acting.

"The one inconsistency I did catch," Laurie noted, "was at first she said she was home because she was sick. Then when I asked how she could have left so quickly for the audition, she said she was going to a frat party but then thought she was sick, and then Frank happened to call when she was still prettied up. It sounds convoluted to me."

"And a frat party?" Grace said skeptically. "Please. I may not have known Madison Meyer twenty years ago, but I can't picture her hanging out with the campus Greeks. Something's not right."

Laurie's thoughts were interrupted by her phone buzzing. Two new voice messages had come in while her cell was turned off during the shoot.

"Hi, this is Tammy from Advocates for God. You left a message last night for Reverend Collins about an old police investigation? The reverend apologizes that his schedule did not permit him to return your call personally, but he asked me to call you. He says police interviewed several of our members at the time, and in his recollection, they verified the whereabouts of the individual you mentioned in your message. He has nothing further to add but suggested that you could contact the police for details."

Laurie skipped to the next message. "Ms. Moran, this is Keith Ratner. I wanted to apologize for losing it yesterday. It's frustrating, to say the least, that people still question me after all these years. But I do want to help if the show will still have me. Give me a call when you have a chance."

She hit the RETURN CALL button, and Keith picked up immediately. "You got my message?" he asked.

"I did, and I feel like I also need to apologize. My tone was sharper than I intended yesterday. And I want to assure you that our show will remain objective. In fact, since we saw you at the bookstore, I looked into your alibi for that night, and we've also been exploring every possible theory with the same amount of depth. For what it's worth, I thought you might want to know that Susan's mother and both of her roommates all said that Susan was much too devoted to have been involved with anyone but you."

She saw no point in telling him that Rosemary's response to the question had been, "Oh, I would have been *thrilled* if Susan had stepped out on that jerk."

Keith confirmed the address for the summit session in Bel Air and then said goodbye just as they were pulling into the driveway.

"Pretty boy is back on board?" Grace asked.

"Careful," Alex said. "I'm starting to think you call everyone pretty. My feelings are hurt."

"Yes," Laurie reported, "Keith Ratner — a.k.a. Pretty Boy Number Two — is back. But I'm starting to wonder whether he has a point about Rosemary suspecting him for no reason. His alibi is at least as good as Frank's. He's got multiple people vouching for him, not just one person who had a lot to gain in sticking by a critically acclaimed director."

Alex unstrapped his seat belt as the SUV

rolled to a stop. "I don't think you can ignore the fact that the multiple people belonged to what some have called a brain-washing religion. Advocates for God doesn't exactly have a squeaky-clean reputation."

The sun felt good on Laurie's face as she stepped down from the front seat. Maybe she could get used to California. The neighborhood was absolutely silent except for the distant sound of a lawn mower and Grace's voice.

"And you heard what Madison said about Susan's car being fickle," Grace was saying. "If she was worried about a breakdown on her way to the audition, who would she ask for a ride? Her boyfriend, that's who. Her agent was on the road, driving down to Arizona. So she called Keith. I still say they got into a fight on the way up there, she hopped out of the car, and it got out of control."

Once again, Laurie felt like she was swimming through mud. The entire purpose of these early interviews was to crystallize the case so Alex could move in for the kill during the summit session. But they were supposed to start shooting in two days, and she still had no clearer picture of who killed Susan than when she'd first spotted the Cinderella Murder case online. Brett Young would never trust her again with this kind of budget. And more importantly, it was possible that this episode would fail by the only measure that really mattered to her — revealing something new about the investigation.

She was so distracted that she slipped her key into the front door without checking the knob first, accidentally locking them out instead of letting them in. She turned the key in the other direction and pushed the door open. It parted a few inches before she felt something blocking the way.

"Hello?" she called out. Jerry must have moved a piece of furniture into the foyer during his staging. "Jerry? We can't get in! Hello?"

"Let me try." Grace jumped in front of Laurie, crouched low, and placed both of her palms against the door, shoving with all her weight like a football player pushing a blocking sled across a field. She grunted from the effort and the door opened enough for her to step sideways through it.

"No!" Grace cried out. Through the crack in the door, Laurie saw her assistant fall to her knees on the hallway floor.

"Grace?"

Alex reached out to grab her arm, but it was too late. Laurie stepped inside and saw

Grace crouched next to the obstacle that had been blocking the door. It was Jerry. His face was barely recognizable through the injuries. Streaks of red marked his journey from the den to this spot on the floor, his cell phone extended in his right hand. Laurie felt her breath leave her chest and leaned back against the door for support. She felt something damp and sticky on the wood behind her.

She heard Alex's fist banging against the door but could not bring herself to move.

Jerry had been here alone. He had tried to call for help and had tried to crawl outside, but despite all of that effort, he was still all alone. And he was covered in blood.

46

Talia Parker tapped on the door to her husband's den. He had been in there for the last three hours, supposedly watching screeners of the ever-growing number of films campaigning for Academy Award nominations. Getting no response, she slowly pushed the door open.

There he was, reclined on the Eames sofa, his stockinged feet crossed at the ankles, his hands clasped just beneath the remote control resting on his barrel chest. On the wide-screen television, an A-list actress had been paused midsentence. A low, steady snore was the only sound in the room.

She gently lifted the remote control, turned off the entertainment system, and draped a light blanket over him. He slept better when he was warm.

Back in their bedroom, she reviewed the wardrobe choices she had made for tomorrow's meeting with the TV people: an open-collar dress shirt, gray slacks, and navy blazer for him; a white sheath dress and neutral pumps for her. Casual, but put-together and respectable. Frank was known for being a demanding and meticulous film-maker, but she knew him to be a solid person. A good, caring man. To her, he looked most like himself in conservative clothing.

When she had first overheard Frank agree to do this show, she'd worried it could be trouble. And now, as production was approaching, she knew she had been right. For days, Frank had seemed distracted and nervous. It wasn't like him. She was used to seeing her husband confident and decisive.

He had been staying up late and then mumbling through the night once he finally fell asleep. And he wasn't murmuring about negotiations with production companies or screenwriters, as he sometimes did. She'd heard the words "police" and "Madison" more than once.

She had finally mustered up the courage to ask him about it this morning. He insisted he had no recollection of whatever dream had provoked the mysterious words, but in the Parker marriage, she was the actor, not him.

Their marriage had lasted ten years in a

town where Botox outlasted the length of the average relationship, and that was because they always fought for what was best for each other. And sometimes that meant Frank doing things she didn't immediately agree with. It was Frank, after all, who'd killed Talia's first and only offer of a starring role in a feature film. He had said the director was "frighteningly unscrupulous, even by Hollywood standards." She had been so tempted to leave, accusing him of not wanting to share the spotlight with her. But then, sure enough, when the film was released, it barely earned an R rating because of explicit nudity that the lead actress insisted was unauthorized. Frank was too decent to say *I told you so,* but Talia had learned a valuable lesson about the give-and-take of a marriage.

Ever since they met — she had a bit part in Frank's seventh movie — he had taken such good care of her, even when it meant upsetting her.

Now it was time for her to return the favor.

47

Laurie hated hospitals, and not for the usual reasons: the chaos, the smells, the reminders at every turn of our fragility and the ticking of the clock. Laurie hated hospitals because they reminded her of Greg. She could not stand beneath those fluorescent lights, surrounded by the odor of disinfectant, without picturing Greg coming down the hall in sea-green scrubs, a stethoscope draped around his neck.

The doctor who walked into the lobby at the Cedars-Sinai emergency room looked nothing like Greg. She was a woman, probably not much older than Laurie, with blond hair pulled into a ponytail. "Jerry Klein?"

Grace's jump from the seat next to her woke Timmy, whose head was resting in Laurie's lap. Timmy rubbed the sleep from his eyes. "Is Jerry okay?"

Laurie had called her father as soon as

the EMTs whisked Jerry away in the ambulance. Leo immediately cut short their visit to the La Brea Tar Pits, dropping Timmy off at the hospital so he could stay with Laurie while Leo tried to get more information about Jerry's attack from the police.

Laurie hugged Timmy close to her chest and patted his head. She did not want him to hear any more bad news.

Alex appeared next to the doctor, two cups of fresh coffee in hand, which he delivered to Grace and Laurie. Laurie was truly impressed at how well Grace was keeping herself together. She was desperately worried about her friend Jerry but had been helping to comfort Timmy and had even thought to call Dwight Cook and inform him of the break-in at his house.

"I'll take Timmy," Alex offered, seeming to read her mind.

The doctor introduced herself once Timmy was out of earshot. "I'm Dr. Shreve. Your friend is stable, but the assault was quite serious, multiple blows from a blunt instrument. The injuries to his head are the most significant. The bleeding impaired his breathing as well, which has led to a coma-like state. He's showing signs of improvement already and seems to be neurologically normal or near normal, but we won't know for certain until he regains conscious-ness."

Grace choked back a sob. "Can we see him?" she asked.

"Sure," the doctor said with a patient smile, "but don't expect too much, okay? It's unlikely he can hear you, and he cer-tainly won't respond."

Despite the doctor's warning, Laurie gasped at the sight of Jerry in bed. His head was swathed in bandages and twice its usual size. Beneath the oxygen mask, his face was swollen like a balloon and beginning to bruise. An IV drip was taped to the crook of his left arm. The room was silent except for the constant hum and rhythmic beep of a machine next to the bed.

Grace reached for Laurie's hand, then rested her free hand on Jerry's shoulder and began to pray. They had just said "amen" when Leo walked in. "I didn't want to inter-rupt, but I said my own words from the hallway."

Laurie gave him a quick hug. "Is Timmy okay?"

"Yep, he's in the lobby with Alex. He's a tough kid."

After his father's murder and the mayhem at the end of filming "The Graduation Gala," Timmy had seen more violence than any person, let alone a child, should experience.

"Any word from the police?"

"I just came from the house. The entire block's covered. The lead detective, a guy called Sean Reilly, seems like a good cop. They're canvassing for witnesses, but I've got to tell you, I'm not optimistic. The lots in that area are so huge, you can't even see your next-door neighbor."

"I don't understand it," Grace said, sniffling. "How could anyone want to hurt Jerry, of all people?"

"I've got a theory on that," Leo said. "The house was tossed. Drawers opened, luggage rifled through. Laurie, you had your laptop with you, but the rest of the computer equipment is missing."

"A robbery?" Laurie asked.

"Except they left behind everything else. They didn't even touch some very expensive speakers that would have been easy to grab. And unless you took the case files with you, I think those are missing, too."

She shook her head. They had stored the files in two large banker boxes. The last time she'd seen them, they were in the den. "So this is related to the show?"

Leo nodded. "It's the show."

"The summit session. We told them all

the address for filming." She was thinking out loud now. "Someone was worried about what we might know. They took the files and the computers to find out what everyone else was saying."

"Or they wanted to scare you into stopping production altogether."

Laurie knew her father could be overprotective at times, seeing danger around every corner. But no one would break into a house that luxurious and leave with only documents and a few inexpensive laptops unless they were interested in *Under Suspicion.*

"Dad, you were worried when Rosemary's neighbor was killed that it was somehow related to the show."

"And I still believe that."

"Can you reach out to the police up there? Make sure that both departments know there's a possible connection between Lydia's death and the attack on Jerry?"

"Absolutely."

She leaned over Jerry, carefully avoiding the tubes and wires, and gave him a light kiss on the cheek. She had spent so much time telling her father not to worry about her while she worked on the show, but she never stopped to think that her production might be putting others in this kind of danger.

She had to find out who did this to him.

48

At nine o'clock, Leo turned off the light in Timmy's room. Timmy had taken the next volume of the Harry Potter books with him to bed, but as Leo had expected, he had fallen asleep on the first page after their long and strenuous day.

He made his way to the hall, leaving the door cracked open in case Timmy cried out in the night.

If there was any sliver of light to be found in the brutal assault on Laurie's colleague, it was that she was finally willing to concede that someone might be targeting people connected to her show. After all, the murder of Rosemary Dempsey's neighbor had been Leo's primary reason for coming to California.

Still, Leo was not happy about Laurie's decision to stay at the Bel Air house. Detective Reilly had cleared them for reentry after the crime-scene unit had finished its work, but the bigger question was whether they'd be safe. "It's obvious the guy was after one thing," Reilly had said, "your computer and research on the show. You say there was nothing pertaining to the show that he didn't take. So presumably he got what he wanted and won't be coming back."

Leo didn't agree with Reilly's logic, but the fact was that they were a large group, and the police planned to drive past the house every twenty minutes to be safe. And, Leo thought, my gun is at the ready in a worst-case scenario.

The police hadn't located any witnesses yet in their neighborhood canvass. Some of the homes had surveillance cameras, but detectives still needed to wade through the footage. If they were extremely lucky, they might be able to locate images of cars or people coming and going from the street.

In his bedroom, he shut the door and pulled up a recently dialed phone number on his cell. It was the number for Detective O'Brien at the Alameda County sheriff's department.

"Detective, it's Leo Farley. We spoke earlier this week about your investigation into the murder of Lydia Levitt."

"Of course I remember. In fact, I happened to touch base yesterday with one of my friends in the NYPD. Name of J. J. Rogan."

"Talk about a blast from the past. I was his lieutenant when he first moved to detective squad."

"That's what he told me. He confirms you're 'good people,' in his words."

In light of what Leo was about to ask of Detective O'Brien, he was grateful for the recommendation on his behalf.

"You mentioned that you had some camera footage from the roads going in and out of Castle Crossings."

"We do, but it's a major thoroughfare. A whole mess of cars that could be heading in any direction. We've got no clear idea who exactly went into the gated community. I've got an officer capturing stills of license plates, matching each car up to a driver, but we're talking about a lot of people to track down. I've been prioritizing the burglary angle, working my sources, but if this was a botched break-in, the person who did it hasn't spoken a word of it on the street."

Leo told O'Brien about the assault on Jerry and his belief that both that attack and Lydia Levitt's murder could be connected to *Under Suspicion*.

"We'll certainly pursue that theory," O'Brien said. "We're looking at every possible lead."

"The gated community doesn't have cameras right at the entry?" Leo asked.

"You'd think, but those places really don't have any major crime. The walls themselves act as their own kind of deterrent, and the guards at the gate have a dog and pony show, but they also wave a lot of people through if they seem to belong."

Leo had been hoping that O'Brien would have gotten further in his investigation since they last spoke, but he knew how slowly things could move when no clear suspects have emerged. "So what you're saying is that your footage from the road outside could be a search for a needle in a haystack."

"You got it."

"Any chance you could use the assistance of a retired cop from New York to wade through that list of drivers?"

"Could I *use* it? I'll pay you back in whiskey at the first opportunity."

"Sounds like a deal."

After a quick discussion that Leo didn't entirely understand involving digitization, file size, and data compression, Detective O'Brien estimated that he could get everything to him by e-mail tomorrow morning.

"I'll probably have to get my grandson to

help me open them," he said before hang-ing up.

Sifting through images of cars on a busy street would indeed be searching for a needle in a haystack, but if Leo happened to find the same needle in two different haystacks on opposite ends of the state, he might just have himself a lead.

49

Four and a half miles away in Westwood, Dwight Cook was pacing at the foot of his bed.

He flashed back to a long-forgotten memory of his father screaming at him in what must have been the eighth grade. *Stop pacing. Just stop. You're driving me crazy. And it's weird. Maggie, tell your son how nervous he makes people when he acts that way.*

His mother grabbed his father's arm and whispered: *Stop yelling, David. You know loud noises make Dwight jumpy. He paces when he's jumpy. And* don't *call your son* weird.

Dwight had trained himself to control the obsessive pacing in high school by sitting on his hands instead. He learned that remaining still, focusing on the feeling of his weight on the back of his hands, didn't make people nervous the way his pacing had. But he was alone in his bungalow now, so he didn't need to worry about affecting anyone else. And he had tried and tried to sit on his hands, but the racing in his head — the *jumpiness* — wouldn't stop.

He momentarily paused at the center of his bed to hit REWIND and then PLAY once again on his laptop.

Dwight had been speed-watching footage of the empty house when the man first appeared on the screen, walking directly through the unlocked front door with a ski mask over his face. Twenty-three minutes. That was the amount of time Jerry had been gone, returning to the house with a bag from In-N-Out Burger. Had he eaten his fast food in the kitchen, maybe the masked man would have snuck out through the front door undetected.

But Jerry hadn't taken his lunch to the kitchen. He walked directly into the den, where the masked man was rifling through the documents Jerry had left scattered across the coffee table.

Dwight continued to pace, clenching his eyes shut as each blow found its target. The weapon was the engraved crystal plaque Dwight had received from UCLA when he donated his first hundred thousand dollars upon graduation.

Dwight watched as the assault ended and

310

the masked man turned to run out of the den, his arms filled with two banker boxes.

He had to make a decision.

If Dwight did not turn over this video, the people investigating the attack would not have it as evidence. If he did, he would reveal the fact that he'd been monitoring the activities of *Under Suspicion.* He could be ruined professionally, not to mention the possibility of criminal charges. More important, he would lose all access to the production team and be cut out of the case.

It was a cost-benefit analysis, a matter of statistics. What had a higher likelihood of being helpful: the videotape of this assault or his continued surveillance of the Bel Air house?

He hit REWIND and then paused on the clearest still image of the masked man. Dwight stared once again at the insignia on the left side of the man's white polo shirt. Even with Dwight's ability to manipulate computer images and search for information on the Internet, the quality of the video simply wasn't detailed enough to make out the logo. The attacker was lean, muscular, obviously very strong, but there was no way to identify him.

This video was useless. But if he kept monitoring the television show's production, he still had a chance of figuring out who killed Susan.

He flipped the laptop closed and stopped pacing. He had made his decision. Now he had to make sure that the gamble paid off.

50

Laurie was finally ready to call it a night when she noticed light glowing beneath her father's bedroom door. She tapped gently on the door and cracked it open.

He was beneath his covers, reading a copy of *Sports Illustrated*.

"Sorry, I saw the light."

He set the magazine down and waved her in. "You holding up okay, baby girl?"

If she had any doubt that she looked like she'd aged a decade in a day, his question sealed the deal. She plopped herself horizontally at the foot of the king bed, her head resting on his blanketed shins. She couldn't think of a more comfortable place at that moment. "I used to hate it when you called me that. And then somewhere down the road, it became music to my ears."

"Sometimes dads do know best."

"Not always. Remember when you tried to push Petey Vandermon on me?"

"I'm not sure I'd agree with that wording, but I'll concede that my matchmaking effort was what Timmy would call a *fail*."

"Petey was the *worst*," Laurie continued with a laugh. "You convinced me to go to that stupid carnival out in Long Island with him. He got terrified in a mirror maze and ran out screaming. He left me bumping around in there for twenty minutes in search of a way out."

Leo chuckled at the memory. "You stormed into the living room, swearing you would never speak to me again if I ever tried to play Cupid. Then I got another lecture from your mother that night before I could go to sleep."

"You had good intentions, though."

"If I recall correctly, Petey was supposed to distract you from that Scott whoever-he-was."

"Mr. Future President. Intern to a congressman. Carried a briefcase to high school."

"I didn't like him. He was . . . weaselly."

"I don't think I ever told you this. He became a lawyer and got indicted for embezzling client funds."

Her father flipped back the covers with excitement. "See? Daddy does know what's best."

"Sometimes I think no one knows best. Look at how I met Greg." The word "met" was an overstatement given that she'd been unconscious at the time. She'd been hit by a cab on Park Avenue, and Greg was the ER doctor on duty. At the time, Laurie's parents — and eventually Laurie — had been grateful for the reassuring treatment, but she wound up engaged to him three months later. Then Laurie's mother had died a year after that, and Greg had been there for everyone.

Her father sat up and stroked her hair. "You only reminisce like this when something's troubling you. I know you're worried about Jerry. He's going to be fine."

Laurie took a deep breath. She couldn't cry again today. "Not to mention, I just got off the phone with Brett. I swear that man might be a vampire — I don't think he sleeps at night. I was the one who had to beg him to cover the Cinderella Murder, and now that someone's coming after the show, he's dead set against canceling it. Part of me is relieved I don't have to make the decision, but he won't even delay the production schedule. He gave me a big song and dance about how Jerry would want us to keep working, but I know it's all about the bottom line."

"I was wondering whether that bottom line had something to do with your decision to stay in this house. If so, I'm going to strangle that man."

"It's just a few more days, Dad, and we're all on high alert now. And you heard what Detective Reilly said about the police keeping an eye on us."

"You do what's right for you, Laurie. You know I've always got your back."

"Thanks, Dad. It's okay. If anything, this attack on Jerry has me convinced that whoever killed Susan is one of our participants. That makes it all the more important to me that we follow through on this."

"I called the police up in Alameda County. They're going to send some surveillance pictures of cars that were near Rosemary's house around the time her neighbor was killed. I'll go through them. Maybe we'll catch a break."

"You don't sound too optimistic."

His shrug said enough. She stood and gave him a hug. "I better call it a night. We meet with Frank Parker tomorrow."

"Tomorrow? You weren't kidding when you said Brett didn't want to disrupt the schedule."

"Hey, we saved the big celebrity interview for last. Then it's on to the big summit session, and then back home to New York."

"You do know you can't set a timeline like that, Laurie. Don't get your hopes up about solving this thing. All I want right now is to keep everyone safe. And don't you dare — not for one second — blame yourself for what happened to Jerry."

"Of course I do. I can't help it."

"If it's anyone's fault, it's mine. We realized after you and the others left to meet Madison that we didn't have enough house keys to go around. Jerry gave me the last copy, assuming it would be fine to leave the door unlocked if he had to run out for a few minutes here and there."

"Dad —"

"My point is that you can drive yourself crazy asking whether things would have been different if *a,* or *b,* or *x, y,* and *z.*"

He didn't need to say any more. How many times had they both wondered if they could have done something to save Greg? She saw the light click off beneath the door as she closed it but knew neither of them would find sleep any time soon.

51

Laurie hadn't expected to be at her best the next morning, but she felt like she was still half-asleep. She had spent the night waking up every twenty minutes, picturing Jerry being lifted onto the gurney by EMTs.

Alex must have had a rough night too. In the back of the van, parked at the curb in front of Frank Parker's former home, a makeup artist was touching up his eyes. He had rightly said to Laurie, "I look like I was on a bender."

For today, it was just the two of them and the camera crew from the *Under Suspicion* staff. Jerry, of course, was in the hospital, still in what the doctors politely called "a comalike state." Grace had stayed at the house to keep Timmy busy while Leo pored through the surveillance footage coming in from Alameda County. If they could somehow connect the murder of Lydia Levitt to the break-in at the Bel Air house, they might figure out who assaulted Jerry. Laurie was nearly certain that person would also turn out to be Susan's killer.

Right now, the immediate goal was to lock Frank Parker down on his timeline for the night of Susan's murder. He and Madison had been consistent in sticking to their stories, but Madison's mention of Susan's car acting up before her death had added a new layer to the mix.

Laurie watched as a cameraman on a wheeled cart backed up to film Alex and Frank walking side by side. They were there now: a turn in the road entering Laurel Canyon Park, just off Mulholland Drive, the exact spot where Susan's body had been found. For Laurie, it was a poignant moment. She couldn't help but think of the playground where Greg had been killed. As she began to tear up, she forced herself to look toward the sky, focusing on the individual branches of a huge sycamore tree towering above them.

Her composure regained, Laurie kept up with the cameraman as he continued to film Alex and Frank walking out of the park and toward Frank Parker's former home. The purported purpose of this stroll had been to get footage of the iconic setting for the show, but she and Alex had another goal in mind: to establish the short distance between the body and Parker's house. It was less than half a mile.

As planned, Alex and Frank made their way past the home's front gate to an interior courtyard, where, with the permission of the present owner, they had staged two chairs next to the front garden. Once they were seated, Alex stole a casual glance at his watch. "Our walk from the scene of Susan's death was only ten minutes, and I think it's safe to say that we weren't exactly hurrying."

Frank gave a warm smile. In the short time Alex had spent with the director, he had already managed to find a camaraderie that was apparent on camera. "You may not believe me, Alex, but I could have told you the number of minutes without even looking at a watch. I have an inner clock that never stops ticking, and I really can pinpoint the time of day — within one to three minutes — at any given moment. It's a useless party trick, but I have a feeling that's not why you brought up the time."

"Susan Dempsey lived on the UCLA campus, more than eight miles from the spot where she was killed. Yet your house is only a ten-minute walk from that spot. Or perhaps five minutes if someone were running from your house in terror. And Susan was scheduled to be at your house the very night of her murder. You must understand why people suspected you."

"Of course I understand. If I had thought the police were unreasonable in initially questioning me, I might have hired a team of lawyers and refused to have anything to do with the investigation. But that's not what I did, is it? Ask any of the detectives who were involved. They'll confirm I was cooperative. Because I had no cause *not* to be. I was shocked, of course, when they told me Susan's body had been found. And *where* it was found. I provided a thorough account of my whereabouts for the night. They confirmed that account, and that really should have been the end of the story."

"But it wasn't the end of the story. Instead, your name is forever associated with the Cinderella Murder case."

"Look, it would be easier if I could take some magic truth serum so people would finally believe me, but I get it. A young, bright, talented woman lost her life — and her family has never gotten the closure they richly deserve. So I have never expected anyone to feel sorry for me. She was the victim, not me."

"Well, let's go over that account you gave the police."

"Susan was supposed to be here at seven thirty, and she wasn't. Her agent surely would have told her that I am absolutely intolerant of lateness by anyone working or potentially working for me. If time is money, it's never truer than in the film business. Once she was fifteen minutes late, I called Madison, who had been my second choice, to see if she was interested. She must have come straight here, because she arrived by eight thirty. She left shortly before midnight. In fact, I even recall her saying, "I can't believe it's almost midnight." His version matched Madison's, minute for minute.

"And you ordered pizza," Alex prompted.

"Yes, the pizza. My order was logged at nine twenty-seven, delivered at nine fifty-eight. Check the records. You know Tottino's still has a copy of the takeout receipt framed on their front wall? They at least had the good judgment to black out my address."

"And how did Madison look when she arrived?" Alex asked. This was a question they had planned in light of Madison's waffling about whether she'd been feeling sick the night of Susan's murder.

"How did she *look*? Like a million dollars.

That role called for an absolute beauty, and she fit the part."

Laurie smiled to herself but was impressed that Alex kept his expression neutral.

"The coroner estimated Susan's time of death as between seven and eleven P.M. She was expected here at seven thirty. You and Madison said Madison arrived here at eight thirty. The assumption has always been that you could not possibly have killed Susan, called Madison, returned Susan's car to campus, and then returned home by the time Madison arrived."

"No, I have not yet found a way to navigate Los Angeles traffic at hyper speed."

"But our research has revealed a new wrinkle to the timeline," Alex said. "We have learned that Susan had been having car trouble prior to her death, so she may have gotten a ride to her audition from someone else. That means you could have had a violent interaction with her upon her arrival and have been home before Madison arrived."

"If I went to a movie studio and pitched a story where a culprit sets an appointment to meet with someone at seven thirty, then phones her dorm room at seven forty-five, and then for some reason chases her into a park and murders her by eight thirty or so,

I would get laughed out of the room. Alex, you're one of the best criminal defense lawyers in the country. Does that really sound plausible to you?"

Laurie watched Frank smile on the screen. She knew how this would play on television. The director was cocky, but he had a point. Unless they broke his alibi, Frank was in the clear. And so far, every part of the evidence supported his alibi: the phone records, Madison's statements, the pizza receipt.

But Laurie still felt in her gut that the evidence was almost too perfect. What was she missing?

52

Talia lingered at the edge of the yard, in her carefully selected white sheath dress, wondering why she had bothered. By the time she met Frank, this was the starter house he would ask their driver to cruise by after he'd had too many drinks, eager to reminisce about his younger, less privileged days. It was probably worth two million dollars by now, but by comparison to their current homes — five total — this place was a shack.

Why had she thought for a second that the producers of *Under Suspicion* would ask her opinion? She wasn't a part of the narrative. When the press wrote about Frank, at best an article might mention that the previously hard-to-get bachelor had now been married for a decade. But they never bothered to name his wife, or to mention that she was the valedictorian of her class at Indiana University, was an accomplished pianist and singer, and had had a semi-promising acting career before she'd fallen in love with Frank.

Though she'd never played out the full arc of her career, she knew enough about show business to recognize that her husband wasn't hitting a home run on the screen right now, answering Alex Buckley's questions. Yes, he had scored a single — maybe even a double — pointing out the ridiculousness of Alex's theory: how could he have decided to kill Susan, executed the deed, and been back in time to answer his door in less than an hour's time? Yet, at the same time, he sounded a bit too much like those guilty guys in bad movies who sneered while taunting, "Too bad you don't have any evidence."

In short, Frank had noted the lack of evidence of his guilt but hadn't offered any alternative theory of his innocence. He had told his version of the story but hadn't helped the show with theirs.

Talia watched the crew pack up the cameras into their overstuffed van. This clearly was not a high-budget operation. Why, oh why, had Frank even bothered participating? It would have been so easy for him to say he was too busy to help.

Their equipment was loaded, and the crew was ready to leave. Alex Buckley and the producer, Laurie, were thanking Frank again for his participation. They'd be heading to their cars soon.

She was about to miss her opportunity. How was she going to catch them without Frank's seeing her?

Just as Alex and Laurie were walking down the driveway toward the black Land Cruiser parked on the street, Frank's assistant, Clarence, stepped out of the production trailer, one hand covering the microphone of his cell. "Frank, I've got Mitchell Langley from *Variety*. He's been trying to reach you all day. I told him there's no truth to the rumors about Bradley pulling out of the project, but he wants to hear it straight from you."

She overheard Frank offer a final goodbye before he followed Clarence into the trailer. She caught up to Laurie and Alex at the end of the driveway.

"My husband is being overly cautious."

When they turned toward the sound of her voice, it was as if they were seeing Talia for the first time. At forty-two years old, Talia knew she was still beautiful, with high cheekbones, catlike green eyes, and shoulder-length waves of dark blond hair.

Laurie said cautiously, "I'm sorry, Mrs. Parker. We really didn't get much of a chance to talk. You have something to add to your husband's replay of the night?"

"Not directly. I didn't even know Frank then. But I'm tired of this cloud hanging over him. I get it — her body was found a hop and skip from this house, and she was killed when she was supposed to be right here, alone with my husband. But, despite that, Frank truly has never understood why his alibi for that night hasn't put him in the clear. In that respect, my husband can be a bit naive. Until someone comes up with a better theory, he will always be suspected. But, I'm telling you, you're on the wrong track with the movie connection."

"I understand your frustration —"

Talia cut Laurie off before she chickened out. "Susan Dempsey had a huge fight with her roommate just hours before her murder."

"With Madison?"

"No, the other one; the third girl, Nicole. At least, according to Madison. You know how after Frank couldn't reach Susan on her cell phone, he called the dorm room? Well, when Madison answered, she said that Susan had a knock-down, drag-out fight that afternoon with their other roommate, and maybe that's why she was late."

"This is the first we've ever heard of this,"

Alex said. "Are you sure?"

"I wasn't there, but I know for a fact that's what Madison told Frank. It was so bad that Nicole even threw something at Susan. Then Susan called Nicole insane and said she was going to get her kicked out of the dorm, maybe even school, if she didn't change her ways. Back when the police were clearly targeting Frank, he hired investigators to look into it. It turns out that Nicole suddenly quit school after Susan was killed. And she didn't just take a semester or school year off. She left Los Angeles entirely and started all over again. Cut off ties with everyone. She was even using a fake name when she first moved. Then she changed her last name when she got married. Look into it: it's like Nicole Hunter died right along with Susan."

"Why didn't your husband ever tell anyone this before?" Laurie asked.

"His lawyers admonished him not to," Talia explained, clearly frustrated. "They were planning to use Nicole as the alternative suspect if he was ever formally charged."

Talia watched Laurie look to Alex for guidance. "It's probably what I would have advised too," he said. "Better to say as little as possible and spring it on the prosecution at trial."

"But there was never a trial," Talia said. "And yet twenty years later, here we are. Formal accusations aren't the only kind of punishment. Maybe now that you know the truth, you can ask the question the police never did: what happened between Susan and that other roommate?"

While Alex was starting the engine of the SUV, Laurie snapped her seat belt in place. "Good timing," she said. "Not even noon, and we're already wrapped up with Frank Parker."

Alex turned to her and smiled. "That means there's no need to rush back. Your dad is at the house with Grace and Timmy, so we know they're all safe. I have a suggestion. Let's drive up the coast for an hour and find a place on the water for lunch. I don't know about you, but my brain is scrambled. It's as though every time we talk to one of the witnesses, a new suspect emerges."

Laurie started to protest that they needed to get back to the house, but Alex was right. It would be good for the two of them to quietly discuss what they had been hearing from the potential suspects these past few days.

And a little time alone with him would be a nice bonus.

53

The next morning, Laurie was on her knees by the front door, buttoning Timmy's jean jacket.

"Mom, are you sure you and Alex can't come to the zoo with us?"

She had the fleeting thought that Timmy had begun to call her Mom instead of Mommy. He was growing up so fast.

"Sorry, sweetie, but we talked about this. Alex and I have to work, just like if I was in New York, but we get the bonus of being out here in California. I'll see you tonight, though. *Dad,*" she called out. *"Are you about ready to hit the road?"*

She looped the last jacket button and glanced at her watch. This was the start of the summit sessions, and today's participants would be here any minute. Up first was Susan's social group: Keith Ratner, Nicole Melling, and Madison Meyer. Rosemary was coming, too, because she wanted to watch. Tomorrow they'd talk separately to the computer crowd, Dwight Cook and Professor Richard Hathaway.

She heard rushed footsteps down the stairs. "Sorry, sorry," her father said. "I'm coming. I got that e-mail I was waiting for from the Alameda police: a list of license plates that were near Rosemary's neighborhood the day her neighbor was killed."

"Dad," Laurie whispered protectively.

"Aw, don't worry about Timmy. Kid's tough as nails, aren't you?" He tousled Timmy's brown wavy hair.

"Nails made of kryptonite," Timmy shot back.

"When we're done with the zoo, I might swing by the local precinct here for a little help running some criminal records. How does that sound, Timmy?"

"That sounds *cool*. And can we go see Jerry too? I want to get him a stuffed animal from the zoo and bring it to his room to keep him company until he wakes up again."

When they had agreed to bring Timmy out to California for an adventure, this wasn't what Laurie had in mind.

"You guys have a good day," she said. "And, Dad, try to take it easy on certain subjects, all right?"

Alex and Grace came out of the kitchen

in time to say good-bye. Just as the rental car pulled out of the driveway, a red Porsche convertible replaced it. Keith Ratner was here. They were greeting him at the door when a black Escalade arrived, carrying Rosemary, Madison, Nicole, and Nicole's husband, Gavin.

Laurie leaned toward Grace to whisper a question. "Madison's staying at the hotel with the out-of-towners? Her house is, like, twenty minutes from here."

"Tell me about it. But girlfriend's agent insisted."

As Keith, Nicole, and Madison exchanged polite hugs and exclamations of *It's been so long* and *You look just the same,* Laurie escorted Rosemary and Gavin into the house to settle in as the day's observers. "Craft services brings in a ton of food throughout the day, so please, help yourself. It's all set up in the kitchen. Gavin, I didn't realize you were making the trip down to L.A."

"It was the least I could do, given how nervous Nicole has been. You're probably used to camera shyness, but I've never seen her like this."

After the bombshell Talia had dropped about Nicole and Susan fighting just hours before Susan's murder, Laurie had to wonder if the cameras were the only reason for Nicole's nerves.

With Jerry still in the hospital, Grace was doubling as production assistant, escorting Keith, Nicole, and Madison to the bedroom they were using for hair and makeup. Once they were camera ready, they'd have a group conversation with Alex in the living room.

"You ready to roll?" Laurie asked Alex. Their lunch excursion to the coast the previous afternoon had been fruitful. They had rehearsed the plan ad nauseam, but now Laurie found herself hoping that their suspicions about Nicole were wrong.

54

As they had planned, Keith was on the far end of the sofa, farthest from Alex's chair, followed by Madison and Nicole.

"I thought we'd start," Alex said, "by having each of you walk through where you were the night of the murder. Keith, would you like to begin?"

Keith explained that he was at a bookstore with several people who had vouched for his whereabouts, and then volunteered that the gathering was an Advocates for God event. "People can form their own opinions about Advocates for God, but I've always been very open about my relationship with AG. I was still learning about the church's mission at the time, but once Susan died, I poured myself into it. I found that I was a happier person when I was providing service through the church. I became less selfish. But, anyway, that's where I was — the whole night."

Alex nodded, satisfied for the moment. "And what about you, Madison?"

"I suspect many of your viewers already know my version, because I'm probably most famous for being Frank Parker's alibi for that night." Laurie was impressed by how quickly Madison changed her affect for the cameras. Gone was the diva striving for a celebrity comeback. Speaking in the serious, measured tone of a news anchor, she repeated her memorized timeline.

"And according to Frank Parker," Alex noted, "you arrived for the audition looking like 'a million dollars.' "

"Well, I'd like to think so. But it was my audition that got me the role."

Alex nodded again. So far, so good.

Next up was the speaker Laurie was most interested in, Nicole.

"That night? I never really think about where I was. When I think of that May seven, I always remember it as the night Susan died."

"I understand. But surely when a close friend — your roommate — is killed, you must go through a process of saying, *What if I had been there? What if I could have stopped it?*"

Nicole was nodding along. "Absolutely." This was how Alex operated on cross-examination. Give the witness easy statements to agree with, and then use those statements to lead the witness in the desired direction.

"So," Alex continued, "you must recall where you were."

"Yes," Nicole said quietly. "To be honest, I'm heartsick and ashamed about that night. I went to O'Malley's, a local bar. I ended up drinking way too much." Without being asked, she added, "I was desperately nervous about a biology exam."

It had only been a matter of seconds, and Nicole already sounded defensive.

"You weren't too upset about your argument with Susan to focus on your studies?" Alex asked sternly.

Even beneath the makeup, Nicole's skin tone faded three shades. "Excuse me?"

"Our investigation has revealed that just that afternoon, shortly before Susan was killed, the two of you had a very significant argument."

"Susan was my best friend. We had the occasional squabble, but nothing I'd call a *significant argument.*"

"Really? Because according to our source, the dispute was so heated that you threw something at Susan. She then threatened to drop you as a roommate if you didn't change."

Nicole was stammering, pulling at the mic looped through the buttonhole of her silk blouse, trying to remove it. Next to her, Madison tried to suppress a smile. She was eating this up.

"Madison," Alex said, shifting his attention, "you seem to enjoy seeing Nicole's feet to the fire."

"I wouldn't say I enjoy it. But, yes, after all these years of being under suspicion, as you call it, I find it a bit ironic that the so-called *nice* roommate was actually throwing things at Susan."

"Some might say it's ironic," Alex said, "that *you* were the one who overheard the fight. So the question I have for you, Madison, is why you never told the police what you heard."

"There was no reason. I was coming down the dormitory hall and heard them shout at each other. I didn't want to get involved. When the door opened, I stepped into the bathroom to avoid the whole scene. Susan left first, then Nicole. That was right around six o'clock. Once I knew the drama had left the building, I went to our room. Then Frank called, and the rest is history."

"You say you resent being under suspicion, but evidence of a bitter dispute between Susan and Nicole might have helped deflect that attention. And yet you never mentioned the fight to anyone." There was a note of astonishment in Alex's voice.

The entire room was silent. Laurie found herself leaning forward, waiting for the next words. She hoped viewers would do the same.

When Madison did not answer, Alex continued to press. "How about this as a theory, Madison? Drawing attention to Nicole as a suspect would have meant deflecting it from Frank. And then your alibi for Frank wouldn't have been quite so valuable."

"The reason I never said anything is because I never thought for a second that Nicole could ever kill Susan."

"*And* you liked being needed by Frank Parker. Isn't that right, Madison?"

55

Laurie could feel the tension in the room. Moments like this were the reason they invited multiple suspects on camera at once. Each person acted as a check on the others, making it harder to sneak in a lie that could easily be disproven by someone else.

Alex continued to press Madison. "Some people have questioned why Frank Parker — a mere fifteen minutes after Susan's expected time of arrival — would invite another actress, who just *happened* to be Susan's roommate, to audition. Tell the truth: When Frank called your dorm room that night, the call wasn't really for you, was it? Isn't it true that Frank was calling for Susan, to see where she was?"

"Fine," Madison conceded. "He didn't actually invite me to audition. But when I realized Susan had no-showed, I saw an opportunity. Susan had told me where Frank lived, so I drove up there. I had *no idea* at the time that she was in danger. When Frank said she didn't show up, I figured she was off crying on Keith's shoulder about the fight."

"And just like you seized the opportunity by auditioning, when you realized that Susan had been killed, you seized the opportunity to be Frank's alibi."

"I *was* his alibi. I was at his house."

"But not by eight thirty. He called at seven forty-five inquiring about your roommate, and it's at least a thirty-minute drive. You'd have to be awfully conniving for your first instinct to be to steal her role."

"I didn't *steal* —"

"But some time must have passed before you *saw the opportunity,* as you described it. To have arrived at Frank Parker's house looking like — quote — 'a million dollars,' I imagine you would have spent some time on your hair and makeup."

"No, in fact, I was already dolled up."

"Right. During our preinterview, you first said you were sick at home when the phone rang. Then you corrected yourself to say you had gotten dressed for a Sigma Alpha Epsilon party and then changed your mind because you weren't feeling up to it."

"That's what happened."

"A fraternity party? Really? Nicole and

Keith, you knew Madison in college. Was she the type to show up for a frat party?"

They both shook their heads. "Absolutely not," Nicole added for emphasis. "She hated them."

"Oh my gosh," Madison snapped. "Can you stop already? Talk about minutiae. Fine, if you absolutely must know why I was home that night, ready to walk out the door, it's because I had been expecting a gentleman caller, so to speak."

"A boyfriend?" Alex asked.

"No, nothing serious — but someone I thought was interested. I had sent him a flirty little note, suggesting it would be worth his time to pick me up at the dorm at seven thirty. I got myself dolled up, expecting him to take the bait. Apparently he wasn't interested, because there I was when Frank called at seven forty-five. Not the kind of thing I wanted to advertise at the time, but not a big deal in retrospect. I got a career-defining role instead. The point is: I was home, the phone rang, and the call records back it up. I saw my opportunity, drove immediately to Frank's house, *begged* for a chance to audition, and then acted my little butt off. I was there from eight thirty to midnight, just like I said."

"And yet you and Frank have always

maintained that he *invited* you to audition. Why the lie?"

"A *white* lie."

"Perhaps, but why stretch the truth at all?" Alex asked.

"Because it sounded better, okay? Susan never came home that night. I thought she was still mad at Nicole and crashing somewhere else. The next morning Rosemary called, completely panicked. She said a body had been found in Laurel Canyon Park and the police thought it was Susan. She was hoping we'd tell her it was all a mistake, that Susan was safe in her room."

"But she wasn't," Alex said. "You'd been to Frank's house. You would have known how close the park was. You must have suspected him."

Madison was shaking her head and starting to cry. She was no longer putting on a performance. "No, absolutely not. I had been at his house, just like I said. And I knew he'd called the dorm at seven forty-five. So I knew for sure it wasn't him. But I also knew I was the only person who could prove that."

"And so?" Alex asked.

"So I went to Frank's. I told him there was nothing to worry about — that I knew he wasn't involved and that I'd back him up to the police."

"But you set contingencies, didn't you? You threatened him. You told him that you'd only support his alibi if he cast you in *Beauty Land.*"

After a long pause, all she could say was, "I *earned* that role."

If this had been a courtroom, Alex would have resumed his seat at counsel table now. His job with respect to Madison was done. She was so conniving that even after she knew Susan was dead, her first priority was becoming a star.

But this wasn't a courtroom, and Madison wasn't the only witness. Alex paused and looked again to Nicole. "Nicole, you must see now that the argument you had that day could be the key to solving her murder. She fled the apartment at six o'clock with every intention of getting to that audition. But she was also having car trouble. We have no idea where she was between that moment and her death. What did you fight about?"

"I remember now that we had some kind of spat, and I went to O'Malley's and started drinking. It was a college hangout, and I got pretty wasted. I'm sure you could find people who'd remember. As for the reason we argued? I have no idea. Something stupid, I'm sure."

"Keith, you've been very quiet during this. Wouldn't Susan have confided in you that she was quarreling with one of her closest friends?"

He shrugged as if this was the first he'd heard of any tension between the two friends. His seeming indifference struck Laurie as odd.

Alex made one more effort. "I want to ask you all, now that the importance of the question is clear. For the first time, we have revealed that Susan stormed out of her dorm room. It is likely because of her car problems that she did not drive herself to Frank Parker's for the audition. That means she may have encountered someone the police never questioned. Where should we be looking? Where would she have gone?"

Madison appeared genuinely perplexed, but Laurie noticed Nicole and Keith exchange a wary glance.

From the first time Laurie had met Nicole in person, she'd believed Nicole was being intentionally vague about her reasons for leaving UCLA. They hadn't yet solved the case, but one thing was clear: Nicole's departure from Los Angeles had something to do with her fight with Susan, and Keith was covering for her.

56

Leo Farley sat back on the sofa to rest his eyes. Detective O'Brien, the lead detective, had e-mailed Leo a list of license plates from camera footage near Castle Crossings, the gated community where Lydia Levitt had been killed. Today, after taking Timmy to the zoo, he had stopped by the LAPD and gotten driver's license photos for most of the cars' owners, as well as their criminal history reports.

He had excused himself from the dinner table early, eager to pore through the materials. This house was luxurious, but at the moment, he missed the bulletin boards and laminate furniture of a police precinct. The documents and pictures were spread around him in layers across the sofa cushions, glass coffee table, and plush carpet.

Two hours later, he had finished his second perusal of every single piece of paper. He had been hoping for an obvious lead: a name associated with the Susan Dempsey case, something to connect the murder in Rosemary's backyard to the murder of Rosemary's daughter twenty years earlier. He had to believe that Laurie's decision to feature the Cinderella Murder case had led to the attacks on both Rosemary's neighbor and Jerry.

But nothing was jumping out.

Timmy came bounding out of the kitchen toward him. "Grandpa! Have you found anything yet?"

"Careful," Leo warned as Timmy tipped over a stack of printouts on his way to Leo's side. "I know this stuff looks like a mess, but I've actually got a system going here."

"Sorry, Grandpa." Timmy reached next to him and began straightening the pile that had been toppled. "What are these?"

"Those are photographs of drivers who were near Castle Crossings on the day I'm interested in but who have prior addresses in Los Angeles."

"And you're interested in that particular day because that's when Mrs. Dempsey's neighbor got killed?"

Leo looked toward the kitchen, where he could hear the others finishing up their dinner. Laurie didn't like him talking so openly about crime with Timmy, but the boy had witnessed his own father's murder and spent years under the killer's threat to come for Timmy as well. As far as Leo was concerned, the child was going to have a natural curiosity about crime.

"Yes, that's why we're interested. And if the person who hurt Lydia has something to do with your mother's case —"

Timmy completed the thought. "Then he might have lived down here when Susan was in college." He was sneaking peeks at the driver's license photos he was supposedly straightening.

"That's right," Leo said. "I tell ya, Timmy. You can do anything you want when you grow up, but you've got the chops to be a better cop than I was."

Timmy suddenly stopped fiddling with the pictures and pulled one from the pile. "I know him!"

"Timmy, we're not playing police right now. I've got to get back to work here."

"No, I mean it, for real. I saw him in the restaurant in San Francisco, the one with the huge meatballs and all the pictures of celebrities on the walls."

"At Mama Torini's?"

"Yes. This man was there. He was sitting at the bar, right above our table. Whenever

I looked at him, he turned around really fast."

Leo took the photograph from his grandson. According to the driver's license, the man was Steve Roman. His current address in San Francisco had been changed with the DMV two years earlier. Before that, he had been a longtime resident of Los Angeles.

"You're saying you saw this man, in person, when we were in San Francisco?"

"Yes. He had big muscles and pale skin. And his head was shaved. Not like bald when the hair falls out, but it was shaved, like when you say you have five o'clock shadow, Grandpa. And I remember thinking it was funny he'd shave his head while other grown-ups complain all the time about their hair falling out. Plus the bartender had long dark hair but kept it in a ponytail, so in a way he was hiding his hair too."

"Timmy, are you sure?" But Leo could tell Timmy *was* sure. As much as he credited Timmy's ability to deal with hardship, the threat of Blue Eyes had trained the boy to constantly monitor any man in his vicinity.

Leo believed that Timmy had indeed seen Steve Roman. Still, he'd like to have something more to connect this man to the case.

"Do me a favor, kiddo. Can you fetch me your iPad from the kitchen?"

Seconds later, Timmy was back with his gadget in tow. "Are we playing a game?"

"Not quite yet." Leo opened the browser, typed in "Steve Roman," and hit ENTER.

He found listings for a Boston Realtor, a New York City investment banker, the author of a book about rain forests. He scrolled to the next page of results.

Timmy touched his index finger to the screen. "Look, Grandpa. Click on that one. Weren't Mommy and Alex talking about that today?"

Leo knew immediately from the name of the website that he had found the correct Steve Roman. He finally had the connection he was looking for between Lydia Levitt's murder and *Under Suspicion.*

"Laurie!" he called out. "You need to see this!"

57

"Alex, that was delicious." Laurie could still smell the aroma of cooked red wine and mushrooms as she filled the cast-iron pot with sudsy water to soak overnight.

"I'll pass the compliment on to Ramon. He's the one who taught me everything I know about coq au vin." It had been Alex's idea to send craft services away early so they could have one home-cooked meal in this gourmet kitchen.

"A five-star dinner," Laurie said, "and then in the morning, little elves will appear to carry away the dirty dishes. I could get used to this."

She had just stacked the final plate in the sink when she heard the sound of her father's voice from the living room. "Laurie!" Was it her imagination, or did he sound excited? "You need to see this!"

She turned off the faucet and ran to the living room. Her father and son were next

352

to each other on the sofa.

"We've got something, Laurie. It was actually Timmy who made the connection."

"Dad, I told you I didn't want him exposed to all this."

Now Timmy was on his feet, extending a printout of a driver's license. "I recognized this man right away, Mommy. His name is Steve Roman. His car was photographed right outside Mrs. Dempsey's neighborhood the day Lydia Levitt got killed in her yard." Laurie could not believe she was hearing her nine-year-old son talk this way about a homicide. "And I also saw him right next to us at the restaurant in San Francisco, at Mama . . ."

He looked to his grandfather for help with the name. "At Mama Torini's," Leo said. "Timmy got a good enough look at him to recognize this picture. The man's name is Steve Roman. He lives in San Francisco, but until two years ago, he was in Los Angeles. And get this."

Her father handed her the iPad. Part of her didn't want to look. She didn't want to believe that Timmy had been sitting right next to someone involved in Lydia Levitt's murder. She didn't want to believe that the woman's death had anything to do with her decision to reinvestigate the Cinderella

Murder.

She saw the name "Steve Roman" multiple times on the screen. The website was for Advocates for God. Someone named Steve Roman was a frequent poster to the community forum.

She shuffled a pile of documents off a chair so she could sit and process the information.

A member of Keith Ratner's church had been watching them in San Francisco and had been spotted near the murder of Rosemary Dempsey's neighbor? This couldn't be a coincidence.

She thought back to that moment at the end of filming today. When Alex had pressed Nicole about her fight with Susan, Keith Ratner appeared to know more than he was saying. Did the fight have something to do with AG?

Laurie stood from the sofa and steered her son into the kitchen. "Grace? Do you mind keeping an eye on Timmy? I have a few more questions for Nicole."

58

When Laurie knocked on Nicole's hotel door, Alex was at her side. He and Leo had insisted that she not leave the house alone. They finally agreed that Leo would stay home with Timmy and Grace while Alex accompanied Laurie to the hotel.

When the door cracked open, it was Nicole's husband, Gavin, who answered.

"Laurie, hi. It's after nine o'clock. Were we expecting you?"

"We need to talk to Nicole."

"I hope this is important. My wife is in bed."

He stepped aside, allowing them to enter. Laurie was surprised to find a large living area, with a separate dining room to the side. Clearly Gavin had used his own money to upgrade them beyond the standard suite provided by the show. "She's not in any danger, is she?" Gavin asked. "She's been so darn nervous ever since Rosemary called her about this show."

Laurie heard Alex intentionally clear his throat. He was reminding her not to slip into her normal mode of trying to comfort her witnesses. "Actually, yes, there's a real possibility she's in danger, Gavin."

"That's impossible," he snapped. "Nicole, you need to get out here."

When she emerged from the separate bedroom, Nicole was wearing a pajama set topped by a robe. "Sorry, I was getting ready for bed."

She did not sound sorry.

"They said you're in danger."

"I said you *might* be in danger," Laurie emphasized. "Have you ever seen this man?" Laurie handed her a printout of Steve Roman's driver's license photograph, monitoring Nicole's face for a reaction.

Her expression was blank. "No, I don't think so."

"His name is Steve Roman. We believe he's the man who killed Rosemary's neighbor, Lydia Levitt."

"How would I know a burglar?"

"We think Lydia interrupted this man snooping behind Rosemary's house, but he wasn't a burglar. He was trying to learn more about the people involved in *Under Suspicion*. In fact, just days after Lydia's death, he was following my family and me in San Francisco. He was probably watching you as well. He could also be the person who attacked my assistant producer, Jerry."

"I'm afraid I'm not following your logic," Nicole said.

"Steve Roman is a longtime member of Advocates for God."

Laurie had been prepared to lay out AG's connections to Keith Ratner and her theory that Keith may have sent one of his church friends, Steve Roman, to sabotage the show and stop production. But the expression on Nicole's face at the mention of Advocates for God made it clear that Nicole already knew something about them.

"Today during the shoot, you said you didn't remember what you argued about with Susan. And when I first met you, you were vague about your reasons for leaving Los Angeles. It has something to do with this church, doesn't it?"

"I don't — I don't know anything about it."

Alex handed her the file folder they had prepared before leaving the house. Laurie slipped the first photograph from the file, an eight-by-ten of nineteen-year-old Susan, smiling up at the camera. Laurie quickly followed it up with a second picture, this one of Lydia Levitt.

"These two women are dead. This is no longer about whatever personal history you want to keep private," Laurie said. "People are being hurt. My friend Jerry is in the hospital right now. And it has something to do with Advocates for God."

Gavin wrapped a protective arm around his wife's shoulder. "Nicole, if you know something —"

"I never meant to hide anything from you, Gavin. I was trying to protect myself. To protect *us.*" Nicole took Gavin's hand in hers and faced Laurie directly. "I'll tell you. But only to help. No cameras."

Laurie nodded. At this point, the truth mattered more than the show.

59

Dwight stepped carefully from the dock onto the stern of his boat, a forty-two-foot cruiser perfect for short trips. He immediately felt a calmness enter his body as he rocked with the sway of the boat on the water. The waves slapping gently against the fiberglass were like a lullaby. Once his scuba partner arrived, he'd be out in Shaw's Cove, diving into the darkness. He loved nothing more than the solitude of night diving.

He would not truly be able to enjoy the scuba dive until he first completed one task. He climbed down into the cabin, retrieved his laptop from his messenger bag, flipped it open, and clicked on the surveillance video of the Bel Air house. It had been two days since Dwight had decided not to go to the police with the video of the horrible attack on Jerry. He had to hope that his continued monitoring might lead him to some answers about Susan's death, and possibly Jerry's attacker.

He sped through the video, slowing down only when something interested him. When he reached the end of the tape, he rewound to the scene that fascinated him most, the joint interview with Madison Meyer, Nicole Hunter, and Keith Ratner.

Alex Buckley had caught Madison in a couple of inconsistencies, but they were small ones. She was still vouching for Frank Parker. The bigger revelation was that Susan had a fight with Nicole and had stormed out of the dorm that evening.

Dwight knew how excited Susan had been about that audition. She wouldn't have missed it voluntarily.

He rewound the video once again, replaying Alex Buckley's final question over and over again: *Where would she have gone?*

He closed his eyes and pictured Susan on the night when he decided that he truly loved her. They had worked so late at the lab that they realized that dawn was only an hour away. They decided to drive to Griffith Observatory, reportedly the best place to watch the sun rise. As they sat in the grass, in the dark, she had filled the silence, talking about how petty girls could be to each other. How the theater department was filled with actresses who had the same amount of talent as she did but twice the ambition. How too many of her friends prioritized their boyfriends over their girlfriends. The way, even with Keith, she always felt she had to boost his confidence. She said there was only one place where she could let another side of her personality take over.

Where would she have gone?

Dwight was pretty sure he knew.

He used his computer to pull up an online calendar from 1994 to refresh his memory. By May 7, it had been weeks since Hathaway had caught Dwight hacking into the university computer system. Dwight remembered the timing because he was counting down the days until the end of the semester. He wanted to go to La Jolla for another scuba trip.

All this time, he had suppressed the connection between the date of Susan's death and another event that had changed his life.

He closed his eyes again and recalled Susan's excitement about her audition with Frank Parker. She always said she liked to feel calm and focused before a performance, trying to channel her character. If a fight with Nicole had forced her from her dorm room at six, that gave her at least forty-five minutes to calm herself down. If she had needed another place to feel calm and safe, Dwight knew exactly where Susan would have gone. And he knew exactly what she would have heard when she got there.

His skin felt hot. He stood up and started pacing in the boat's cabin. He was having a hard time controlling his own breathing. He needed his own safe place now. He needed to be in the water.

But he also wanted to get his thoughts out. His plan had worked: he finally believed he knew who had killed Susan.

He pulled up Laurie's number on his cell and hit ENTER. *"You've reached Laurie Moran . . ."*

"Call me ASAP," he said at the tone. "I need to talk to you."

He was so focused on leaving a message that he did not hear the footsteps on the deck.

60

Gavin led his wife to the sofa and held her hand protectively. "I'm here for you," he whispered. "Always. No matter what. If there's anybody you're afraid of, I'll protect you."

Nicole spoke quickly, focusing on some random spot in the distance. "The fight with Susan was about Advocates for God. I'd been a member of the church for months, and Susan didn't approve. She said they were crooks, that they used religion to bilk people of their money. She said I was getting brainwashed. And it didn't help that I was . . . in a relationship with Martin Collins. I thought he was the most generous, inspiring person. I thought I was in love with him, but I was so young and impressionable."

The moment was disrupted by the buzz of Laurie's phone. Laurie fumbled in her purse and glanced at the screen. It was

Dwight Cook. She did not want to interrupt Nicole, so she hit the REJECT CALL button. "If you'd been with the church for months," Laurie said, "why did you fight about it that day?"

"The argument was about Susan's boyfriend, Keith. I took him to a new-member party. Susan was furious, saying I was out to convert him. The fight was as bad as Alex described earlier — even worse. I felt attacked. I threw a book at her. I can't believe that's the last time we saw each other." She dropped her head into her hands.

"You realize, Nicole, that some people might not believe that. If Susan was threatening to kick you out of the dorm —"

"No, she never would have done that. It was an ugly fight, but honestly, I think she only snapped at me because of the culmination of everything at once: the audition and her agent leaving for Arizona because of his mom's heart attack, and she was harried, rummaging through her drawers in a mad search for her lucky necklace. I walked in, and she lashed out at me about taking Keith to an AG event. I think it was just the icing on the cake. We would have been fine. And I would certainly *never* have hurt Susan."

Something about Nicole's version of the argument was bothering Laurie. "You say you wound up at O'Malley's drinking too much. If it wasn't truly a blowout, why were you so upset?"

"After Susan stormed out, I walked to Martin's to vent about our argument. Whenever I was with Martin, he had this way of making it all seem okay." She whispered to Gavin, *"I'm so sorry I never told you, please forgive me,"* before continuing. "When I got to his house, the lights were on, and his car was in the driveway. He didn't answer the door, so I just walked in, assuming he couldn't hear me knocking. When I got to his bedroom —"

Her voice broke, and she started to shake. Gavin pulled her close and told her that everything was going to be all right. "These secrets are torturing you, Nicole."

"When I walked into his bedroom, he was with a little girl. My gosh, she couldn't have been more than ten. They were . . . in the bed. I ran from the house, but he caught up to me in the driveway. He told me if I ever breathed a word of what I'd seen, he would kill me. And not just me. The girl, too. He threatened to kill anyone I loved — my parents, my friends. He said he could find me forty years later and kill my children and grandchildren. And I could tell he meant it. I think he would have killed me on the spot if that little girl hadn't been there to witness it."

"And you never said a word to anyone?" Laurie asked.

Nicole shook her head and then looked down, sobbing into her hands. "You have no idea how much guilt I've carried. Every time I see him on television, I feel nauseous, wondering how many others he has victimized. I was tempted so many times to tell you, Gavin, but I was ashamed. And afraid for both of us. And I had no idea who the child was, and no proof. Martin is powerful. At the very least, he would get other church members to say I was crazy. And I didn't doubt for a second his ability to carry out his threats. It's why I was always afraid to have children, Gavin. I didn't want to spend every moment terrified about Martin coming after them."

Laurie knew the fear of knowing that someone wanted to hurt your child. "Do you think Martin had something to do with Susan's death?" Laurie asked.

"I'm sure he's capable of murder," Nicole said. "But he had no reason to harm Susan, and I saw him at his house that night with my own eyes."

"But if Martin found out you were doing our show," Laurie said, "he'd worry that

366

you might end up saying too much about the past."

Nicole wiped away a tear. "Yes, that's how he operates. He's insular and deeply paranoid. That's why I've kept such a low profile all these years. The thought of me on television, talking about my days at UCLA? He would have gone nuclear. That man in the picture is probably one of Martin's henchmen, sent to shut down your show."

Laurie was having a hard time processing the new information. She had been so certain that if they found the person who attacked Lydia and Jerry, they'd also find Susan's killer. And there was still something nagging at Laurie about Nicole's description of her argument with Susan that afternoon.

Alex had been quietly allowing Nicole to answer Laurie's questions. Now he spoke up. "Let's talk about Keith Ratner. We know he's still active in the church. He knew who the other show participants were. He probably told Martin that Nicole had signed on to appear. Then Martin could have asked Steve Roman to keep an eye on her, which could have led Roman to Rosemary's neighborhood. You two see each other, right?"

"Yes," Nicole said excitedly, "that's it! Rosemary came to my house the day before

Lydia was killed. This man could have followed her from there."

"Our best shot at finding anything on
Martin would be to go through Keith Ratner," Laurie said.

Dwight Cook and Richard Hathaway were
supposed to be coming to the house for
their interviews in the morning, but their
scenes would be short. Laurie pulled her
phone from her purse. Ignoring the alert of
the missed call from Dwight, she composed
a text to Keith, reading aloud as she typed
with her thumbs. *Thanks for all the help
today. I hate to tell you this, but a technical
glitch swallowed up some of the footage. Any
chance you can reshoot the part about your
bookstore alibi in the morning? I promise it
won't take long. — Laurie*

She hit the ENTER key and breathed a sigh
of relief when he immediately texted back:
No problem. Just tell me the time.

*Great, thanks. Be sure to wear the same
shirt.*

"Add a smiley face for good measure,"
Alex suggested, reading over her shoulder.

"Got him," she said.

"We should have Leo fill in the LAPD on
what we've got," Alex said. "Nicole, we can
keep what you've told us confidential, at
least for now. If the police agree, they can

368

monitor the questioning of Keith while disguised as camera crew."

"Maybe Rosemary was right about Keith all along," Laurie said. "He could have sent one of his church buddies to shut down production on the show."

"You guys are the experts," Nicole said. "But if any of this is related to Advocates for God, I wouldn't bother worrying about Keith Ratner. Martin Collins is the truly dangerous one. If this Steve Roman works for Collins, he'd be the kind of person willing to do anything for him. Trust me, I know."

On her way to the car, Laurie was replaying Nicole's description of Susan in a frantic search for her necklace, stressed out about her audition and lashing out at Nicole for introducing Keith to her fringe church. There was something about the scene that was bothering her.

Her thoughts were distracted by a new voice mail alert on her phone. It was Dwight. *Call me ASAP. I need to talk to you.* He would have to wait until morning. They needed to find an LAPD detective willing to help them corner Keith Ratner.

61

The next morning, Laurie stood in the driveway of the Bel Air house, watching for cars. She checked her watch. It was 9:58 A.M. Dwight Cook and Richard Hathaway were scheduled to arrive at ten, so she had asked Keith Ratner to come at eleven thirty. She figured he would be less likely to be suspicious about being called back in if he were one of multiple witnesses at the house.

She snuck a glance through the door into the living room. LAPD detective Sean Reilly blended in with the camera crew, wearing blue jeans, a baseball cap, and the black *Under Suspicion* T-shirt Laurie had provided. He was the detective assigned to the assault on Jerry. He was young, probably early thirties, the only lines on his face the kind that came whenever a cop took his job seriously.

It had taken a long late-night phone call to explain the connection from Lydia Levitt to Steve Roman to Advocates for God to *Under Suspicion* to Jerry, but Reilly finally agreed to come to the set to hear what Keith Ratner had to say about the church's involvement in all of this.

Nicole Melling was already waiting in the house. Laurie had to hope that when the time came, all the pieces to the plan would fall into place.

A white Lexus SUV pulled into the driveway at 10:02. Hathaway was driving. No one else was in the car.

"I thought you and Dwight would come together," she said as he opened his door.

"My place is in Toluca Lake." Hathaway must have registered her blank expression because he added, "It's in Burbank. Great place. Private lake. One of the best golf clubs in the state. Anyway, Dwight still has his student crash pad in Westwood. Driving out of your way during the L.A. commute? No one's that good of a friend."

"We'll get you in and out quickly, just a little background about Susan's technology interests. Her father was a successful intellectual property lawyer, and they shared an excitement for the tech world. You can talk about that side of her in a way our other witnesses can't."

Dwight still hadn't arrived by the time

Hathaway had been miked and powdered by the makeup technician. It was 10:20. Laurie listened as Hathaway left yet another voice mail message for Dwight: "Hey, man. Laurie and I have both been calling you. Hope you're on your way."

"I don't get it," Hathaway said, slipping his phone in his sports coat pocket. "He's usually so prompt."

Laurie was kicking herself for not finding the time to return his "ASAP" call last night. She now had a feeling that he had been calling to cancel. "I wonder if the idea of the cameras scared him off on the eve of the shoot," she said.

Hathaway shrugged. "Maybe. But he had been so eager to help with the show."

Laurie had planned to get Dwight and Hathaway out of here shortly after Keith arrived. Otherwise, Keith might lose patience and leave.

She made a quick decision to proceed with Hathaway alone. He was telegenic. He had cachet, having earned his tenure in his early thirties and then moved on to help a protégé form a groundbreaking company. If she could rope Dwight back in later, Alex could question him separately. It was more important not to ruin their plans for Keith Ratner.

■ ■ ■ ■

As she had expected, Richard Hathaway was a natural on camera. "I had a lot of talented students at UCLA," he told Alex, "but Susan was among the best. When she died, there was so much talk about her promising acting career, but I've always believed she could have gone on to be a star in the tech world. She could have been another Dwight Cook. Such a tragedy."

His handsome face furrowed in thought, his voice resonating with the authority of a man who had been a professor, with step-by-step reasoning, he continued to talk about Susan and then, under Alex's questioning, the night of her death.

"I remember the absolute shock of hearing on Sunday that her body had been found. Dwight was only nineteen years old then, the brain of a wizard but still adolescent in his relationships. It was impossible not to realize how he felt about Susan. Whenever they were in the lab together, his eyes were shining and he was smiling. When he got the awful news, he tracked me down at my home and cried in my arms."

"Do you happen to know where Dwight

was on the night Susan died?" Alex asked quietly.

"With me, actually. Dwight was in the throes of writing code for his project, and I knew he wanted to talk to me about it. I didn't have any plans for the evening, so I called Dwight and asked him if he wanted to join me for a burger."

"What time was this?" Alex asked.

"I called him around seven. Met him just after that at Hamburger Haven."

"One more thing," Alex added. "I wouldn't be doing my job if I didn't mention the fact that you were very popular among female students and had a bit of a reputation as a Don Juan."

Hathaway laughed. "Ah, yes. Most crush-worthy professor, according to the campus paper. All rumor and innuendo, I assure you. I'm convinced it's inevitable when you're a young, single academic."

"So anyone who suggested you may have taken a more-than-professional interest in Susan . . . ?"

"Would be deeply mistaken. Not to mention, Susan was very clearly taken by her boyfriend. It broke my heart watching poor Dwight pine for her."

Hathaway had been perfect, providing the touch of personality she'd been looking for.

Dwight Cook was the face of REACH, but Hathaway was a hundred times better on camera than Dwight would have been.

She had just yelled *"Cut!"* when she heard the purr of a sports car outside the house, followed by the sound of a car door slamming. Keith Ratner was here. She could send Hathaway home. Perfect timing.

62

Laurie placed Keith in the same spot on the sofa where he'd been the previous day, wearing the same shirt, as requested.

"Again, I'm so sorry," she apologized. "We lost the footage of you telling us where you were the night of Susan's murder. If you can just repeat that, we'll shoot you close in. It will look just like you're sitting next to Madison and Nicole."

"Sure, no problem."

She double-checked that Detective Reilly was positioned with the camera crew, then gave the signal to start filming.

Alex started with the identical line he'd used the previous morning. "I thought we'd start," Alex said, "by having each of you walk through where you were the night of the murder. Keith, would you like to begin?"

Keith repeated the same story he'd given many times over the years: he'd been at a bookstore with fellow AG members.

"Now, speaking of Advocates for God," Alex said, "do you know this man?" He placed a photograph of Steve Roman on the coffee table in front of Keith.

Keith shot Alex, and then Laurie, a confused look. He picked up the picture for closer inspection. "Never seen him."

"He's a member of your church, and we believe he is determined to shut down this show's production — using violence when necessary."

Keith reached for the mic clipped to his shirt collar. They'd assumed he would try to leave once he realized they were departing from yesterday's script, but at least they had him here. The LAPD was here. All they had to do was get him to say something that would give Detective Reilly probable cause to detain him.

"Keith, it's important," she said. "There are things about the church you don't know."

Keith's gaze suddenly darted away from Laurie. She turned to see Nicole stepping from the kitchen. Nicole was terrified of retribution from Martin, but Laurie, Leo, and Gavin had convinced her the previous night to be present at the house, listening from the next room, in case she decided to help confront Keith.

"I told them about my fight with Susan," she said. "They know I was the one who introduced you to Martin and AG. You know I left the church. Los Angeles, too. But I never told you my reasons."

"You left because Susan was killed. She was your best friend."

As Nicole took a seat next to Keith on the sofa, Laurie noticed Detective Reilly take a step forward. He was paying close attention.

"No, that wasn't it. Keith, Reverend Collins is not the man you think he is."

63

Keith Ratner could not believe the words that were coming out of Nicole's mouth.

First Nicole claimed to have had a secret relationship with Martin, and now she was saying he abused a little girl?

"Nicole, these are crazy accusations. No wonder Martin was so worried about you being a part of this show."

"I saw him with my own eyes, Keith. And you would not believe he was a good man if you heard the threats he made against me. Some part of you must see the truth. Look at his lifestyle. All that money he raises isn't going to good works. It's lining his pockets. And think about those families he chooses to help — always with young girls, always with vulnerable parents. I didn't see the pattern either until that night. But I couldn't prove anything. Who knows how many other victims he's had? You can help. You're in his inner circle."

Keith covered his face with his hands. This was absolutely insane. "I haven't seen you in twenty years, Nicole. Why should I believe you?"

"Ask yourself: How did Martin feel about your doing this show? Did he want you talking about AG?"

"Yes, in fact. I didn't even want to do it. Martin's the one who *pushed* me to accept." But as Keith finished the sentence, he felt a tug of doubt. He recalled the moment he first mentioned *Under Suspicion* to Martin. Keith had wanted no part of the show. He hated the idea of having his name dragged through the mud again. Martin had been the one to steer him here. Martin had wanted to know what Nicole was up to. His exact words had been, *You let me worry about my own enemies.*

But child abuse? Was it possible that Keith had devoted his entire adult life to a church led by a man who would do something so heinous? It was unimaginable.

He cleared his throat, as if it could somehow clear his thoughts. "What do you people want from me?"

A cameraman in a baseball hat lunged forward, a badge in his hand. When were the surprises going to stop?

"Mr. Ratner, my name is Detective Sean

Reilly with the Los Angeles Police Department. Let me be straight with you. I've got Ms. Melling's twenty-year-old recollection of an unconfirmed observation. I don't have the name of whatever child she saw with your reverend. It's not even close to the evidence we'd need for a prosecution. But I think you'll agree that a person of good conscience can't ignore this. You asked what we want from you? Under California law, police can monitor a telephone conversation with the consent of one party."

"You're asking me to turn on Martin."

"You're not *turning* on anyone. Just tell him two things." Reilly ticked off his points on his thumb and index finger. "The police asked you about this man Steve Roman. And they raised the possibility of child abuse in the church. If he's innocent, we'll find that out. But if he's not?"

Keith thought of all the hours he had spent at Martin's side, delivering food to needy families. Without the church, Keith would still have been the shallow, insecure kid he used to be. Then he pictured all the young girls he'd seen in the families Martin helped. He hadn't seen Nicole for twenty years, but she was right about the type of family Martin preferred. And he couldn't imagine Nicole lying about something so awful.

"Okay, let's do it." He said a silent prayer that this was all a misunderstanding.

While Detective Reilly prepared Keith for his phone call to Martin Collins, Laurie walked Nicole to the driveway, giving her a brief hug before turning her over to the care of her husband, Gavin. Two weeks ago, when Laurie first met the couple in their gourmet kitchen, Nicole had seemed distant and cold, still trying to cover secrets that were two decades old. Now Nicole couldn't stop sobbing, and Laurie wondered whether the woman would ever regain control over her emotions.

But Laurie forced herself to focus on the hard facts. Even twenty years ago, Nicole had been mature enough to begin a relationship with Martin, an adult man. She had ignored Susan's warnings about Martin and his so-called church. Even after she caught Martin inflicting perhaps the worst harm imaginable, she had buckled under his threats, running away and leaving the child behind.

Laurie could empathize with Nicole, but she couldn't sympathize.

64

Laurie was surprised at how simple it was for Detective Reilly to record Keith's call to Martin Collins, with a simple cord from Keith's cell phone into a laptop's microphone port. After considerable negotiation, Reilly agreed to let Leo and Laurie listen in on the call, but with no cameras or recording on their part. If the call panned out, Laurie could find another way to report the facts for the show. Right now, she just wanted to hear what Martin Collins had to say.

With the help of an audio splitter, Leo, Laurie, and Detective Reilly were all plugged in with their own earphones. She gave Keith a thumbs-up as he hit the dial button. The man was far from perfect, but today he was doing the right thing.

"Hey, Martin, it's Keith," he said when the call connected. "You got a sec? I had a weird visit from the police."

"The police?"

"Yeah, asking about a Steve Roman. Bald, muscled, maybe in his forties. They said he belonged to Advocates for God, but I told them I didn't know him. Does the name ring a bell?"

"Sure," Martin said nonchalantly.

Laurie arched an eyebrow in her father's direction. They had just connected the head of AG to a man spotted near Lydia Levitt's murder, a man who was monitoring their movements just days prior to the attack on Jerry. Was it really going to be this easy?

Through her headphones, she listened as Martin continued. "I told you I wanted to know what Nicole was saying to those TV people? I asked Steve to lend a hand. He's helpful that way."

"Helpful? The police think he killed a woman in the Bay Area while he was snooping on one of the show's participants. And three days ago, someone broke into the show's set, stole a bunch of equipment, and nearly killed a member of the production team."

There was a long pause on the other end of the line. "Steve used to be a violent person. But that was a long time ago. I don't know anything about a woman in the Bay Area, but, yes, he did tell me about the unfortunate situation at the house in Bel Air."

Laurie clenched a fist in celebration. *Yes,* they had identified Jerry's attacker.

"An unfortunate situation?"

"He crossed a line. He said he found a door unlocked. He went in. Then someone came home and found him there. He told me he panicked, but he didn't tell me how bad it was until I read about the assault in the paper. I've been counseling him, but it may be time for me to call the police before he hurts someone else."

As Keith had explained it to them, Advocates for God encouraged all members to open up fully to the church but did not observe the traditional priest-penitent privilege. Instead, it was for the church to decide when disclosure of the information was necessary to "advocate for God's goodness." It sounded like Martin was getting ready to use what he knew about Steve Roman to distance himself from the man's crimes, depicting Roman as an out-of-control lone wolf.

"Martin, it gets worse. The police also asked me whether — I feel gross even saying it. They asked if I had ever seen you be *inappropriate* with children."

The line fell silent.

"Martin? Are you there?" Keith asked.

"Yes. This has to be coming from Nicole. She's crazy. She fabricated something like this when she was in college. That's why I wanted to keep an eye on her during the TV show. Obviously it's not true, so don't repeat that to anyone. Now, I better track down Steve. He's clearly become a problem."

When Martin hung up, the kitchen immediately broke into cacophony as they all spoke at once, rehashing every last word of the conversation. Detective Reilly formed his hands into a capital T to quiet them. "Good work, Keith. We've got what we need for an arrest warrant for Steve Roman. I'll follow up with Martin Collins to get him locked down on the details of whatever Roman told him about the assault on Jerry."

"Wait," Laurie said. "You're not arresting Collins?"

"I've got no probable cause. It's not against the law to ask someone to keep an eye on a situation. If it were, there'd be no private investigators."

"But Steve Roman's not a PI. He's hurting people. He probably *killed* Lydia."

"And that's why we're going to arrest him. But until we can prove Martin Collins solicited Steve Roman to commit these crimes, he's an innocent man."

Laurie started to argue, but Leo interrupted. "He's right on the law, Laurie. But a running start is just the beginning, right, Reilly?"

"Absolutely." Reilly's brow momentarily unfurrowed. "Once we get our hands on this Steve Roman character, he might have a different story to tell. Happens all the time. We'll get the phone records, search his apartment, the works. I'll get the arrest warrant out pronto. We can apply over the phone now. Trust me, we'll get to the bottom of all of it."

Laurie tried not to be disappointed. After all, they had probably solved Lydia's murder and the attack on Jerry. But they still had no idea how any of this connected to Susan's murder.

Reilly had just finished packing up his recording equipment when Grace came running into the kitchen. "Turn on the television!" she yelled, reaching for the remote control on the counter.

Laurie placed her hand gently on Grace's forearm. "Hold on a just a minute, Grace. I'm about to walk Detective Reilly out."

"No, it can't wait." She fumbled with the buttons and began flipping channels until she reached her destination. "Look!"

On the screen was a helicopter's aerial footage over bright blue water. An anchor's voice said something about a "thirty-nine-year-old genius" and the "revolutionizing of the Internet." It wasn't until Laurie read the text at the bottom of the screen that she understood what she was watching: *REACH founder and CEO Dwight Cook's body recovered from a scuba accident, sources say.*

No, not Dwight. Please don't let it be him, Laurie thought.

65

Laurie didn't want to believe that Dwight was dead. Three hours after Detective Reilly's departure, she wanted to hear that this was all some misunderstanding. When Dwight had called last night, she was so wrapped up in tracking down Steve Roman and his connection to AG, she hadn't even found the time to return his phone call. Now that sweet man — that sweet, overgrown boy — was dead, and she was convinced that his death had to be connected to her investigation into Susan's murder. And she was wondering if she could have stopped it.

Timmy was upstairs playing video games, but the adults all huddled in the den to watch the television coverage. Between Keith's phone call to Martin Collins and the news reports of Dwight's death, they were on edge. The LAPD had obtained a warrant for Steve Roman's arrest, but he was still at large. Was he still in Los Angeles, on his way back to San Francisco, or on the run toward the Mexico border? Could he return to target the team again?

At the sound of the doorbell, Grace let out a yelp, then placed a hand to her chest. "Oh my Lord. I'm like some girl in the middle of a horror movie."

Leo went to the front door, gun in hand, and gazed through the peephole. "It's Detective Reilly," he announced.

Laurie could feel their collective relief.

"Sorry to disturb you," Reilly said, entering the den with a laptop already in hand. "First I'm afraid I have some bad news. Dwight Cook's body has been positively identified. I'll spare you the physical details, but there's no question that it's him."

Laurie blinked back the tears that were starting to form.

Alex leaned toward her and whispered, "Are you okay? We can take a break."

She shook her head. "No, I'm okay. Please, Detective Reilly, tell us the rest."

"I didn't realize this when I was here earlier, but apparently this house is owned by Dwight Cook?"

"Yes," Laurie said. "He lent us the house to help us out."

"*Help you out,* huh? See, one of my fellow

detectives was going through Mr. Cook's computers as part of their investigation. Apparently Reverend Collins wasn't the only person keeping an eye on your production. Cook had every inch of this place wired for surveillance."

"Like, spying on us?" Grace asked. "Not to speak ill of the dead, but that's straight-up perverted."

"Not your showers or anything like that," Reilly clarified. "But pretty much everything that has happened in this house since your arrival is on video."

"The house is usually vacant," Laurie said. "It would make sense he'd have a state-of-the-art security system in a high-end property like this."

"It's not only a matter of the equipment," Reilly explained. "Given how the video files are set up, we can tell that Dwight actually viewed them. We can also tell when he was watching and what footage he watched. Apparently he stopped watching last night at nine twenty-three P.M."

Laurie checked the voice mail log on her own cell phone. "He called me just a few minutes later. He said he needed to talk ASAP."

"And . . . ?"

"We were in the middle of trying to figure

out Steve Roman's connection to our case. I didn't have time to call. Obviously if I had known . . ."

She felt her stomach drop as Reilly rolled his eyes, clearly frustrated by the dead end.

"Well, here's the thing." Reilly flipped open his laptop on the coffee table and began tapping away. "Dwight watched a couple of clips repeatedly."

He turned the screen so they could all see it. "One clip was the attack on your friend," Reilly said. Laurie felt sick as they watched the brutal assault on Jerry. Reilly paused the tape just as Jerry's masked assailant rose from his bloodied body. "See that insignia on his shirt? We've got a tech trying to sharpen the image, but at least the body type is consistent with Steve Roman."

"So Dwight must have called me because he had Jerry's assailant on video," Laurie said.

Reilly was shaking his head, fast-forwarding through the video. "I doubt it. He saw the assault for the first time three nights ago and has replayed it multiple times since. He would have called you earlier. But here." He slowed the tape. "This is the segment Dwight watched right before he called you."

Laurie immediately recognized the scene

from yesterday: Keith, Madison, and Nicole, side by side on the living room sofa, discussing the day Susan was killed. Reilly played the interview to its end and then paused it. "It looks like he kept replaying the very end. Is there some reason he'd be interested in that scene?" Reilly asked.

"I have no idea," Laurie said. "He wasn't really friends with any of them apart from Susan. I've got to ask, Detective Reilly. If you have colleagues searching Dwight's computers, are they certain Dwight's death was an accident?"

"No. If anything, it looks like the scene was staged to seem accidental. They found traces of bleach throughout the entire interior of the boat, and according to the medical examiner's initial inspection, the nitrogen levels in his tissue are inconsistent with having scuba dived that night. The current theory is that he was already unconscious when his body hit the water."

"Could this be more of Steve Roman's crime spree?" Laurie was thinking aloud, wondering if Roman would have a reason to go after Dwight. "The alternative is that Dwight knew something about one of the other suspects."

"That's our theory," Reilly said, "especially if he figured it out as he was watching the end of this video. I thought you might realize its significance."

Laurie shook her head. What are we missing? she thought.

The buzz of Laurie's cell phone broke her concentration. She wanted to throw the thing across the room until she saw that the call was from Rosemary Dempsey.

"Hi, Rosemary. Can I call you right back —"

"Are you watching the news? They're saying that Dwight Cook is dead. And now there's a warrant out for some man named Steve Roman, and it has something to do with the attack on Jerry? Are we in danger? What in the world is going on?"

66

Steve Roman rocked back and forth, shirtless, on the motel bed.

His name was all over the news. The police would be monitoring his credit cards as they searched for him. The second he heard his name on the car radio, he made a quick cash purchase on the streets of South Central L.A., then found a fleabag dive willing to accept cash for a room, no ID necessary. He counted the remaining bills in his wallet. Twenty-three bucks. Not much he could do with that.

A used-car ad blared at him from the crummy television set on the dresser. He flipped the channel in search of more news about his arrest warrant. He halted at the sight of a familiar face. It was Martin Collins, standing in his front yard in a throng of reporters.

"It has come to my attention that the LAPD is searching for a man named Steve Roman.

Some of you have already gleaned from the Internet that he is a member of Advocates for God. I founded this church a quarter century ago. In that time, Advocates for God has gone from a car full of good people willing to help the downtrodden, to thousands of believers who sacrifice every day to help their fellow man. I do know Steve Roman and truly believed he had reformed himself through the healing power of God's goodness. But I've been speaking with the police, and, unfortunately, it seems that a disturbed individual found his way into our flock. But that shouldn't reflect on our group as a whole. Our church is doing everything within our power to apprehend this criminal."

"**Reverend Collins,**" a reporter called out. "*We have sources who say the arrest warrant for Steve Roman is related to the attack this week on a producer for the show* Under Suspicion. *They are in town covering the Cinderella Murder. What is the connection between your church and the unsolved murder of Susan Dempsey?"*

Martin placed his hands on his hips, as if this were the first time he had really contemplated the question. "*It's not my place to speculate about the motivations of a sick mind. But our best guess is this person — obviously ill at some level — was making a misguided attempt to protect Keith Ratner, another AG member who has been unfairly under suspicion all these years in the death of his former girlfriend. That's all I have for now, folks."* He gave a friendly wave and retreated into his mansion.

Steve pulled on a white undershirt, warming himself as the air-conditioning unit rattled in the wall beneath the motel window. *A disturbed individual? Criminal? Ill? Misguided?*

Steve had always done whatever Martin asked of him. Yet now Martin was selling him out, feeding into the worst stereotypes of their church, for his own benefit.

Steve clenched his fists. He felt old impulses rising in his blood, the way he felt when that neighbor found him in Rosemary Dempsey's yard, when the production assistant had surprised him in the house in Bel Air. He needed a punching bag. He needed to run.

He left the motel room, checking first that no one was watching. He made his way through the parking lot to his pickup truck and then popped the glove box.

He retrieved his newly purchased nine-millimeter. It was small for his hands, but it had been cheap. He tucked the gun in the back of his waistband.

He had made some mistakes in recent weeks, but that was because Martin Collins had treated him as an errand boy. He was feeling levelheaded now. He was in charge.

67

Laurie's first instinct was to rush to the hotel after Rosemary's panicked phone call. This woman, whom she'd convinced to trust her with her daughter's case, had learned the news of both Dwight Cook's death and an arrest warrant being issued for Jerry's attacker from the television. Laurie owed her an in-person update.

Alex insisted on coming with her, while Leo stayed at the house with Timmy and Grace. "Alex, thank you for keeping an eye on me," Laurie said once they were in the hotel lobby. "But I think I should speak with Rosemary one-on-one."

"No problem," Alex said. "I'll check in with hotel security to make sure they're on the lookout for Steve Roman."

Outside Rosemary's hotel room, Laurie heard the muted sounds of a television. She took a deep breath and knocked on the door. Rosemary answered immediately.

"Laurie, thank you for coming. I'm so afraid. I don't understand what's happening. Yesterday it was that whole scene at the house with Susan's friends. I can't believe Nicole, after all these years, never told me about that fight. And now Dwight Cook is dead? And the police think this man who attacked Jerry, who's on the loose, is connected to Advocates for God? Now I'm wondering if I was right all along: maybe Keith Ratner is behind everything — Susan's murder, the attack on Jerry, now Dwight."

On the television screen behind Rosemary, Laurie spotted Martin Collins at an impromptu press conference in front of his house.

"Hold on," she said. "Can you turn up the volume?"

"It's not my place to speculate about the motivations of a sick mind," he was saying. *"But our best guess is this person — obviously ill at some level — was making a misguided attempt to protect Keith Ratner, another AG member who has been unfairly under suspicion all these years in the death of his former girlfriend. That's all I have for now, folks."*

Martin Collins was attractive and charismatic. He duped thousands of people into turning over their hard-earned money to him every year. Now he was using those skills to sweet-talk the viewers watching him on television.

Laurie muted the volume and led a ghostly pale Rosemary to a wing chair in the living area of the suite. Laurie sat on the couch facing her. "I wish I had all the answers," Laurie said. "But we don't know much more than you do, and new information is coming in fast. The reports about Dwight Cook are true, but police suspect foul play. We think this Steve Roman person is trying to shut down the production, but on whose behalf? We're not sure."

"Because of Susan? Is this the man who killed my daughter?"

Laurie reached out and held Rosemary's hand. "We honestly don't know. But the LAPD is on top of this. They're going to search Steve Roman's apartment tonight in San Francisco, and they've got out a high-priority arrest warrant throughout the state. Alex is downstairs right now speaking to security. We'll be sure there's security around the clock for you, Rosemary. And we'll all breathe a sigh of relief — and hopefully learn more — once Roman is caught."

As she made her way to the elevator, Laurie checked her phone. There was a text from Alex: *All set with security. Waiting in lobby.*

She almost missed the familiar face of the man exiting the room at the end of the hall. Richard Hathaway.

On instinct, she turned her back, continuing to check her phone, until she heard the *ding* of the elevator. What was Hathaway doing here? He had turned down the offer of a hotel room.

Laurie walked quietly to the end of the hall, pressing her ear gently to the door of the room he had left. She could hear music playing inside. Before she could even think about what she was doing, she was tapping on the door.

When it opened, Madison Meyer appeared in a white robe.

68

Madison tightened her robe's sash around her waist. "Laurie. Hi. What are you doing here?"

"Um, I was here to see Rosemary," she said, pointing down the hall. "I — Did I just see Richard Hathaway leave your room?"

Madison's face broke out into a wide smile, then she let out a girlish giggle. "Fine. I guess there's no harm in admitting it now that we're both grown-ups."

"You and Hathaway?"

"Yep. I mean, not this whole time, of course. But let's just say those rumors about the handsome young computer science professor were true. I heard he was down here for the production, so I figured I should say hi — see how my older crush turned out. I'm actually surprised myself, but we're . . . *rekindling.*"

Laurie found herself with nothing to say.

There was too much happening on the case right now to carry on with Madison about her love life. Madison wanted to know if the search for Steve Roman was going to affect the filming schedule. "Just so I can tell my agent," she added.

Laurie refrained from rolling her eyes. "We'll know more soon, Madison. Congratulations on your romance with Hathaway."

As Laurie pressed the elevator button, she realized that something was bothering her about discovering Hathaway in Madison's room. The facts themselves certainly weren't surprising. After all, Hathaway had a reputation as a ladies' man, Madison was an obvious flirt, and they were both extremely attractive.

But, still, something was nagging at her. She'd had this same feeling the previous night when she'd spoken to Nicole about her fight with Susan. Maybe this case had her second-guessing every conversation.

As she stepped onto the elevator, she noticed the eye of a security camera in the upper corner to her left. Surveillance was ubiquitous in the modern world, she thought, shuddering at the idea of Dwight's secretly monitoring them these past days.

Secretly. The cameras. Unlike this hotel

security camera, Dwight's equipment had been hidden behind the walls.

Once she stepped from the elevator, she pulled up Detective Reilly's number on her cell and hit ENTER. Come on, she thought. Please answer.

"Reilly."

"Detective, it's Laurie Moran. I've got something for you —"

"Like I said, Ms. Moran. We're working every angle. It takes time. Just ask your dad."

"Dwight Cook had the house in Bel Air wired for surveillance."

"I know. I'm the one who told you, remember?"

"But the equipment was hidden behind the walls, and he only offered us the house last week. He didn't rebuild those walls on a week's notice. This has to be his regular MO."

"The boat," he said, following her logic.

"Yes. Be sure to check the boat for hidden cameras. If Dwight's death wasn't an accident — if he really was murdered — you might have it all on video."

"I'll call the team at the boat and have them check. And good work, Laurie. Thanks."

She had just hung up from Reilly when

her cell rang. It was Alex.

"Where are you?" she asked. "I'm in the lobby but don't see you. You won't believe who I spotted Madison with —"

Alex interrupted. "I pulled the SUV around out front. You ready for some good news?"

"After the last couple days? Definitely."

"It's Jerry. He's conscious. And he's asking for visitors."

69

Steve Roman sat behind the wheel of his pickup truck outside the soup kitchen. He knew Martin Collins would be inside. He had photographers here every week to make sure they caught him on film, feeding the needy. Steve also knew that the millions of dollars Martin had raised for this center far exceeded what AG actually spent here feeding the homeless.

He had seen over the years the way Martin's excesses had grown. Early on, Martin would offer explanations for his seemingly small indulgences — a fine meal was the ultimate pleasure, a custom-cut suit would make him more presentable to donors, and so on. But over time, the indulgences became larger and more frequent — the mansion, trips to Europe, vacation homes — and Martin stopped making excuses for them.

But Steve had always truly believed that

Martin's impact on the world — and guidance of Steve personally — made him a genuine leader. That's why he had always been willing to do everything the church had ever asked of him.

Steve felt his grip on the steering wheel tighten as he replayed Martin's words to the media that day. He had described Steve as a "disturbed individual" who had "found his way into" Advocates for God. He had assured the press that AG was doing everything in its power "to apprehend this criminal."

Steve knew he'd messed up — bad. He hit that man who interrupted his break-in at the *Under Suspicion* house harder, and more times, than he should have. And that neighbor lady back in Oakland — that had gone really wrong.

But if Steve was such a disturbed, ill criminal, shouldn't Martin Collins have to take some responsibility for his conduct? Martin, after all, had known Steve's struggles with his temper. And yet who had Martin turned to when he needed someone to get to the bottom of what Nicole Melling was saying about him to *Under Suspicion*? That's right: Steve. As far as Steve was concerned, his actions — right or wrong — belonged to Martin just as much as to him.

He felt the comfort of the nine-millimeter in the back of his waistband as he spotted Martin exiting the homeless shelter. Because Martin was a firm believer in what he called "the strengthening power of routine," Steve knew that Martin's next stop would be home. Steve also knew that Martin would spend several minutes shaking hands and posing for photographs before getting in his car.

That would give Steve plenty of time.

He started the engine and drove to the hills, parking one block away for safety, even though he'd stolen the blue pickup he was now driving. As he strolled on the sidewalk, he kept alert, checking for any police or security guards circling the neighborhood. If necessary, he could crouch in a nearby garden, posing as a landscaper. Steve knew how easy it was to hide in plain sight, simply by looking like someone who belonged in a setting. But the block was quiet. There was no need for camouflage.

Within seconds, he slipped right through the front door, using tools he'd wielded so many times on Martin's orders. All these years, he had looked to Martin for guidance about what was right and what was wrong. Now Martin had turned that entire world upside down.

It was time for both of them to be judged by the only voice that counted.

He made himself comfortable on the living room sofa, placing his gun on the coffee table in front of him. He could not recall ever being so self-assured inside Martin's home.

When he heard the mechanical rumble of the garage door, he rose and picked up his weapon. It was showtime.

Fifteen minutes later, a reporter named Jenny Hughes was jogging in the Hollywood Hills, admiring the homes as she passed. Her own digs were quite different, a converted warehouse in downtown Los Angeles. But on most days, Jenny's runs doubled as a chance to check out how the other half lived. She had a serious case of real estate envy.

She used the approaching hill as an interval opportunity, breaking into a full sprint. By the time she reached the top, she was gasping for breath, and her pulse had spiked to maximum capacity. She slowed to a casual walk, feeling the endorphins surge with each deep inhale. There was a reason she had a resting heart rate of fifty-one.

She found her pace slowing further as she neared the next house on the block, an all-white modern number, chock-full of floor-to-ceiling picture windows. Her particular interest in this house wasn't limited to the property itself. The home's sole resident was Reverend Martin Collins, founder of the Advocates for God megachurch. Before she'd left for her run, the newsroom had been abuzz with reports that one of the church's members was on a one-man crime spree.

She'd watched the reverend's impromptu press conference. According to Collins, the man wanted by the LAPD was a free agent — a rogue who had gone off the deep end. But some in the newsroom speculated that the man's arrest might be a chance for police to peer behind the church's carefully crafted façade. There had been rumors for years that the church and its charitable activities were all a front for financial shenanigans. What would this Steve Roman say about AG now that Collins had thrown him under the bus on live television?

Jenny felt her pulse dropping beneath cardio level. Time to get back at it.

She gave a final look at Collins's house as she picked up the pace. Just like her dream of owning a mansion was a distant fantasy, so too was a world in which she'd be trusted to write a front-page article exposing corruption at a megachurch. Jenny was a reporter in title, but so far her bylines were limited to human-interest stories, "personality" features, and other lightweight fare. If Collins had a dog who could ride a skateboard, that would be the kind of thing her editor might send her way.

Her thoughts were broken by the sound of two quick blasts, back to back. On instinct, she dove to the grass median next to her, seeking shelter behind a station wagon parked on the street. Were those *gunshots*?

The sounds were gone now. The distant hum of a lawn mower reminded her that she wasn't exactly in East L.A. She was rising to her feet, laughing at her own wild imagination, when she heard one more blast.

This time she was certain. It was gunfire. And unless her ears were playing tricks on her, it sounded like the shots had come from Martin Collins's house.

She entered 911 in her cell phone but then deleted the numbers for a quick call to her editor first. She finally had dibs on a major story.

70

Madison Meyer slid into the booth at one of her favorite Italian restaurants, Scarpetta, careful of her extra-short hemline. "Did you miss me, Professor?" she asked coyly. She had excused herself to the powder room to reapply her lipstick. Men had a tendency to stare at her lips when they were coated in cherry red.

Richard Hathaway smiled at her from across the table. "Terribly. And you missed the dessert tray. The waiter was a minute into his elaborate descriptions before I finally pointed out your absence. I think there might be an inverse correlation between basic common sense and the ability to go on and on about a tray of food. But I did ask him to come back once you returned."

"I love it that you use terms like 'inverse correlation' in everyday conversation."

When she first got the letter about *Under*

Suspicion, she'd had a fleeting hope of reconnecting with Keith Ratner. At one point, they'd been so well matched. Both actors. Both driven. Both a little bit sneaky. Maybe she could finally get Keith to love her the way she had once loved him.

But now she wasn't the least bit interested in Keith. She'd always thought that his connection to AG was a gimmick, as if the do-gooder, Bible-thumping image would compensate for the he-might-have-killed-his-girlfriend stigma. But nope, apparently he really was a changed man. Good riddance.

Then it turned out that Keith wasn't the only former flame at this little UCLA reunion. The years had been kind to Richard Hathaway. If possible, he had even gotten better with age. Of course, the millions of dollars he'd earned certainly didn't hurt. He had the kind of money that made A-list actors feel broke. Plus he was smart. There was a reason all the female students had been so drawn to him in college.

She was trying not to get her hopes up, but she couldn't help it. He was planning to return to Silicon Valley in a couple of days. She just needed to plant the seed that she was available to go with him if he wanted company.

"I've been meaning to tell you," she said

breezily, "my agent wants me to audition for a play in San Francisco. It's a small production, but a few movie stars are interested in the lead, so it will get plenty of attention." There was no play, of course, but she could always tell him later that the funding fell apart.

"Sounds like a good opportunity." His gaze wandered around the restaurant. "I'm starting to think that waiter's never coming back. The desserts really did look spectacular."

"I'll be going up next week," Madison continued. "You know, if you want to get together."

"Sure thing. Let me know what hotel you'll be at, and I'll find a restaurant nearby."

Well, dinner was better than nothing. Madison could swing a couple nights in a hotel if it meant a chance at landing a man like this one. "Oh, speaking of hotels, I almost forgot to tell you: Laurie Moran saw you leaving my room today. I guess the cat's out of the bag."

"Not much of a cat: we're two consenting adults."

"True, but it still feels a little naughty, doesn't it?" Madison took another sip of the red wine Hathaway had ordered without even looking at the list. It tasted expensive. "Anyway, you wouldn't believe how out of control her production has gotten. Did you see there's an arrest warrant out for that guy from Keith's church? Plus I heard some of the crew at the hotel saying that Dwight had that house in Bel Air seriously wired up for surveillance. Totally creepy, right?"

"Surveillance?"

"Yeah, and not just normal security cameras, either. Like hidden cameras and microphones in every room. I know he was your friend and everything, but that seems pretty stalkerish. Made me remember how he used to look at Susan all weird and dreamy in college. Did you know him to be the type to spy on people without telling them? Maybe it was his way of having control. Ah, here he is!"

The waiter was back, and as Richard promised, the choices looked delicious. She never ate dessert — sugar was a surefire way to bloat, which the camera magnified tenfold. But maybe she'd allow herself just one bite of that amazing-looking chocolate torte.

The waiter was midway through his tour of the tray when Richard suddenly dropped three hundred-dollar bills on the table. "I'm terribly sorry, but I'm afraid my stomach is having troubles."

"Sir, is everything okay?" the waiter asked. "I can call for medical assistance if it's serious."

"No." He was standing up already. "I just — I need to go. Can you please make sure she gets a cab?" He was stuffing fifties in the waiter's hand. "I'm terribly sorry, Maddie. I'll call you tomorrow. And, please, if it's not too forward, I'd like you to stay with me when you come up for your audition, okay? It's a ways from San Francisco proper, but we'll get you a driver."

He blew her a kiss, and then he was gone.

The waiter looked at her apologetically. "So, should I call you that cab?"

"Sure. But first, I'll have the chocolate torte. And a glass of your best champagne."

"Very good, ma'am."

Twenty years ago, Richard had stood her up for a date, and look what happened. She'd won a Spirit Award. He may have left tonight's dinner early, but he had invited her to his home. He had called her Maddie.

Before he knew what hit him, she'd have him wrapped around her little finger. Madison Meyer Hathaway. It had a nice ring to it.

71

The mood in Jerry's hospital room was as bright and celebratory as the last visit had been terrifying and dreary. He still looked weak and his head was still bandaged, but the oxygen mask was gone. The bruises were deep purple but beginning to fade ever so slightly.

Laurie and Alex had driven straight here from the hotel, arriving at the hospital's parking garage just behind Leo, Grace, and Timmy. They'd only been in Jerry's room a few minutes, and already the nurse had popped in twice to remind them not to get "the patient" too excited.

Jerry pressed an index finger to his lips. "Keep it down," he said groggily, "or Nurse Ratched will send me to sleep without a martini." He glanced toward a tiny stuffed panda bear resting on a nearby tray. "Timmy?"

Laurie nodded.

"I thought so. One of the nurse's aides said the 'sweetest little boy' had brought it."

"He's just outside." Laurie sent a quick *OK* text message to Grace, who was waiting in the hall.

"You were afraid the bruised and battered mummy might scare a nine-year-old?" His voice was still weak but growing stronger by the minute.

"Possibly," she admitted.

Leo's cell phone rang at his waist. He silenced it as he took a seat in a chair in the corner. "I keep telling her the kid's probably tougher than she is."

"And I keep telling you he's only a nine-year-old."

"Speak of the devil," Jerry said as Grace and Timmy rushed in. Jerry managed to hold up his wired fist to Timmy, who "bumped" it with a grin. "I've got a bigger crowd here than I get for some of my parties."

"Yeah, right," Grace said, leaning in for a gentle hug. "I've seen your parties, honey. You'd need a larger dance floor."

"I have a feeling it will be a while before I'm doing any dancing." His tone suddenly became more serious. "I can't believe I was out for three whole days."

"How much do you remember about what

happened?" Alex asked.

"I left the house to pick up some lunch. When I came home, a man with a ski mask was in the den. I had this second where I thought there was some explanation, because his shirt said 'Keep-safe' on it. Then I thought, Why would a guy from a security company wear a mask? I remember trying to run, then blackness. You know the worst part of it? Now you guys know I sneak greasy fast food when no one's looking."

Laurie was pleased to see Jerry hadn't lost his sense of humor in the assault.

Leo's cell was buzzing now. He glanced at the screen and then slipped out to take the call while Jerry continued to talk.

Laurie and Alex were still filling Jerry in on everything they had learned from Nicole about Steve Roman and Martin Collins when Leo returned to the room and asked Grace if she could take Timmy downstairs for some frozen yogurt in the hospital cafeteria.

Laurie was worried. If her father didn't want Timmy to hear, whatever he was about to say was going to be bad.

"But you said I was tough as nails," Timmy complained. "Why can't I listen?"

Grace responded matter-of-factly, "Because your grandpa said so."

"That's just what I was going to say," Laurie told him.

"And I'm backing them all up," Alex added.

"Hospital patients get to vote, too," Jerry said.

"Not fair," Timmy sighed. His feet dragging, he left the hospital room, shooed out by a determined Grace.

"What's up, Dad?" Laurie asked once her son was out of earshot.

"Those calls were from Detective Reilly. There was a shooting at Martin Collins's house. Steve Roman is dead — a self-inflicted gunshot. He left a note confessing to both the attack on Jerry and the murder of Lydia Levitt. As we thought, he was spying for Collins, starting first with Nicole and then moving out from there to see what she had said to others."

"Was Collins there?" Laurie asked.

"Two gunshot wounds. Steve Roman was trying to kill him, but they think he'll live. The police found a videotape collection in Collins's bedroom. It looks like whatever child Nicole saw him with twenty years ago wasn't his only victim. Collins may survive, but he'll never get out of prison. And speaking of video, Reilly said to thank you, Laurie, for the tip about Dwight Cook's boat. Turns out it was packed with surveillance equipment too, just like the house. Once again, *Under Suspicion* is bringing some much-deserved justice."

"So does it show what happened the night Dwight died?"

"Not yet. It's all digital, so they've got a computer tech trying to find where the video files may have been uploaded. If you don't mind getting everyone back to the house in the SUV, I'll take the rental car to meet Reilly. I want to make triple sure there's no reason for us to fear some other crazy church member following in Steve Roman's footsteps."

Laurie assured him they'd be fine in one car. He hugged her good-bye, whispering, "I'm proud of you, baby girl."

When she turned back to Jerry, his eyes were closed. It was time for them to go, too. She gave him a gentle kiss on the forehead before following Alex into the hall.

Laurie was quiet as they rode the hospital elevator to the lobby level. She was elated that they'd nailed Collins, a fraud and, worse, a pedophile. But when this all started, she had made a promise to Rosemary to do her best to find Susan's killer.

Laurie couldn't imagine losing a child. Twenty years later, and Rosemary still went to bed with haunting images of her only daughter running through a park with one bare foot, her necklace being torn from her throat in a violent struggle for her life.

The realization came with the *ding* that sounded as the elevator doors parted. "The necklace," she said aloud.

72

"What about a necklace?" Alex asked as they stepped out of the elevator.

"I don't know. Not yet, anyway."

"Come on, Laurie. I know you. I can tell when you're working on a theory. It's that kind of hunch that Leo calls your cop instinct. Is this about Susan's necklace? The one found near her body?"

"Just give me two minutes to work it out in my head, okay?" She could barely hang on to the various threads of thought starting to knit together in her mind. She didn't want to lose her momentum by trying to spell it all out prematurely. "Can you round up Grace and Timmy from the cafeteria? I'll get the car from the garage and swing around front."

"Aye-aye, Captain. But I'm dragging that hunch out of you once we hit the road. You know my interrogation skills," he added with a smile.

As she walked to the parking garage, she pulled up Nicole's number on her phone and dialed, holding her breath, hoping that she would answer.

She did. "Laurie, did you hear the news? Martin Collins was shot."

"I know, but I need to talk to you about something else." Laurie got right to the point. "You said that Susan was rummaging for her lucky necklace when you argued about Keith and the church. Did she find it?"

There was a pause on the other end of the line. "I really don't remember after all these years. So much else happened later that day."

"Think, Nicole. It's important."

"Um, she was running around, opening drawers and searching in her bedsheets and behind the sofa cushions. That's right: she was digging through the couch in our common area when I got so mad I threw my book at her. Then she stormed out. So I'm just about sure she didn't find it."

"Thanks, Nicole. That's a big help."

Susan had fled her dorm room without her necklace but had been wearing it by the time she was killed. *Where would she have gone?* That had been the question that Alex had pressed with Keith, Nicole, and Madison. And that had been the question that Dwight Cook kept replaying on the surveillance video before his death.

Laurie thought about her own habit of taking off her jewelry when she was busy at her desk. She believed she knew where Susan had found her lucky necklace.

She pulled up another name on her phone and hit ENTER.

Alex answered after two rings. "Hey, I just found Grace and Timmy. We'll meet you out front."

"Okay, I'm walking into the garage and am about to lose my signal. Can you do me a favor and call Madison? Remember how she said she sent a sexy note to some love interest to pick her up at the dorm but he never showed? Can you ask her who the guy was?"

"This is for your theory, right? Just tell me, Laurie."

"Call Madison first. It's the last piece of the puzzle, I promise. See you in a jiff."

As she beeped the Land Cruiser's locks open, she already knew in her gut what name Madison would give Alex.

Richard Hathaway.

73

Richard Hathaway stepped out of his SUV. He could not believe his good luck.

He had dashed from the restaurant after Madison mentioned the hidden cameras at the Bel Air house. Two years ago, Dwight had installed the same technology at the REACH offices and his Palo Alto home. Now it turned out that he'd also wired his parents' house in L.A. Had he gone so far as to wire his boats?

Yes, Hathaway thought, it would be exactly like Dwight to order the job for all his property at once, and he cared about his boats at least as much as that empty house in Bel Air.

And if the boat Dwight had used last night was equipped with hidden cameras, had they been on when Hathaway stepped onto the cruiser for his scheduled dive with Dwight? Had the cameras recorded Dwight as he angrily accused Hathaway of killing

Susan, insisting nonsensically that he'd figured it out by watching "the video"? Had they filmed Hathaway as he smothered Dwight with a life vest and then staged his body to appear in the water as a scuba accident? Had the police found the footage yet?

These were the questions that had swirled through his head as he drove from the restaurant, circling aimlessly through Hollywood, too panicked to go home or even to REACH's jet in case the police were waiting for him.

Instead, he'd gone to the storage unit he'd been renting for two decades to grab his "go bag," containing false identification, fifty thousand dollars, and a gun. He had identical bags in separate storage facilities in five different California cities, waiting in the event this day ever came.

But now that the moment he had been dreading was actually here, he realized he did not want to run. He had enjoyed the success of the last twenty years, and it was all about to improve further, as he was poised to become the new CEO of REACH. If he had even a shred of a chance to stay in this life, he was going to seize it.

At least he now understood Dwight's reference to a video. Something Dwight saw on the surveillance footage of that stupid TV production had alerted him to Hathaway's role in Susan's death.

He had to figure out what Laurie Moran knew and then silence her — and anyone else necessary — for good.

Parked on the street outside the Bel Air house, he saw an older man, a little boy, and the woman named Grace pile into a car. It was simple enough to follow them.

Once in the parking garage outside the hospital, Hathaway watched as Laurie and Alex pulled in a few minutes later in a black Land Cruiser. Since then, he'd been waiting, planning his next move.

Now Hathaway had caught two lucky breaks. The first was when Laurie's father, an ex-cop who was probably armed, had driven away from the hospital alone. At the sight of his leaving, Hathaway had experienced the same sense of relief he'd felt the moment Susan strapped on her seat belt on the night she died.

It had been May 7, a Saturday. Hathaway had asked Dwight to meet him in the lab because no one else would be there that night.

He wanted to talk to Dwight alone about REACH. Hathaway had created a search technology with the potential to revolution-ize the way people found information on the Internet. It was worth thirty times more than a professor could make in a lifetime of teaching. But technically, even though Hathaway had invented REACH, the idea didn't belong to him. He was owned by UCLA, which in turn owned anything he created during his employment there.

But students were in a different position. Students, unlike faculty who were paid a salary, owned their own intellectual prop-erty. And given Dwight Cook's invaluable assistance with the code, who was to say that REACH wasn't the sole invention of the young genius?

Hathaway had been so focused on making his pitch to Dwight — convincing him that this technology could change the world and that it would be wasted in the hands of UCLA — that he almost didn't notice Susan watching them in his peripheral vi-sion. But then he turned to see her standing by her desk near the door, looking as he'd never seen her before — her hair and makeup perfect, in a yellow halter dress. He had known immediately from the way she was rushing out of the lab that she had overheard their conversation.

Why had she been there on a Saturday?

Why did she have to walk in unexpectedly at that very moment?

Hathaway knew he needed to stop her. He needed to provide a context for what she'd overheard. He said, "Dwight, stay here where it's quiet and think about it. I'll call you later." Hathaway then ran after Susan, catching up to her as she was walking toward Bruin Plaza.

"Susan, can I have a word with you?"

When she turned, she had a necklace in her hand. "I have an audition. I have to go."

"Please, I just want to explain. You don't understand."

"Of course I do. Everyone I know is disappointing me today. It's like I don't really know anyone. I can't deal with this now. I have to be in the Hollywood Hills in an hour. And my jinx of a car is back at the dorm and probably won't even start."

"Let me drive you. Please. We can talk on the ride there. Or not. Whatever you want."

"How will I even get home?"

"I'll wait. Or you can call a cab. Whatever you'd like."

He thought back to that two-second pause as she pondered her options. He just needed her to get in the car, and he was certain he could convince her that what he was doing was the right thing.

431

"Okay," she agreed. "We can talk. And honestly, I just need a ride."

When Susan strapped on her seat belt and began putting on her necklace, he was certain he'd avoided a potential crisis.

But that moment of relief had been fleeting. Once he started to drive, he laid out the same argument for her that he'd offered to Dwight Cook. The bureaucrats in the UCLA administration could never begin to understand the potential of this technology. It would be tied up for years awaiting layers of approval, while competitors in the private sector worked at a rapid-fire pace. Besides, crediting Dwight with the technology was only a thin stretch of the truth, given how much programming work he'd put into the project.

He was certain Susan would go along, either out of dedication to technological development or to support Dwight. If worst came to worst, he would offer her a cut of the action. But Susan was too principled and, more important, too smart. Her father was an intellectual property lawyer. She knew from his work how important the creator of technology was to its development. In her eyes, Hathaway's plan was not only stealing from the university but from potential investors.

"With dot-coms," she had argued, "the face of the company is half of the product. You're leading people to think that a creative genius like Dwight — someone who doesn't care in the least about money, someone who looks at the world and sees only the best — was the seed for all this. That he'll be calling the shots. That's fundamentally a different company from one run by you. It's *fraud.*"

He began to slow at the curves, buying time to build his case. "But a company run by me would be worth more," he had insisted. "I have more experience. I'm a tenured professor. I don't have Dwight's personality quirks."

"The tech market loves quirks," she had said. "Besides, it's not simply a matter of dollar value. It's just dishonest. Aren't we getting close now? Why are you slowing down?"

When they were half a mile from her audition, he pulled the car to the side of the road. "Susan, you can't tell anyone what you heard. It will ruin my career."

"Then you shouldn't have done it. You offered to drive me to my audition. I've heard you out. Now I need to get to my appointment."

"Not until you understand —"

Just like that, she was out of the car, determined to make the rest of the trip on foot. He had to go after her. She ran faster in those heels than he would have thought possible. By the time he caught up with her in the park, one of her shoes had fallen off.

His first move had been to grab her by the arm. "You're being naive." He was still trying to persuade her. Why couldn't she be as gullible as Dwight?

And before he knew it, she was beneath him, hitting him, kicking at him. Sometimes he even convinced himself he couldn't remember what happened afterward.

But of course he did.

Once it was over, he made a quick decision that his best option was to leave her body. All her friends knew she was coming up here for an audition, so hopefully that would distract the investigation.

He called Dwight immediately, not long past seven o'clock, asking him to meet at Hamburger Haven to explore his suggestion further. If anyone ever asked, Dwight could vouch for his whereabouts for all but this short window of time.

Just as he hoped, the investigation had focused on Frank Parker, with Susan's boyfriend, Keith, the alternative suspect. For twenty years, he was convinced he'd gotten away with it, until he arrived at Dwight's boat last night. Now here he was, wondering how much Laurie Moran knew.

And that was the second piece of good luck to come in Hathaway's direction. First, the ex-cop had driven away. And now here was Laurie Moran, keys in hand, all by herself.

74

As Laurie walked through the parking garage toward the Land Cruiser, she realized that the clues pointing to Hathaway had been there all along. Susan had fled her dorm room after her fight with Nicole, eager to find her lucky necklace before her audition. Where would she have gone? To her desk at the lab.

And what would she have seen when she got there?

Laurie wasn't certain about this part yet, but if Susan went into the lab on a Saturday, she could have walked in on a moment that Hathaway assumed would be private. Maybe she'd caught him in one of those rumored liaisons with a female student or in the midst of some kind of academic impropriety. Hathaway could have talked Susan into getting into his car to discuss whatever she'd seen, especially since her own car had been acting up and she was set on getting to her audition.

Hathaway claimed to have been with Dwight the night Susan was killed, but the timeline was hazy, and now Dwight was dead. There was no way to know with certainty where Hathaway was that evening, but that's where the phone call to Madison came in.

Laurie realized what had been nagging her about her conversation with Madison after Laurie spotted Hathaway leaving Madison's hotel room. Madison had said that she had nothing to hide *now* that they were both grown-ups. She said they were *rekindling*. This wasn't a new relationship for them.

Laurie was certain that once Alex called Madison, she would confirm that Hathaway was the love interest who never showed up to her dorm room the night Susan was murdered. He never showed up because he was killing Susan in Laurel Canyon Park.

She opened the car door and paused to glance at her cell phone. No signal, as she suspected. Oh well, she thought, once I pull around to the hospital entrance, Alex can tell me if he reached Madison.

She had just slipped her cell phone in the pocket of the driver's-side door when she felt a hard object pressed against her back. In the side-view mirror, she saw the reflection of Hathaway standing behind her.

"Get in," he ordered, shoving her behind the wheel. Keeping the gun on her, he climbed over her into the passenger seat. "Now drive!"

75

Alex knew there was no stopping Laurie once her mind was on a mission. So when she asked him to call Madison about the identity of the love interest who turned down her invitation the night of Susan's murder, he did, even though he did not understand the significance.

"Madison," Alex said once he had her on the phone, "you sent a note to someone inviting him to see you the night Susan was killed. We'd like to know who that was, if you don't mind."

Alex was shocked when she responded, "Professor Hathaway. We'd had some flirtatious interactions already, so I thought we might spend a Saturday night together. But he was a complete and total no-show. No phone call, no nada. It's the kind of slight I take seriously — I blew him off after that and never spoke to him again. Until two days ago."

"Thanks, Madison," Alex said. "That's helpful."

Alex could see now the theory Laurie had been mulling over. From what they'd heard about Hathaway, he wasn't the type to have ignored a beautiful young woman's overture.

Then Alex realized why Laurie had mentioned the necklace. Susan had been searching for her lucky necklace during the argument with Nicole. From there, she might have gone to Hathaway's lab to look for it.

He found himself fiddling anxiously as he waited for Laurie to pull the car around so they could connect all the dots.

"Mom just turned the wrong way," Timmy said.

They were standing just inside the double doors of the hospital exit.

"You saw your mother?" Grace asked.

"She's over there," he said while pointing to an SUV heading to the hospital exit. "Is that Grandpa in the car with her?"

Alex pulled up Leo's number on his phone and hit ENTER. "Leo, it's Alex. Are you with Laurie?"

"No, I'm just pulling into the police station to catch up with Detective Reilly. Is everything okay?"

"I have a horrible feeling," Alex said.

"Laurie figured out who killed Susan. And now he has her. Richard Hathaway has our Laurie."

76

Laurie felt a surprising sense of relief when Hathaway ordered her to turn left out of the parking garage, away from the hospital. No matter what happened, at least Timmy, Alex, and Grace, who were waiting for her, would be safe.

"Up here," Hathaway barked. "Take a left at the next light."

This was not the same cool, confident man she'd seen over the past week. He was ranting to himself under his breath. She could almost smell his desperation.

"You must have access to cash and a plane," she said. "Just let me out. You take the car."

"And give up everything I've worked for my whole life? No, thank you. Take a right up here, after we pass Santa Monica Boulevard."

She did as instructed.

"Tell me about the video, Laurie. What

exactly did Dwight see? And don't play stupid or this will be worse for you than it needs to be. Tell me what Dwight knew."

"I'll never be certain," she said. "He left a message but died before I could speak to him. But I think he was calling me about you," she added. "To tell me that Susan went to your lab before her audition."

"And the boat?"

"What boat?"

"Were there cameras on Dwight's boat?" Hathaway yelled. "And don't forget, I can go back for your son if you need an incentive to talk."

Not Timmy, she thought. "Yes," she blurted, "Dwight had hidden cameras on his yacht."

"What do they show?"

"I have no idea. The police haven't found the digital upload yet."

"Take the next left."

As she hit her blinker, she could feel him calming down in the passenger seat. He mumbled something about his ability to find the data files before the police.

She slipped a hand into the pocket of the door to awaken her phone. She risked a glance at the screen and saw a list of recent calls.

As she took the turn, she let her hand

drop into the door pocket one more time. She tapped the screen to redial her most recent caller.

Please, God, she thought, *please let this work.*

77

Alex had never heard Leo sound so panicked. "What do you mean, Hathaway has Laurie?" Leo demanded.

"She thinks Hathaway killed Susan Dempsey, and Timmy just saw her drive out of the garage with someone in the passenger seat. She was only alone for a minute —"

Alex heard the beep of an incoming call. He checked the screen and saw one name: *Laurie.*

"Wait, that's her now," Alex said. "I'll call you right back." He clicked over to the incoming call. "Laurie, where are you?"

But he didn't hear Laurie's voice in response. He heard silence, then eventually the sound of a man's voice. It was Hathaway. "Slow down," he ordered, "and stop swerving. I know what you're doing. If you get pulled over by a cop, I'll shoot you both, and that's a promise."

"Where are you taking me?" Alex heard

Laurie say. "Are we going to your house? Why are we heading into the Hollywood Hills?"

Alex hit the mute button on his phone to block his end of the line. "Grace," he said, waving her over to the alcove. "Call Leo back and have him put Detective Reilly on the line. Laurie's giving us clues about their location."

Within seconds, Grace handed Alex her phone.

"Reilly," Alex said, "I'm certain of it now: Hathaway has Laurie and is taking her to the Hollywood Hills."

If something happened to Laurie, he would never forgive himself.

78

Laurie didn't dare steal another glance at her phone. She just had to hope that the call had connected and that Alex was able to hear her.

"Just do what I say, and no one else will be hurt," Hathaway said. "Your son and your father will be fine."

But not me, she thought. You have other plans for me.

Maybe if she kept him talking, she could buy herself more time. "Why did you do it? What did Susan see in the lab that afternoon to make her such a threat to you?"

"It didn't need to be such a big deal. Dwight had already done so much of the code work. Whether REACH was his idea or mine was just a matter of semantics. She overheard us and completely overreacted. It was worth millions. Did she really expect me to turn it over to a bunch of academic know-nothings?"

Hathaway was almost talking to himself at this point, but Laurie was able to piece the story together. She remembered the article published in the campus newspaper when Hathaway retired. It mentioned that, as a faculty member, Hathaway did not own any of his own research. She pictured Susan walking into the lab as Hathaway enlisted his favorite student to take the credit for his work so they could both profit from it.

Hathaway suddenly stopped muttering and told her to take another turn. His expression was cold and determined.

"Don't do this, Hathaway." She made it a point to say his name. If nothing else, maybe Alex would know who did this. "You'll never get away with it."

"I may live my life under suspicion, as you call it," Hathaway said, "but I won't be convicted. There's no real proof I killed Susan. As for Dwight, I can find the video files from his boat faster than any low-level hack working for the LAPD. And once I'm done with you, my next stop will be to Keith Ratner. He'll kill himself, leaving behind a distraught note confessing to the murders of both you and Susan. This entire thing will go down in the history books as being wrapped up with Advocates for God."

Laurie remembered taking this exact route

when they'd driven to the spot where Susan Dempsey's body was found.

"You're taking me to Laurel Canyon Park, aren't you? We're going to the place where you killed Susan."

"Of course that's where we are going," Hathaway said. "It's exactly what Keith Ratner would do in a meltdown over the downfall of his beloved church leader — a demise that *you* brought about."

Laurie thought about the terror Susan must have felt when she realized Hathaway was trying to kill her. It was about to happen to her, too.

She had to find a way to save herself.

79

Alex felt helpless as he continued to listen to the open line. Hathaway was forcing Laurie to drive to the spot where he killed Susan Dempsey.

Good, Laurie, he whispered. *Just keep talking.*

She had already gotten Hathaway to admit to killing Susan Dempsey, and now he had a plan to kill Laurie and pin all his crimes on Keith Ratner.

"He's taking her to Laurel Canyon Park," Alex said to Reilly, who was doing his best to overhear through Grace's phone. "You have to send police cars there now, Reilly. You have to find Laurie."

Laurie could see the park entrance approaching. They were just seconds from what Hathaway intended to be her final destination.

Just as she knew he would, Hathaway

instructed her, "Take the left turn up here, into the park."

She turned slowly, hoping to see a cavalry of police cars waiting for them, but the park was empty, dark as pitch.

This was it — her one chance. She remembered the exact location of the sycamore tree she'd noticed when they were filming here with Frank Parker.

She thought about making a quick move to latch her seat belt before impact. But she did not want to risk alerting Hathaway to her plan. If she was unable to buckle the seat belt, she wanted to have two hands on the wheel when they hit.

As they approached the sycamore she gunned the gas as hard as she could. Hathaway began to yell — "What are you — ?" She swerved left and piloted the front side of the SUV squarely into the tree.

Laurie cringed when she heard the loud bang, at first believing that Hathaway had shot her. The bang was not a gunshot but the sound of the airbag deploying. Laurie felt a jolt in every part of her body as the airbag flung her back against her seat. For a moment she wasn't sure where she was.

As Laurie's head began to clear she looked over at Hathaway. He too had been stunned by the impact but was beginning to stir. She looked in his hands and on the floor for the gun but couldn't find it. Should she try to fight him now? No, if he woke up quickly, he would easily be able to overpower her. There was only one thing to do: run!

Detective Reilly spoke quickly as Alex pressed his ear to the cell phone. "We dispatched all local units to Laurel Canyon Park. One unit is in the park interior. I've been tracking the movements of Laurie's cell phone. It stopped moving about one minute ago. Either the phone is no longer in the vehicle or the vehicle has stopped."

With her body protesting every move, Laurie managed to open her door. She slid out of the car's raised seat and briefly lost her balance as her feet hit the sandy soil. She heard a groan and saw Hathaway raising his hand and massaging his forehead. Reaching into the driver's door side pocket, her hands groped for the cell phone in the darkness. It was gone.

Laurie ran a few strides until she felt her feet on pavement. Disoriented, she looked up and down the road, which was faintly illuminated by the moonlight. She wasn't sure which direction would take her toward Frank Parker's former house or deeper into the park. Her time to decide ended when she heard the crunching squeal of metal from the car. The passenger-side door was beginning to open.

Laurie began running as fast as her bruised legs would allow. How many times had she wondered what her beloved Greg was thinking in the final moments of his life? In trying to understand Susan Dempsey she had imagined Susan's terror as she fled through Laurel Canyon in a desperate attempt to outrun her killer — Our killer, she thought — Richard Hathaway! She thought of Timmy. She could not let him go through the loss of another parent. She had promised him she would always be there for him. She then heard Richard Hathaway's footsteps growing ever closer.

Highway Patrolman Carl Simoni had been inside Laurel Canyon Park investigating a complaint about illegal campers when he received the emergency dispatch about a carjacking. It had taken him several minutes to hustle back to his cruiser from the elevated campground. He was now pushing his cruiser as fast as he dared through the winding roads that led to the entrance of the park.

■ ■ ■ ■

Laurie wasn't sure if the burning feeling in her chest was the result of the jolt from the airbags or if her lungs were unable to accept more air as she approached exhaustion. The quiet of the canyon was no longer disturbed only by her. Interspacing the sound of Laurie's footsteps was the faint wail of a siren.

Patrolman Simoni rounded a winding curve as the latest dispatch cackled from this radio. The carjacking victim's cell phone signal had been traced to an area just inside the park. He would be there in less than a minute. He squinted as he believed he saw a silhouette moving on the park road.

As Laurie ran, she looked back over her shoulder. The hulking figure of Hathaway grew larger every time she turned. Without realizing it she stepped on the border of the road and the soft soil to the side sent her sprawling to the ground. She flipped over and tried to get up. Hathaway had stopped a few feet away. She watched as he extended his arm toward her. There was a glint of moonlight off the gun in his hand. "Laurie, would you prefer that I shoot you or do you want to die the way Susan Dempsey did? Either way, they'll find your body in the same spot they found hers."

Before Laurie could respond, a bright light briefly covered her body from behind. It then moved quickly over to Hathaway, who raised one hand to shield his eyes from the blinding glare. Over a megaphone she could hear a voice echoing across the canyon ordering him to put his gun down and drop to his knees.

The gun was still pointed at her head. He was laughing, a maniacal, defiant sound. With all the strength she could muster, she swung her leg up and managed to kick his hand. The gun went off, with the bullet exploding in the sand next to her. The patrol car was rocketing toward them. Before Hathaway could aim again, it had slammed into him, knocking him to the ground.

As a swarm of patrol cars thundered down the road, she struggled to her feet. The force with which she had kicked Hathaway's hand had caused her shoe to slip off. As she reached for it, she could only think of the shoe Susan Dempsey had lost when she was trying to escape her killer.

80

Laurie had assumed that her next visit to Cedars-Sinai hospital would be to escort Jerry from the ICU. But she was back in the lobby again, Alex at her side. Once the doctors pronounced Laurie in good health after the collision, Grace had taken Timmy back to the house. Now she was waiting to hear about Richard Hathaway's injuries.

"I was so afraid," Alex said, "and then when your cell phone stopped moving, it was unbearable."

"I didn't think I'd make it," Laurie said. "I counted on you to pick up the phone." She managed a laugh. "Thank God you didn't put me on hold!"

Leo appeared from the ICU, his expression ambiguous. "Hathaway's got two broken legs but he'll make a full recovery."

"You sound disappointed," she said.

"He killed two people in cold blood, then came after my only daughter tonight," Leo said. "I wouldn't have lost sleep if he'd broken every bone in his body."

"He's only fifty-seven years old," Laurie said. "There's plenty of time for karma."

"The prosecution has a slam-dunk case against him," Alex said. "Kidnapping and attempted murder for tonight. Plus he confessed to killing both Susan Dempsey and Dwight Cook."

"And," Leo added, "Reilly says his techs found the camera feed from Dwight Cook's scuba boat. When Hathaway showed up to dive with Dwight, Dwight confronted him about Susan's murder. He'd figured out that Susan went to the lab after arguing with Nicole and overheard them talking about REACH. Hathaway admitted catching up to her and driving her up to the hills, but he tried to make her death sound like an accident. When Dwight didn't believe him, Hathaway smothered him and then faked the supposed 'scuba accident.' "

"And the police have the whole thing on film?" Laurie asked.

"In living color."

EPILOGUE

Two months later, Alex Buckley looked out from the television screen in Laurie's living room. "She became known to the public as Cinderella," he said solemnly, "but to a mother, she was always Susan. And tonight, on May 7, exactly twenty years after her death, we hope you feel you know her as Susan, too. Her case is now officially closed."

A round of applause broke out as the program ended. They had all gathered here to watch together: Laurie, her father, Timmy, Alex, Grace, Jerry. Even Brett Young had joined them. He was so happy with the show that he had flown Rosemary, Nicole, and Gavin to New York for their viewing party.

"Congratulations," Leo declared, holding up his beer bottle for a toast. "To *Under Suspicion*."

They all clinked glasses — Timmy's filled

with apple cider — and then someone yelled out, "We need a speech, Laurie."

"Speech, speech," they all began to cheer.

She rose from her spot on the sofa. "Talk about a demanding crowd," she joked. "First off, *Under Suspicion* has always been a group effort. The show wouldn't be the same without Alex, and probably wouldn't have been *made* if not for Jerry and Grace. And I think it's safe to say that Jerry took an extra *hit* for the team this go-round."

They groaned at the pun. Two months ago, she couldn't have imagined making light of the horrible assault. But Jerry had recovered fully, and the man who'd assaulted him, Steve Roman, was dead. Jerry himself jokingly referred to the beating as a reminder that he shouldn't sneak out for junk food.

"And Timmy and Leo," Laurie added, "I'd say the two of you should have pushed the studio to be listed in the credits."

"That would've been *cool,*" Timmy announced gleefully.

"Hey, don't forget a shout-out for the guy who signs the checks," Brett jokingly chided. "And who made sure you aired on May seventh."

"Thank you for that gentle reminder, Brett. And I'm sure the fact that May

459

seventh fell during sweeps was completely a coincidence. But most of all," Laurie said in a more serious tone, "I want to thank Rosemary."

They all gave another round of applause.

"You were our inspiration throughout the entire production — from the early research to Alex's closing line. I don't often talk about the loss we suffered in my own family." She smiled gently at Timmy and Leo. "Losing a loved one is hard enough, but not knowing who did it, or why, is its own kind of torment. For me, every day has gotten just a little better since we finally got our answers. I only hope the same will be true for you."

Rosemary wiped away a tear. "Thank you so much," she said quietly.

Laurie noticed Nicole pat Rosemary soothingly on the back. Rosemary had vowed to forgive Nicole for the long delay in discovering who had killed Susan, but Laurie knew true forgiveness would take time.

Grace, always quick to lighten the mood, jumped from her chair and began topping off glasses. "So am I the only one who caught Keith Ratner on *Morning Joe* today? Seems like he's had a conversion of a different kind."

Undoubtedly timed to coincide with the airing of *Under Suspicion,* Keith's tour on the talk-show circuit was billed as an "insider's view" of Advocates for God. Martin Collins was already facing multiple abuse charges stemming from the videos discovered at his home. According to Detective Reilly, federal prosecutors were also putting together a racketeering case, alleging that Collins had used the church as a corrupt enterprise to cover criminal activity ranging from theft to bribery to extortion to his own predatory acts against children. Keith was not only cooperating with police but also using his disenchantment with the church to get back in the spotlight.

"Well, his PR tour is working," Laurie said. "A publishing friend told me there's a bidding war for the memoir he's pitching. Madison and Frank Parker are using the case as publicity, too. *Variety* reported yesterday that Frank has given Madison a small but 'come-back-worthy' role in his next film. She'll be playing a ruthless businesswoman willing to do anything to get ahead."

"Talk about typecasting!" Leo said.

When Rosemary went to leave, she gave Laurie a long hug at the door. "I think you and Susan would have been such good friends. Please, stay in touch. It would mean so much to me."

"Absolutely," Laurie assured her. Rosemary's approval meant more to her than any ratings or awards her show might earn.

Alex was the last to leave. At the door he said, "Congratulations, Laurie. The show was spectacular." He started to kiss her cheek, then involuntarily reached out his arms, and she stepped into them. His lips found hers and, for a long minute, they clung to each other.

Then as they stepped apart, he said, "Laurie, get something straight. I'm not a man about town. I'm a guy who's desperately in love with you and willing to wait."

"I don't deserve that," Laurie said.

"Yes, you do. And you'll know when the time is right."

They smiled at each other. "Not too much time," Laurie whispered, "I promise."

They both became aware of a small figure in the hallway to the bedrooms. Timmy was smiling happily. "Awesome!"

ABOUT THE AUTHOR

Mary Higgins Clark, #1 international and *New York Times* bestselling author, has written thirty-three suspense novels; three collections of short stories; a historical novel, *Mount Vernon Love Story*; two children's books, including *The Magical Christmas Horse*; and a memoir, *Kitchen Privileges*. She is also the coauthor with Carol Higgins Clark of five holiday suspense novels. Her books have sold more than 100 million copies in the United States alone.

Alafair Burke is the bestselling author of ten novels, including the thrillers *Long Gone*, *If You Were Here*, and the latest in the Ellie Hatcher series, *All Day and a Night*. A former prosecutor, she now teaches criminal law and lives in Manhattan.

The employees of Thorndike Press hope you have enjoyed this Large Print book. All our Thorndike, Wheeler, and Kennebec Large Print titles are designed for easy reading, and all our books are made to last. Other Thorndike Press Large Print books are available at your library, through selected bookstores, or directly from us.

For information about titles, please call:
  (800) 223-1244

or visit our Web site at:
  http://gale.cengage.com/thorndike

To share your comments, please write:
  Publisher
  Thorndike Press
  10 Water St., Suite 310
  Waterville, ME 04901